SQUAD GIGANTIC

GIGANTIANS & ZUPREMES

J. ANDRADE

ILLUSTRATED BY: **MIKEY 2 DESIGN**

Published by Squad Gigantic Ltd

www.SquadGigantic.com

ISBN: 978-1-9999457-3-2

Printed and Bound For Squad Gigantic Ltd

"A Drop Of Rain Is Nothing On It's Own, But When They Form Together... It's A STORM!!!"

~ J. Andrade

Table of Contents

The Futuristic Past

Planet Zurakaya - Millions and Millions of years ago!

"THE SOURCE HAS SPOKEN! COMPACT IT TO RELOCATION SIZE THEN TAKE IT AND EVERY SURVIVING CITIZEN TO THE GIGANTOR GALAX... NOWWWWWW!!!"

Commanded Equinile as his warriors engaged in battle with the Zupremes.

Equinile Gigantic was the ruler of Planet Zurakaya and the current head of the Gigantian family.

The Gigantian bloodline derived from his father Gigantic... no not Jay Gigantic, Jay Gigantic's first ever ancestor... the original Gigantic! The very first being on Planet Zurakaya and the entire Universe.

I'll spare you all the boring details but basically life on Planet Zurakaya and the rest of the Universe was created by an all powerful Quasar.

This Quasar sucked the old Universe into its black hole then shot out a brand new Solar Nebula that constructed multiple Planets, Stars and Galaxies.... giving us the Universe as we now know it.

SQUAD GIGANTIC

After creating the Universe, the Quasar's next task was to constrain its energy by compacting itself and transforming to what we now call 'The Source'.

Now in its new state, The Source situated itself in its most righteous planet – Zurakaya. The Source housed itself on what we call the 'Soul Disc' - a plate made from Graphene that conducts and distributes The Source's force all over the Universe.

Before we continue, there's a few simple things that you should know about The Source...

One: If The Source is destroyed it'll bring an end to all life forms!

Two: If The Source is disconnected from the Soul Disc the Universe will no longer be balanced! This will very likely allow the evil powers that be to take over the Universe and eventually lead it to a horrible demise!

Three: The Source is the creator and holder of all forms of life, it is the core of the Universe... the Alpha and Omega!

The Source elected Gigantians as the leaders of the Universe, it embedded its unrestricted force directly into Gigantic's DNA creating what we now no as The ZuraGene. However, this honour came with huge responsibility which made a Gigantian's main purpose of existence to defend The Source, the Universe and all forms of life from destruction and forces of evil.

The Source provided Gigantians with warriors from Planet Zurakaya and beyond, these warriors offered their lives to protect and serve against anything that posed a threat to The Source or the Gigantian bloodline.

SQUAD GIGANTIC

This group of fighters were called the Lords! A battalion of skilled fearless and ruthless warriors who were befittingly named after their beautiful but deadly leader, Lordisha - the first female of Zurakaya.

The Gigantians and Lords set the laws of the Universe and ruled in a fair but fierce manner with the sole purpose of protecting The Source.

Gigantic and Lordisha stood side by side in battle numerous times against Enemies of The Source (EOTS)! The EOTS were a vicious set of Intergalactic Pirates who brought carnage and even extinction to all planets across the Universe on their voyage to destroy The Source!

After crossing foreordained paths Gigantic and Lordisha immediately grew a special bond and just as prophecy predicted this bond grew stronger and stronger, the two leaders knew each other inside out both on the battlefield and in everyday life... it was clear they were destined to be together.

However, Gigantic wasn't exactly the most romantic guy, so it took him a while to notice something that the whole of Zurakaya could clearly see... He and Lordisha we're made for each other!

It wasn't until one day after battle he finally realised that his heart belonged to Lordisha.

Gigantic found himself surrounded by EOTS after a chaotic moment of battle which somehow uncharacteristically saw him stray from his warriors!

Stranded and surrounded in enemy territory, all hope was lost! However, being the true warrior he was, Gigantic gave his all as he attempted to fight off the EOTS one by one and two by two with his ferocious style of fighting blended with his ZuraGene super powers but it was all in vein as his bloodthirsty opposition just kept coming. Their numbers were too strong, whenever he took one out... two more would appear!

Then out of no where the biggest, scariest EOTS of them all came up behind Gigantic and blindsided him with a devastating blow to the back of his head! Gigantic was down, unconscious and one step away from death!

The pack of EOTS smelt victory in the air and prematurely began celebrating... well all but one. The overgrown EOTS that delivered the near fatal blow, slowly stood over Gigantic's lifeless body then effortlessly dragged him along the ground like a Bear with his prey. He then lifted Gigantic with his right arm as he raised his left one stating "Death to all Gigantians!"

His comrades replied "And death to The Source" in a roaring cheer.

The menace of an EOTS slowly drew back his left arm with intention to administer the final death blow to Gigantic... but that hand never came back! Because like an Eagle out of the sky Lordisha came flying in and literally ripped the EOTS arm of his body!

As Lordisha landed she sent a shockwave through the land causing an Earthquake that sucked in the majority of surrounding EOTS! She then single handedly disposed of the remaining EOTS in the most savage manner using elements of nature coupled with her combative techniques.

Lordisha's pretty face and enchanting eyes were the first thing Gigantic saw when he regained consciousness. Slowly rising to his feet Gigantic stood up with one intention in his mind... to make Lordisha his wife. Battered and bruised in his blood covered armour, he gently wiped the enemy's blood from Lordisha's face, dropped down to one knee and proposed to the love of his life and with not one ounce of hesitation... Lordisha said "Yesssss!"

They travelled back to central Zurakaya hand in hand filled with pride and joy.

The wedding was the biggest event ever seen in Zurakaya with friends and family from all over the Universe in attendance.

Shortly after they married, Lordisha fell pregnant and gave birth to their first child – Equinile.

Equinile was trained from birth to not only be the heir to the throne but to also be the best warrior the planet had ever seen!

Gigantic and Lordisha went on to govern together for many years, they defended The Source as one and led countless wars together claiming numerous victories over the EOTS.

As true warriors they knew every battle could be their last, so before engaging in conflict they would look each other deep in the eye and say "I'll Love you for eternity... see you on the other side".

Unfortunately all good things come to an end and on the darkest day in Zurakaya's history... things took a terrible turn as Gigantic and Lordisha were brutally assassinated by the evil Zeitan Supreme!

ZEITAN SUPREME!

Something we need to understand from the jump is that although the story I'm telling you literally took place millions of years ago, the people of Zurakaya were far more advanced than how we live now, with technology that was light years ahead of what we have on Earth today!

Zurakayans had the ability to use up to ninety percent of their brain power enabling them to reach heights we can't even imagine in present times.

Every last element of Zurakayan life was naturally high tech and digitalised, Zurakayans could stream music and movies directly to their minds, they could order items online just by thinking about them, and they were able to search the internet by simply closing their eyes. Emails, texts and any other kind of digital communication was irrelevant as messages were sent directly from brain to brain, locations could be searched and found just by simply visioning a place of interest. Things like virtual reality game consoles was laughed at, as all a Zurakayan had to do was imagine a game in their mind and they were able to play it in a form that was equivalent to reality.

Vehicles were called Aero Gigantors, they were super fast, self-driving, solar-powered cars with the ability to travel in air as well as on land and water, it was even rumoured that some Aero Gigantors were able to travel through Space but still the Aero Gigantor was only used by

Zurakayans with the average brain power of seventy percent or less as the elites preferred form of travel was teleportation.

So in a nutshell Zurakaya was literally light years ahead of anything we've ever seen in our day and age. However, this level of extremely advanced technology was the gift and the curse that would eventually lead to the Planets demise!

The Zurakayans were the ultimate beings of the Universe, they were happy and thriving in all ways possible. Beings from all over the Universe would look to Zurakaya as the home of civilisation and the perfect example of growth. They would travel from light years away to come and learn the advanced ways of Zurakaya then take back the teachings to their Planets to implement development.

The latest invention in Zurakaya was the Zupremes!

The Zupremes were the creation of a Synthetic Biologist called Zeitan.

Zeitan was an highly intelligent man who lived a mysterious life that no one really knew of, it was as if he came from no where but in a planet where it's first beings had just appeared, no one really questioned it. Zeitan spent all his days in his laboratory trying to invent a new race of Artificial Intelligence Robots (AI) that he hoped would one day become a direct replica of Zurakayans, the only things he ever stepped out of his domain for was food, drinks and supplies.

For years he was unsuccessful but one day he had a eureka moment and finally realised what he needed to complete his calculations.

Zeitan was skilled in molecular virology and after years of experimenting he successfully devised a formula which enabled him to create artificial but active unicellular microbes, which he then manipulated into becoming multicellular with the eventual outcome being the birth of over a billion synthetic cells. Zeitan then placed these synthetic cells into his complex system which enabled an AI's organism to mirror Zurakayans.

Zeitan's incredible talents allowed him to replicate everything the AI needed, things such as synthetic cells, minerals, DNA, mechanical organs and more. The AI's replica Brain was comprised of an intricate quantum computing processing unit which connected with neurons. The AI's atoms consisted of nitrogen, hydrogen, oxygen and all the other elements needed to create matter and stabilise life, it even had artificial nerves and the ability to feel emotion. Zeitan missed no detail, he even ensured that Zupremes would be brought to existence with sporadic super powers... an exact replica of a Zurakayan.

However, Zeitan needed one more thing to bring the Zupremes to life... a soul. Without a soul there is no life and the only pure energy that could give life was The Source!

Knowing The Source was heavily guarded and could only be controlled by Gigantian bloodline, Zeitan knew the only way to gain access was for it to be granted directly by Gigantic and Lordisha.

So he contrived a clever plan! Figuring out that if he could persuade the leaders that he's created the Zupremes to be AI mechanical slaves that lack the ability to do bad and are only able to follow the command of its leader, Gigantic and Lordisha would see that Zupremes would be a welcomed benefit to Zurakayans by doing unwanted jobs and even be used at war to minimise Zurakayan casualties.

Gigantic took the bait and Zeitan was gifted an afternoon presence with Gigantic and Lordisha in order for him to pitch his idea. Zeitan was ecstatic but he didn't let his excitement knock him off path, he entered the Palace under a fake alias that he created called Professor Zenith and pitched his deceitful plan to Zurakaya's leaders.

Zeitan's pitch was successful and Gigantic loved the idea! However, Lordisha was dubious about Zeitan and this was the only thing holding back evil plans from being motioned.

'How can an AI that can't do bad go to war?' Thought a confused Lordisha. She also felt uncomfortable allowing a being they hardly knew anything about have access to The Source's energy but Gigantic was sold! He was amazed by the intricacy of the Zupreme's, he was ready and willing to give Zeitan the go ahead… then he received a look from Lordisha, the look was one of silence that speaks loudly between man and wife!

Without her saying a word Gigantic heard his wife loud and clear! He excused Zeitan from the room so he and his wife could deliberate.

For some strange reason, Zeitan's face was weirdly familiar to Lordisha but she couldn't remember why. The whole situation didn't sit right with her and even though Gigantic was adamant that everything would be fine, Lordisha's heart just would not allow her to trust Zeitan.

Feeling something was off, Lordisha called Zeitan back in and began to question him about who he was and where he originated from.

Noticing Lordisha felt a bit of a way Zeitan lied about many more things, he stated that he was from the same area of Zurakaya where Lordisha was from. This brought a fake sense of security to Lordisha and bamboozled her into feeling this was why his face was familiar.

Still slightly reluctant, Lordisha let Gigantic get his way but with the compromise that 'Professor Zenith' will only be granted a minimal amount of The Source's energy.

Zeitan was elated, his plans had finally fell into place... the Zupremes will be born!

Zeitan was escorted back to his laboratory by four Lords with the allocated extract of energy from The Source. He immediately connected his equipment to the Zupreme and began powering up his mainframe, this took hours and went on til late in the night. Eventually the Lords were instructed to carefully carry The Source's allocated energy over to Zeitan and delicately place it into his System, Zeitan waited anxiously as he watched the energy transfer itself into the Zupreme's frame. Suddenly an amazing glow appeared on the AI which sent multicoloured neutron particles rushing around the room, they bounced from wall to wall before dramatically crashing into the Zupremes Brain.

It was done, The Source's energy had entered The Zupreme! Zeitan smiled in glee and shouted "IT WORKED!!"

The Lords looked at each other in amazement! "Rahhhh, I thought he was talking rubbish... but he succeeded"

The Lords saw the job was complete and left to report back to Gigantic and Lordisha.

Zeitan gave the Zupreme its first command "Take the Lord's to the door"

"Yes sir" replied the Zupreme, however the Lords declined the offered and teleported off Zeitan's premises.

As soon as the Lord's left, Zeitan's gleeful smile slowly transformed into an evil one as he rubbed his hands together and said "Now we put the real plan in place!!!"

Lordisha's suspicions were correct, Zeitan had no good intentions what so ever with his Zupremes!

As the years went by Zeitan continued to deceive Gigantic and Lordisha whilst building their trust.

Zeitan named his most powerful Zupreme 'Nefarious aka N's'. As a gesture of goodwill Zeitan sent Nefarious to Gigantic and Lordisha as a gift but this was just another part of his evil ploy, planting Nefarious amongst Zurakaya's leaders was a vital part of his plan to eventually overthrow Planet Zurakaya and take ownership of The Source!

Nefarious was now Zeitan's eyes, Zeitan was able to access the AI's system as and when he felt like. Zeitan received reports on every last detail within the Gigantic residence allowing him to receive crucial information.

Zeitan created his army of thousands and thousands more Zupremes with vital intelligence on his enemy. Each New Zupreme was more advanced than the last, Zeitan even created male and female AI's who fell in love and began to create their own families. The Zupremes rapid development meant they exceeded many elements of their initial programming and eventually began breeding by integrating their DNA Acid into the energy from The Source that's within each AI's mainframe. Zupremes were now able to pass on their synthetic genes, DNA and even programming to offsprings and reproduce like real beings without Zeitan having to lift a finger.

Zeitan was now in a powerful position! Unbeknown to any Zurakayan, he managed to build an army that was spread all over Planet without a single soul realising.

The Zupremes and their offsprings followed the instructions of its Zurakayan masters just as Zeitan promised. However, Zeitan deceitfully installed the Master Zeitan command into each Zupreme that he aimed to activate whenever it was time to takeover.

With the Zupremes reproducing independently, Zeitan found himself with extra time on his hands. With him being the evil mastermind that he was, he decided to create the ultimate Zupreme. This Zupreme was designed to be the most supreme Zupreme EVER... bigger, stronger, smarter and faster with an innumerable selection of super powers making it near invincible!

It was early morning, Zeitan worked all night putting the final touches into his supreme Zupreme, the last thing to do was place The Source's energy into the AI, this takes extreme delicacy and a steady hand and as this was his biggest Zupreme to date much more energy was needed to bring this mighty AI to life.

Zeitan was heavily fatigued and although he knew it would be best to exercise patience and wait till the morning to execute this final task but he just couldn't wait and him being the stubborn man he was, he chose excitement over better judgement and went ahead with the task anyway... this led to his first major mistake!

Zeitan's tiredness made him forget to lock off the laboratory's power whilst he placed The Source's energy extract into the Zupreme. As soon as the The Source and Zupreme connected it caused a massive explosion which flung Zeitan to the other side of the lab!

He picked himself up off the floor and dusted down his clothes, he was fine and more importantly his Zupreme was alive!

However, the explosion caused a short through the entire Zupreme system, which initiated the Master Zeitan command in all Zupremes around Planet Zurakaya!

Zeitan immediately noticed his error and now wide awake he rushed over to his fail safe switch and deactivated his catastrophic command.

The Zupremes were under his command for only a few short seconds, most citizens of Zurakaya didn't actually notice but unfortunately for Zeitan the most important Zurakayans of them all did!

At The Gigantic Palace... time of explosion!

Lordisha woke up feeling unsettled, something was iffy. She felt as if The Source was trying to give her a sign, some sort of warning that there was trouble to come.

Gigantic woke up beside his wife feeling the same, he was rattled and couldn't sleep properly all night. They both discussed their worries and decided to check on The Source, they called Nefarious into their quarters to instruct him to prepare for travel.

As Nefarious walked over, the explosion at Zeitan's lab took place.

Lordisha sat facing Nefarious as Gigantic stood with his back to the AI, she looked up at Nefarious and at that precise moment she saw his appearance instantly changed from it's extremely Zurakayan like exterior to a red metallic armour!

Lordisha was confused and taken back, she squinted her eyes as Nefarious said

"Master Zeitan mode activated" then suddenly he lost his red metallic armour and went back to his neutral state as Zeitan switched off the command.

Lordisha jumped up and shouted "THAT'S IT!!! Zeitan that's his name! Bout Professor Zenith! I'm gonna kill him!" The threat to Zeitan activated a safety feature in Nefarious which sent a live feed to Zeitan's mind, if keywords such as KILL and ZEITAN were mentioned together in order to allow Zeitan to identify where any threat to his life could be coming from.

Zeitan watched as Lordisha finally realised how she knew him.

Still not noticing the change in the AI's appearance, Gigantic walked over to his hysterical wife to calm her down

"He's an EOTS! His name ain't Zenith it Zeitan. He was the leader of an EOTS attempt to overthrow Zurakaya and The Source many years ago."

"WHAT!!!" Shouted Gigantic

Lordisha went on to explain "It was a crazy war... one of my worst ever! Those EOTS were fighters... serious fighters! They almost took us but eventually their attack collapsed cos' our numbers were too strong. It took a whole ten days but finally we had them captured and at the face of defeat. Then you know what that little coward done! He tricked his own soldiers and sent them right into our arms just so he could escape, then the punk deserted his army and fled! We executed his whole squad and went in pursuit of him but we never saw him again. The whole of Zurakaya was searched and he didn't surface... we assumed he left the planet"

"Well boy he's here now so I'm going for him!" Forcefully stated Gigantic

"Babes I'm coming... let's done him together" said Lordisha

Zeitan watched the whole conversation through Nefarious, Gigantic and Lordisha were oblivious to the danger they were actually in!

Lordisha's blood was rushing! She only had one thing on her mind... destroy Zeitan!

After what she had just seen happen to Nefarious's body, she decided not to allow the AI to accompany them. Lordisha and Gigantic suited up immediately and headed towards their warriors quarters commanding Nefarious to stay put.

Unfortunately, that ended up being some of Lordisha and Gigantic's last words!

Zeitan recognised the seriousness of the situation and decided he must act now!

Whilst their backs were to Nefarious, Zeitan discreetly switched him back to Master Zeitan mode and commanded him to execute both Gigantic and Lordisha!

Nefarious switched back to the cold hearted, red metallic exterior then his arms slowly transformed to blasters.

Gigantic and Lordisha felt a cold chill run through the hallway and feeling something was terribly wrong, they simultaneously turned to each other as they both sensed this would be the last time they were to set eyes on one another.

Staring deep into each others souls, Gigantic and Lordisha held hands and softly said "I'll Love you for eternity... see you on the other side"

Nefarious aimed his blasters at Gigantic and Lordisha as they both looked back just in time to see their assassin's menacing face, then without any hesitation the now ruthless Nefarious let shots rip!

The exact second the shots hit Gigantic and Lordisha, Equinile jumped out of his sleep sensing his parent's danger! He immediately suited up and called for his guards. Just as they were about to teleport to Gigantic and Lordisha's quarters, Equinile heard their feeble voices in his mind as they used their last breaths to send a message to their son "My beloved child, the future of Zurakaya and the Universe is now in your hands, protect and lead just how we've trained you and you will all be fine... you're build for this!"

Lordisha then gave one last deep gasp and passed over. Struggling to inhale breath Gigantic managed to pronounce three last words... "Go Get Em!"

"NOOOOOOOOOOOOOO!!!" Blustered out Equinile, as he fell to his knees and broke down unable to accept that this was his parent's last words. The Lords surrounded him and lifted him to his feet.

Then in a calm voice of disbelief he muttered "They've killed my parents!"

"WHO?" Said his guard

"I don't know yet but when I find out... everytings' DEAD!" Vowed Equinile.

Equinile and his guards finally arrived at his parent's quarters only to find them lifeless on the floor in a pool of blood surrounded by weeping Lords and Gigantians. Nefarious was no where to be found, Zeitan ordered the Zupreme to return to the labs in double-time!

Everyone gathered together in the Palace grounds baffled to how this had happened, they collectively tried to figure out who could've committed this crime of treason.

Filled with grief and sorrow, Equinile pushed through the crowd and threw his body onto his parent's corpses. As they peacefully laid side by side he huddled them together and hugged both parents with each arm.

Equinile eventually pulled himself together and stood tall, every Zurakayan fell to one knee as he said "I'm am the new leader of Zurakaya and I swear to protect The Source, Zurakaya and the Universe with every resource available to me, today is a sad day in our history but this will not destroy us! I swear on the souls of my parents that I will find out who assassinated our leaders and get revenge... NOW RISE!!!" Every last Zurakayan jumped up to their feet and cheered in agreeance, pledging their allegiance to their new leader – Equinile.

Equinile commanded his guards to take his parents to The Source and prepare them for Ascension. The Ascension Ceremony was the original way to deal with any Zurakayans that are of high esteem when they die. At an Ascension a dead person's consciousness, memories, mind and soul is digitalised by The Source and beamed into its core, the body then follows as it's absorbed by The Source's energy force. Once the process is complete it's said that the Zurakayan has now Ascended.

Moments before the ceremony, Equinile cleared the area so he could have one last moment alone with his ever so loved parents. As he said his goodbyes to his parents, he asked them to guide him and stand by his side from the beginning of his leadership until the day comes for him to join them in Ascension. Not knowing the full extent of his telepathic and farsighted abilities, what happened next was a major shock to Equinile. As he gently leaned to his mother and gave her one last kiss on the forehead, a vision shot into his mind... It was his parents last moments!

In a rapid flash of visions, Equinile saw everything that morning which led to his parent's death! Startled and confused he jumped back as his expression of love and affection changed to incredulity. Equinile couldn't believe it, he thought he was going crazy. Slightly intrigued and empowered, Equinile dubiously went over to his father's body and slowly kissed his forehead too and it happened again! Recognising this wasn't insanity and it was actually a vision, Equinile returned to the bodies and tried to focus on the visions in the hope of seeing exactly who killed his parents. He placed his hands on each parent's chest and sunk his fingertips into the soft luxurious material they were clothed in.

This vision was even more clear and powerful, he saw it all! Equinile now knew everything, his blood was boiling and the only thing that could cool it down was revenge on Zeitan!

Equinile stormed out fuming, he was ready to align his squad and go to war. However, as he paced outside, he saw the whole Planet was watching, using wisdom over brawn he decided that the most sensible thing to do was keep the information to himself for now as he didn't want to tarnish his parents Ascension Day with more bloodshed.

The whole planet stood still in awe, as they watched the beautiful moment when Lordisha and Gigantic peacefully ascended into The Source. This was the first ascension to ever take place, the ceremony was projected into the clear and majestic sky of Zurakaya for all to see from anywhere in the Planet. Rather than filling the streets with tears, the Zurakayans and their guests cheered and smiled with joy as The Source taught that Ascension ceremonies were a celebration of life, not a sad remembrance of death.

THE ZUPREME RISING!

On the dawn after Ascension, Equinile gathered five of his best Lords with the intention of travelling to Zeitan's lab and executing him!

But little did Equinile know, Zeitan was one step ahead of him!

Zeitan knew it was only a matter of time before the Lords and Gigantians figured out he was behind the murders and would come seeking revenge. So whilst the whole planet was focusing on the Ascension ceremony, he took drastic measures to make himself the most powerful being on Zurakaya, and becoming the universe's first ever Cybernetic Organism... a Cyborg.

These drastic measures was the final piece of his evil plan to overthrow Zurakaya and finally control or destroy The Source!

THE MORNING BEFORE

Nefarious came running back in from committing the brutal murder on the Gigantian grounds to find Zeitan swiftly connecting his latest invention, a central processing and data transfer system which merges the mind and soul of any natural being into the body of a Zupreme. The machine amalgamated the two whilst creating and implementing a new unique bandwidth for Zeitan's brain to perform on. This bandwidth allowed

Zeitan's brain to connect and communicate with the Zupreme's synthetic body and take control of all the super powers the Zupreme possessed... basically making both entities become one!

Zeitan instructed Nefarious to grab two connectors and attach one side of each to The Source's energy extract, then place the end of one to the supreme Zupreme's artificial jugular and the other directly into the back of Zeitan's brain! Nefarious followed his orders, then fired up the extracted energy from The Source to begin the transfer.

IT WORKED! After a few gruelling hours the transfer was complete, Zeitan was now the most powerful Zupreme in Zurakaya!

The new powerful Zeitan Supreme stood tall in all his glory, admiring his new form, he just stood and laughed as he looked at his former mortal body which had now reduced to dust.

"I dare them to come for me now!" Gloated Zeitan Supreme.

As a reward for the perfect annihilation of Gigantic and Lordisha, Zeitan Supreme granted Nefarious the position of Captain, second in command of the "Zupremes" that he was now ready to unleash on Planet Zurakaya and the rest of the Universe!

DAWN AFTER ASCENSION

Zeitan Supreme was in his lab testing out his new strength and abilities, when his systems suddenly alarmed, warning him of great danger coming his way!

After investigating, Zeitan saw the threat was coming from none other than Equinile himself. Zeitan watched through the eyes of a Zupreme, as Equinile and his five Lords loaded up and prepared for capture. Not grasping that every Zupreme was under Zeitan's control, Equinile ignorantly still believed that Zupremes could be trusted. He assumed Nefarious was simply corrupted or had a data bug placed in him by Zeitan... his naivety as a new leader immediately showed!

Again one step ahead of his opposition, Zeitan Supreme declared war by activating every last Zupreme and authorising the death of all Zurakayans!

A war for Zurakaya had begun and the Lords, Gigantians and civilians of Zurakaya had no idea. Zupremes from all over the planet ruthlessly slaughtered any Zurakayan they came in contact with, creating an instant genocide by wiping out a large number of Zurakayans! The Zupremes centralised and made their way to protect their master, Zeitan Supreme.

Equinile and his five men teleported on to Zeitan's grounds, only to be welcomed by a barrier of at least fifty blood thirsty Zupremes!

However, Equinile and his men were fearless! Totally unfazed by the Zupremes numbers they dived in and made light work of the frontline Zupremes, then they charged on through to Zeitan's lab.

Upon approach of the lab, Equinile looked back and saw hundreds, if not thousands of Zupremes racing towards them in defence of their leader!

Equinile was still wet behind his ears in regards to leading a war, rather than retreating and returning with the full force of his army, he decided to take his chances of a quick attack on Zeitan, assuming he would be able catch Zeitan slacking and put him to death before Zeitan's back-up caught up with them.

This was the wrong decision! As two of Equinile's men boomed off the laboratory door... they were greeted by a flurry of mighty blasts from both Zeitan and Nefarious, they were obliterated to ashes! In less than a split second Equinile's elite squad was reduced to almost half!

Time stood still for Equinile, the moment he set eyes on the new ominous, towering and intimidating figure of Zeitan, he froze up!

He now had a platoon of Zupremes rushing towards him and the scary Zeitan Supreme standing in front of them. Equinile and his remaining men finally understood they were in way over their heads. Knowing Zupreme's couldn't teleport, he immediately retreated, as Zeitan Supreme laughed at their meager attempt of capture "You're nothing to me... I'm a GOD!"

Equinile beamed back to his quarters and saw the carnage that was taking place all over his land. With out any further delay, he transmitted a declaration of war to all the remaining Lords, Gigantians and Zurakayans! A distress signal was also sent across the universe and received by allies all over, who also loaded up arms and sent some of their best fighters to defend Zurakaya and The Source! However, many of these warriors were located on the other side of the universe, with the quickest estimated arrival time being at least a day! Lords and

Gigantians couldn't wait this long, they didn't have the luxury of time... they had to begin retaliation now or risk being completely annihilated!

Equinile's main priority was to defend and protect The Source, then the Zurakayans and Planet Zurakaya itself!

He made his way to The Source with a squad of fierce and skilled men! The Zupremes were now flooding in from every direction like ants but this didn't bother the Lords and Gigantian warriors at all, if anything the Zupremes were more of an annoyance than a threat, as the Zurakayan warriors ferociously ripped through every last evil AI that crossed their path.

Eventually Equinile and his warriors arrived at The Source.

"Secure the perimeter" instructed Equinile, finally finding his feet as the leader of his army.

"Perimeter secured and locked down... nut'um' ain't getting in here now" replied a Lord, assuring his leaders safety.

Understanding the severity of the situation, Equinile humbly addressed The Source, begging for strategy and instruction from the elders within – his parents and The Source itself.

As Equinile dropped to both knees and prostrated to The Source, the room lit up and The Source spun at hypersonic speed, then shot out an enormous ray of light which then transfigured into visions of prophecy.

The Source began to communicate using the voice of Gigantic, Equinile couldn't believe what he was hearing but with no time get emotional, he focused himself and listened attentively as The Source spoke.

"The land is filled with the enemy and although to fight will be honourable, it will also be foolish... you are severely outnumbered by these disgusting machines and there is no way to win through direct combat but don't worry because this is nothing but prophecy for filling itself.

Your adversary Zeitan Supreme is the last surviving EOTS, he was the EOTS Chief Commander until the Lords and Gigantians eradicated them. Zeitan has managed to infiltrate the land of Zurakaya with the aim to overthrow the kingdom and control or destroy The Source! This is just the beginning of his evolution, the only chance of defeating him is by making the major sacrifice of Zurakaya itself!"

"What, no way we will all die!" Interrupted Equinile.

"Now is not a time for hastiness and rude childish interruptions... conduct yourself correctly when speaking with the all!" Responded The Source

Equinile instantly fell back in line, he dropped his head and apologised.

"You will not have to sacrifice Zurakayans, just the land... sometimes you have to lose a battle to win the war.

An evacuation plan has been put in place many years ago in preparation of this day coming.

Head over to the valleys and you will see large Mountains, in actuality these Mountains are just a smokescreen. When you arrive at the Mountains, place both hands on any section of the rock and your Gigantian

DNA will activate the transformation. The Mountain shield will decline to uncover the Gigantor Galax an advanced intergalactic vehicle that will transport you and thousands of Zurakayans to a planet called Earth.

Earth is a planet on the hidden solar system which I created" said The Source

Equinile was shocked to hear of this planet and new solar system, he stood there dumbstruck but still continued to listen attentively.

"I've purposely hidden this planet from the rest of the Universe in anticipation of this evacuation day coming." Said The Source then it went on to give clear instruction to Equinile.

"Zurakayans will inhabit Earth until eventually returning to Zurakaya once the land is replenished. Earth is a primitive land which has none of our advanced ways. Earth is currently inhabited by a race of beings I've created from the flesh and blood of Zurakayans called Humans, they are the current rulers of this land although they have been invaded by a pesticide called Dinosaurs, they're a violent creature but they have played their part in preserving the land for our arrival.

As soon as you land, you are to purify the Earth which will get rid of the Dinosaurs, then you will impose your Zurakayan authority on the Humans and become the leaders of Earth." Informed The Source.

"How will we purify this Earth place? Through combat?? Because our numbers are already low and once we leave here it'll probably be even less" said Equinile in response, fearing his armies current state may be too inadequate to perform an extermination mission so soon.

"The Gigantor Galax is equipped with a Land Purifier which will release appropriate defence mechanisms, to wipe out any threat to Zurakayan life on any surface" replied The Source.

Equinile gave a smile of relief

"The Land Purifier is built into the Gigantor Galax's underside with its trigger mechanism being located within the spacecraft" The Source continued.

"Before leaving Planet Zurakaya, unleash the Land Purifier and it will leave a viral data bug, that will run a fatal virus to disable the Zupremes. Then a radiation fireball will be dispatched, burning everything above the ground to ashes, leaving no trace of the Zupremes.

Zurakaya will then use these ashes as compost to replenish itself back to its former glory and in due time, come back as strong as ever... this is when the original people of Zurakaya will be able to return." Said The Source.

The Source, then went on to give further instructions on what to do when touching down on Earth.

"The second the Galax lands on Earth... pull the trigger! This will initiate the scanning process enabling the Land Purifier to identify the appropriate method of purification across the entire planet. The Land Purifier will then request your confirmation to perform the cleanse, at this point you will pull the trigger once again and wait for the contraption to let you know when the task has been successfully executed. On completion, all the Dinosaurs will be terminated, leading them and any other threat to Zurakayan and Human life to extinction. The land will stay habitable and you will reside in the centre of the planet in a place concealed from Humans and any other being called Paradise Mountains. You must divide the Zurakayans into different sets of tribes where you will all develop the Earth to its prophesied glory." Instructed The Source.

"And what about the Humans, are they gonna' be a problem or will they just fall in line?" Asked Equinile

"The Human race have many similarities to Zurakayans, from their appearance, their mother tongue and much more... they are literally made from you. However, the crucial difference is, although I've placed the superior ZuraGene in each one of them, the gene has been hidden deep within their DNA behind an encrypted code of algorithms, which can only be unlocked by The Source itself or once their kind has advanced to the level that's needed to correctly control and utilise such powers.

This has been done to avoid the immediate demise of their kind. During the Human race's infancy they'll only know greed and destruction! This will lead to nothing but war and conflict... this will divide them as a people and in return bring nothing but destruction to themselves! This will go on for many years until one day in the very far future, they will mature and finally realise their true path to becoming a successful race of beings, can only be obtained through love and unity, this is when they will be at the level of humanity needed to be able to unlock the DNA code and release the ZuraGenes and become ZuraHumans... a race fathered by the child of a future

Gigantian descendant named Jay Gigantic and his wife Tanya. The ZuraHumans will be the most powerful beings ever known to the Universe!" Stated The Source.

The Source was then interrupted by a BANG!

"The Zupremes has breached the perimeter we haven't got long before they are in!" Shouted the Lord Commander.

"You must condense me now and get me to the Gigantor Galax, I will power the systems and you will all escape" stated The Source sensing the urgency.

As Equinile and his army of Lords got into position for combat, The Source shouted one last set of instructions

"I must warn you, removing me from my natural place of existence here on Zurakaya will unstabilise my energy and temporarily weaken my strength! So once you've landed on Earth you are to find the most fertile piece of land in Paradise Mountains and place the Soul Disc there, then uncondense me and house me on the Soul Disc, I will eventually stabilise and return back to full power."

"THE SOURCE HAS SPOKEN! COMPACT IT TO RELOCATION SIZE AND TAKE IT TO THE GIGANTOR GALAX WITH EVERY SURVIVING CITIZEN... NOWWWWWW!" Commanded Equinile to his warriors.

Equinile transmitted a message to every Zurakayan, directing them to find safe passage and reconvene at the Valleys. Everyone else in the room anxiously looked around at each other until the Lord Commander came forward and said

"But Equinile, The Source can only be touched by Gigantian bloodline... yeah we can use the energy if permitted but if we touch the actual Source directly... we die! You're the only Gigantian left... only you can move The Source".

"This is true" replied The Source, then it went on to say "Equinile, remember your DNA is combined with my core... you can conduct the energy. Approach me with your bare hands and perform the compression, then give safe passage to the Gigantor Galax without the use of teleportation as the quantum physics will prove too risky in transporting my infinite energy"

Mildly trembling with fear, Equinile moved towards The Source. He was still a little unsure of his abilities and worried that The Source would demolish him if he touched it.

Sensing the fear in Equinile The Source yelled out "MAN UP, what you shook for... Gigantians and The Source are one... how can you be afraid of yourself? One day you will ascend and enter my mainframe!"

Slightly gaining in confidence, Equinile whispered under his breath "Yeah I ain't trying to make that day today though!"

As he drew nearer to The Source he asked "How do I do it, is there a button or something to press?

"Since an infant you've been taught... if you can see it you can be it and this situation is no different! Place your hands on The Source and whatever your soul visions will become my form for relocation" stated The Source.

31

As Equinile positioned himself in front of The Source he closed his eyes and stretched out his arms, he felt an overwhelming feeling of power as The Source omitted a phenomenal energy like no other into his anatomy, then all bared witness as The Source formed into the biggest Diamond ever!

It was truly was an amazing sight, everyone stood in awe of this astonishing Red Diamond with veins filled with highly charged waves of energy that ran through to its core, creating a cosmic multi coloured glow that shun with a magical balance of elegance and power.

BOOOOOOOMMMMMMMMM!!!!!!!!! As they all stood distracted by The Source, a Zupreme's blast narrowly flew past Equinile's face! This sprung the Lords back into action.

The close call made Equinile mad! He quickly attached The Diamond shaped Source on to his dangling necklace then somersaulted over his Army whilst dispersing plasma shots at the Zupremes before landing.

The Lords followed his lead and attacked the Zupremes.

"YOOOOO... GET TO THE VALLEYS BY ANY MEANS NECESSARY!" Commanded Equinile as all the citizens of Zurakaya battled on towards their target destination.

The Lords built a wall bodies around their leader and charged through the Zupremes using an array of fighting techniques and super powers! On their war filled journey to the Valleys they united with intergalactic allies and fellow warriors.

The Valleys were a fair distance away and without being able to use teleportation powers they were forced to

32

travel by the royal fleet of Aero Gigantors. Zupremes took flight in drone mode and the conflict took place in both land and air, it was gruesome! Bodies from both sides dropped like flies, the death toll was uncountable and a vast majority of Zurakayans were wiped out!

After hours of bloodshed and combat, Equinile and the Lords finally arrive at the Valleys to find Zeitan Supreme pulling up at the exact same time!

When he found himself close enough to make contact, Equinile launched a swift attack on Zeitan with a flurry of blasts followed by a combination of punches. Zeitan laughed as he simply brushed aside the attack... Equinile's nemesis was too strong!

Zeitan was done playing with Equinile, he grabbed Equinile by the scruff of his neck and delivered three devastating blows to his face... Equinile was down!

Recognising the fragility of The Source, the Lord Commander and a few of his men immediately jumped in to defend Equinile, they knew that one strike to Equinile's chest area could agitate The Source and create a catastrophic outcome for all!

As The Lords launched a relentless attack of both Zeitan and Nefarious, the Commander fell back and lifted Equinile off the ground, she then looked back at the remaining Zurakayans and shouted

"A drop of rain is nothing on its own, but when they form together..."

"...IT'S A STORM!!!" Replied all the Zurakayans, letting out a mighty synchronised roar, as every last one or them charged towards Zeitan and his Zupremes.

The Lord Commander told Equinile "Get to The Gigantor Galax, we'll handle this!"

After checking The Source was still intact Equinile spudded the Lord Commander then made his way to the Mountains making light work of any Zupreme that got in his way!

Equinile arrived at the Mountains and did exactly what he was instructed to do by The Source. The Mountain's structure crumbled and vanished into the air revealing the massive Gigantor Galax, it was an astonishing sight.

Equinile transmitted a message to the Lord Commander "I've located the Gigantor Galax... it's nuts still!" He couldn't wait to get in and navigate the stunning spacecraft through the Universe.

"Get everyone here now, it's time to go!" Said Equinile

"Arrrr it was just getting good, I'm sure we can done this punk and his little sen' outs in five minutes tops" responded the Lord Commander.

"It's not worth putting anyone else at risk, let's stick to the script... the Land Purifier will deal with them, don't worry" said Equinile as he boarded the Gigantor Galax.

The Gigantor Galax's interior was just as amazing as the exterior, it was literally a mini city with the necessary amenities to preserve the life of all passengers for a long period of time, and it even had a fleet of mini Gigantors. The technology was crazy, there was a range of machines that done everything you could imagine from regenerating fuel to generating food and drink just from a mental vision.

The Lord's left Zeitan and Nefarious for dead on the battlefield and made their way to the Gigantor Galax but the Zupreme's were persistent and continued swarming towards the Zurakayans.

Once arriving at the Gigantor Galax, one hundred Lords got in position to guard the entrance and fight off Zupremes as they loaded their people and animals onto the spacecraft.

Seeing how strong the oppositions numbers were, the Lord's second in command shouted "Get the children and women on first, we'll make sure everyone else is safe Commander"

"There's too many of them... you lot need to get on board!" Replied the Lord Commander

"I'mma be real, that was never gonna happen!" Replied the loyal second in command as he looked and saw thousands of Zupremes still coming towards them.

"These Zupremes ain't backing down, we're gonna have to stay and fight or they'll overthrow the spacecraft before we even get to launch!"

In the Commander's heart she knew the warriors were correct but it was still hard to accept.

"That's suicide!" Replied the Lord Commander

"Narrr... that's honour my G!" Said the Lord's second in command "One hundred lives to save a whole universe... sounds like a good deal to me".

Finally, the last Zurakayan was on the Gigantor Galax ready to migrate to Earth.

"LOCKDOWN THE ENTRANCE" Demanded the defending Lord's, they were losing the bout and Zupremes were seconds away from intercepting the Gigantor Galax and destroying the mission.

Two Zupremes managed to breakthrough the wall of guards! Just as they were about to set foot on the Gigantor Galax the Lord Commander spotted them and with a tear in her eye she flipped over and ruthlessly ripped the heads from both AI's bodies! She then battered the Zupremes down to cubes releasing all the pain she had inside from knowing she's about to lose her loved ones but there was no other realistic choice but to seal the entrance and ensure the safety of all, she took one last look at her brave and loyal warriors fighting with honour as they gave everything last thing they had... they were outnumbered but not out-hearted! Then with the heaviest heart the Lord Commander pulled the switch and locked down the spacecraft in preparation for take off.

Equinile kept The Source attached to the necklace under his armour and made his way to the cockpit, confused and bemused he frantically searched for an ignition switch to power up the Galax but his search was a waste of time! As he sat in the pilots seat to try and figure out where the ignition could be, The Source began to glow and the Gigantor Galax stated "Gigantian captain and Source detected". The Source's glow shot around the spacecraft and powered up its signals, the Gigantor Galax was ready to take off.

"Coordinates to Planet Earth locked in... self piloting activated, pilot to take position at the trigger of Land Purifier on the bottom deck" instructed the Galax.

Equinile followed the instructions and made his way to the bottom deck where he instantly noticed the Land Purifier trigger. He placed his hand on the mechanism's protective shell then a two handled blaster emerged from within the casing.

Equinile located the trigger and squeezed it, the mega purification shot came bursting out as they took flight.

Zeitan Supreme got back on to his feet and looked up just in time to see the purification discharging from the spacecraft... it was coming right at him!

Zeitan instantly managed to identify the threat and shouted to Nefarious "That's a viral bug, it'll destroy us all!"

"Follow me we need to get underground ASAP!" commanded Zeitan.

Nefarious and the remaining Zupremes obeyed their leader and sped towards refuge as the purification bug rushed towards them.

Zeitan and a number of Zupremes made it to his underground headquarters just in the nick of time!

He locked down the HQ and tried to log into the eyes of remaining Zupremes but he was unsuccessful, the purification had already began with the bug colonising in the motherboard of the Zupremes who never made it to safety. Zeitan quickly hacked in to surveillance systems all over the planet to get a full view of the situation, he couldn't believe his eyes as he witnessed the demise of his precious invention. The infected Zupremes were doomed, they ran around in circles like possessed dogs until finally collapsing and shutting down.

"WHAT THE... NO WAY! We're dropping like flies out there..... NOOOOOOO!" screamed Zeitan in disbelief as he ran around the room frantically pressing random buttons and switches in hope to stop this decimation.

Every Zupreme above Land was now dead, Zeitan's creation was mulled down to nothing more than the Zupremes, who managed to get underground with him. He determinedly battled for a solution. He put together numerous codings and algorithms, in the hope of overriding the fatal malware that the viral bug had placed in the Zupremes.

Just as he felt he was close to combating the virus "BOOOOOOOOOOOMMMMMMM".

The second stage of purification took place, this time in the form of a radiation blast that burnt everything above ground to ashes!

Zeitan tried everything to save the Zupremes above ground but the blast was the final blow... he was officially done! All he could do was watch the end as every last surveillance camera went down one by one, his last sight was a Planet full of ashes with not one sign of life.

As he was just about to except defeat, he noticed his Source extract glowing and becoming stronger, all the energy that was previously released into each Zupreme was being returned to the extract as they died, this regenerated the extract to a high level of energy.

'There must be a way I can manipulate The Sources power to build back this planet and my creation' thought Zeitan Supreme, as he picked himself up finding a whole new lease of life.

Not knowing if it was safe to go above ground, Zeitan stayed in his dungeon and worked all round the clock trying to find a way to use The Source to his benefit, this proved to be a hard task! He lost a number of his remaining Zupremes as he sacrificed them to make physical contact with The Source but he didn't care, he would just instruct the others to reproduce.

After months of failed attempts, Zeitan had a breakthrough! He decided it was best to change his approach, so rather than keep trying to access The Source, he thought it'll be better to make his Source extract activate itself by somehow communicating with the main Source.

Even though the extract grew stronger each day, The Source's mainframe was still unstable as it was recovering and embedding itself fully into Earth. This enabled Zeitan to create a programme that could enable his extract to hack into the main Source whilst it's security walls were still vulnerable. The outcome of this discovery was more fruitful than Zeitan could have ever hoped for, The Source was like the gift that kept giving. Zeitan wasn't able to get full access as The Source was still way too powerful for him. However, he was able to go through the majority of The Source's data like a file on a computer, he saw many things from the past and even a little from the future! This made Zeitan extremely dangerous as he was now armed with parts of the truth, whilst thinking he knew it all. Eventually Zeitan came across a section called Earth, this section was the most dangerous of all, it had the Earth's blueprints... literally how The Source created it! There was also the equivalent to a live stream of Earth which gave him access to how the planet develops each day, this meant he could now know nearly everything about the land where The Source and all the Zurakayans were located! Zeitan dug a little deeper and found out pieces of the prophecy plans for humanity. Armed with all this knowledge, he vowed to one day make his way to Earth and completely devastate his enemies but first he was well aware that he had to deal with his immediate problems at hand... building back Zurakaya and his army of Zupremes.

PLANET ZURAKAYA aka THE SUPREME EARTH!

Without realising he had the perfect solution right at his finger tips, Zeitan Supreme wrecked his brain in the hope of figuring out a way he could use all the information he ascertained regarding Earth.

Then one day Zeitan sent out a few Zupremes to do the routine checks on the habilitation levels of Zurakaya, the results were still negative. This made him even more angry and frustrated! Then as per usual, he took it out on Nefarious by aggressively blaming him for everything and throwing objects at him, before screaming like a spoilt five year old who couldn't get their own way.

"You lot are useless! I should've left you lot as scrap and went to Earth too!" Shouted Zeitan insulting his Zupremes.

Then whilst in that moment Zeitan stopped in his tracks and had a lightbulb moment

"That's it, Earth... Earth is our survival".

Remembering he had the full blueprint to Earth, he felt he must be able to use his Source extract to some how replicate Earth right there on Zurakaya. It was a tall order but he was completely out of any other reasonable and realistic ideas.

Zeitan ran over to his system and went straight to work and after a number amount of sleepless nights... Zeitan Miraculously did it!

Somehow, he managed to manipulate the data files he had on Earth, this allowed him to connect to the main Source and gain access from literally light years away. This enabled Zeitan to create a direct stream feed from the main Source on Planet Earth to his extract on Planet Zurakaya. Zeitan took this feed and manifested it into a real time simulation of the Earth, then he shot it out to Planet Zurakaya... it sounds complicated I know but basically Zurakaya was now a direct replication of Earth!

Zeitan jumped around like a mad man, he made Zurakaya habitable again. The Gigantians plan to destroy them had failed and Zeitan now felt stronger than ever with an arrogance that could not be defeated!

"MAAADDDDD!!! I DID IT! This place ain't called Planet Zurakaya no more... from now on it's called SUPREME EARTH" enforced Zeitan. Zeitan was so proud of his achievement, he felt he deserved to have the planet named after him.

"We're gonna take this planet to a next level, I'm gonna learn every last piece of this land then take that knowledge and slaughter The Source and anyone on Earth brave enough to protect and as for them Zurakayans...

Gigantians... Lords or anything else they call themselves...
I'm gonna murder every last one of them... WATCH!"
Vowed Zeitan.

Zeitan felt unstoppable but little did he know he was
missing the most important piece of Earth... The Paradise
Mountains!

Paradise Mountains was hidden in the core of Earth
and where the Zurakayans migrated to and housed The
Source. Paradise Mountains was now the most powerful
place in the universe, the designated place where The
Source chose the Gigantians to lead mankind and build
Earth.

The Source felt Zeitan's hack to the system when he
first accessed the files, and although it was still to
unstable and weak to completely nullify the attack, The
Source's firewall was able to gather enough power to
respond with a virus that it placed in Zeitan's Source
extract, the virus's sole purpose was to eradicate Paradise
Mountains from Zeitan's Source extracts data. This meant
Zeitan was only able to clone the land, ocean and its
technology within but not the people and even more
importantly... not Paradise Mountains.

Unfortunately, this caused The Source to become
even more unstable than it had ever been but the silver
lining was that this also allowed the new citizens of Earth
to be in a powerful position because The Source being
reconnected with the extract gave a reverse effect too.
Paradise Mountains was now also able to have eyes on the
Supreme Earth and all Zeitan's goings on.

Unknowingly to Zeitan, he opened up portals between the two planets which at this point neither party knew existed, these portals allowed travel between the two worlds in a matter of seconds but they were risky if not navigated correctly!

Zeitan's arrogance made him naive, he was so impressed at what he managed to achieve that he didn't realise that he had strengthened his enemy!

Over the years to come Zeitan grew stronger and stronger. The powerful Cyborg discovered the portals and learned how to use them at will, using his EOTS technology!

He made many attempts to overthrow Earth and with each attempt he got closer and closer to succeeding but was never successful as The Source was always able to identify these attacks and purify the land just in time to foil Zeitan's plans.

However, every time the Land was purified, every where on Earth except Paradise Mountains was reset! The Source would always instruct the Zurakayans to leave signs behind to help the next generation of humans continue building the race.

The Gigantians protected their anonymity by disguising these events in history as end of ages such as the Ice age... Stone Age... and many more. Humans even labelled the first arrival of Zurakayans as something they called the Big Bang and continued to give false explanations of many historical events and eras, all the way up to the times of the so called Ancient Egyptians which was the era of the last attack attempt from Zeitan

Supreme. After purification pyramids, artefacts and even hieroglyphs were left behind to give guidance for humanities future development.

After his latest pursuit of war, Zeitan was severely hurt! His only option was to retreat back to the Supreme Earth and rebuild everything... his army, his powers, his strength and even his planet!

Zeitan has grown wiser, so this time rather than rushing, he showed patience and promised the comeback was going to be much greater than his knock-back. He took his time to create his strategy and after seeing his error in committing to so many rushed attempts, he identified the best times to invade and conquer Earth.

Zeitan meticulously planned every last piece of his battle strategy. He opened portals and sent infiltrators to live on Earth amongst humans for hundreds of years before he planned to set upon his enemy.

Zeitan Supreme took time to intricately study his Source extract and gather as much knowledge of the prophecy as possible, he then used this information to discover ways to manipulate the prophecy in attempts to change its path.

Zeitan eventually recuperated all his power and felt in the best shape ever but the time still wasn't right, so he demonstrated even more patience and wisdom as he decided that the next time he strikes, he will strike hardest!

Zeitan unearthed files on the Chosen Ones who would arrive in the future, he studied their abilities, their strengths and also their weaknesses, Zeitan knew they would be the biggest threat ever to him overthrowing Earth and destroying The Source! Zeitan decided he had to nip them in the bud and get them whilst they are teens because waiting until they were adults may be a fatal mistake as their full powers and abilities would be matched with wisdom.

Zeitan learnt that these Chosen Ones would have a unique connection to The Source and The Source will distribute energy directly to each Chosen One through what they would call SG Gems, Zeitan also found out about the other Source energy conductors which were effectively weaker gems, that'll be placed around the Earth. Zeitan figured out that his Source extract provided him with enough power to manipulate and communicate through these weaker gems. Zeitan also knew that if he could get in possession of these weaker gems, he could connect them to his Source extract and gain even more power!

After many years of studying his enemy, Zeitan had finally found himself in a position to launch his attack and take on The Source and its new chosen protectors... Squad Gigantic!

Chapter 1 – It's Mad Out Here!

Present day – Planet Earth... London

"Yoooo! Just one more day then no school for six weeks likkle' man" said Kyron aka Younger Burst as he ran over and jokingly placed his arm on Chunksta's shoulder, Kyron was excited to break up for summer holidays.

"Bout' likkle' man, your dad's a likkle' man" Replied Chunksta

"He probably is hahaha, it ain't like I know him" said Kyron whilst he put Chunksta in a little head lock.

Chunksta shrugged him off and asked "Why you always so gassed fam?"

"Urrr why you always so serious G... smile or sutum' you're not that butters hahaha, nar but for real tho' schools done tomorrow fam, then it's holidays bro... that means no waking up early, no more detentions and no teachers wassin' all the time and most importantly... nuff links bro" said Kyron whilst laughing his head off.

"All you ever think about is chicks G'" said Chunksta

"That's a lie... I think of food and P's too hahaha" responded Kyron

Chunksta broke out a little smile.

"Anyway have you counted that change yet? It must be a bag at least, we sold out everyday this term" said Kyron

"Be easy bro, I'll count the P's later and drop you your ting tomorrow" said Chunksta

Chunksta finally settled into school and was starting to enjoy living in London, he now had a little crew it only consisted of a few close friends and out of all of them Kyron was his closest companion.

Kyron and Chunksta were hustlers, they never sold anything illegal but they still made good money. They moved every and anything that was on trend from sweets to clothes, if you wanted it... for the right price you got it.

Chunksta made a rule that they were to wait until the end of each term to distribute the profits and then they stack a third, reinvest a third and then splash a third! Kyron was impatient and had no discipline, he always wanted his cash weekly so he could stunt and waste it on things that'll make him look rich but Chunksta wasn't having none of it and he never give in, Kyron had to follow the rules and wait.

This would wind Kyron up at times but deep down he knew it was for the best, plus he was always able to make more money this way then do something big with his cash when it was time to split the profits.

"It's about being rich not just looking rich" is something Jay Gigantic always drilled into Chunksta's mind and Chunksta made sure he passed this valuable advice on to his friends.

Kyron was a real character, he was cheeky and charming with a fun loving personality that drew people around him. His life wasn't straight forward and even though went through a lot of things at home he still loved life and lived it to the fullest. Kyron was a bit of a thrill seeker which meant he was always getting up to some sort of madness! If he weren't getting in trouble at school, he'll be getting caught up in fights or some sort of beef in the ends.

Kyron was born into the road life, his family is well known by the roads and the Police! Kyron constantly heard stories about family members and eventually began to enjoy the hype that his surname carried, his older brother was a main member in Da Grabberz! Yep, Da Grabberz were back!

In fact there was a number of gangs now! Bang was no where to be found but his name was still running strong. Bang's disappearance was a bitter sweet situation, on one hand it was great to be rid of him but on the other hand this left the gang world in disarray. With no real underworld structure gangs started popping up from everywhere making the crime rate go crazy! The London City Police (LCP) couldn't handle it and half of their officers were corrupt with their dirty mitts deep in London's criminal activity.

There's also many little silly wannabe gangs running around trying to make some sort of name for themselves, but the real active ones were:

Bangz Army – currently led by a few of Bang's loyal soldiers that stayed behind.

Spade Gang – led by Dealer with Elisha by his side.

Rock Ard Thugs aka RATs – led by Thug Rock and his Rock Ard Security firm.

Unknown Hittaz – who was anonymously led! Their leader was basically a hood myth.

Da Grabberz – led by Young Rowdy and Lil' Swarvez, although they have a legendary name they're actually a relatively young gang but that recklessness added to their rep and has them making major waves in the under world.

The only real resistance was Squad Gigantic!

Da Grabberz were re-formed by Young Rowdy and Lil' Swarvez, the sons of Rowdy Renzo and Swarvez! They both linked up and vowed revenge on Bang and his army for the death of their fathers. Young Rowdy and Lil' Swarvez had a lot of ratings for Kyron's big brother Burst, as he was a good money earner for them.

One thing Burst knew how to do was hustle! He always had the flyest clothes and the latest cars with the sweetest girl from ends in the passenger seat... everyone loved him. Kyron didn't only want to be like his big brother, he wanted to be ten times bigger and badder! From a young age Kyron had always asked to go on missions, but Burst would always laugh and say "One day bro" then go into his pocket and give him some cash to go spend with his friends. Most of Kyron's friends thought Burst was the coolest thing ever and would always hype up his name to Kyron. The only friend who wasn't impressed was Chunksta, Chunksta would always turn down anything Kyron tried to buy him with his brother's money, then they'll both have a long deep conversation with Chunksta hoping he could get through to Kyron and make him see why he should walk the straight path in life.

Kyron knew that everything Chunksta told him was true but he lived a different life from Chunksta, Kyron's household didn't have money like that, he grew up in a council flat on ends and saw his mother struggle daily in order for them to survive. Kyron's mother was a proud woman, she refused to accept cash from Burst, as she didn't agree with his gang banging. Burst and his mum would always get into arguments over his choices and after being constantly raided by the LCP, Burst's mum eventually got fed up and told him he could no longer live with them in the family home, so after the last time Burst was released from prison, he had to go into a hostel and live independently.

Kyron's Mum worked every hour she could just to pay bills, often the fridge was empty and they were threatened with eviction and as for Kyron's dad... he was a waste that left when Kyron was a baby, it was literally just Kyron and his mum in the house trying to get by.

Chunksta always told Kyron that he's like a brother to him and one day he'll get investment from Jay Gigantic then they will start their own record label and be rich. Although Kyron loved the dream, to him it was just that... a dream and right now the only real money he saw was from his brother's life of crime, so in his mind the only way to make life better for him and his mum was by taking a position in Da Grabberz as soon as he could.

This always upset Chunksta as he knew one day he may have to go against his best friend.

Chunksta and Kyron walked out of school and decided to go grab some food.

"I'm hungry G" complained Kyron

"Me too, come we go StackTown and get sut'um" replied Chunksta

"Boyyyy, I would mash up some wings and chips but that's a mazza' still" said Kyron looking rather worried

"Why?" Asked Chunksta

"We gotta' go through them Bang youts' block to get there... that's slippin' G" said Kyron

Kyron's links to Da Grabberz meant that he wasn't safe going through any area where Bangz Army controlled.

"That's your brother's argument tho', mans just going to get chicken G! But since them man got you that shook... we can go the long way" Chunksta replied mockingly

"About shook, you really think that?" Said Kyron

"Yep" bluntly responded Chunksta.

"Never that likkle' Jerome but big and serious broski, them man don't care who's argument it is! Plus my brothers argument is my argument anyway... them man bodied Swarvez and Rowdy Renzo, they can't get away with that... you nuts! Watch, imma' ride on every one of them pagans" replied a now hyped up Kyron.

"Bro you know how dumb you sound right now, them man we're like my Dad's age or older! You didn't even know them... how you gonna put your life on the line for man you never even met?" Asked Chunksta, he had enough of hearing about people from his area wasting their lives defending the name of people that they never even knew... it made no sense to Chunksta.

"Urggghh I knew Swarvez, once when I was mad young I was on ends about to link like four chicks at the same time and he drove past me and stopped to let me cross... must've been cos he recognise a real brudda', then I looked at him and said respect big man and he nodded back... he could see I was on stuff from early!" said Kyron lying through his teeth, trying his hardest to convince his friend of his acquaintance with Swarvez.

Chunksta erupted with laughter "Are you serious fam, on a level... are you ok? Even if that was true, you really think that means you know him, furthermore you really think that's enough of a reason to ride for him and mess up your life? Man are really out here putting themselves on the line for some old dead beef that had nothing to do with them... are you not seeing how stupid that is?!"

Kyron realised how silly he sounded and started to laugh too, "For real that's silly, come man just go StackTown and beat some wings".

Kyron's hype behaviour slowly disappeared as they got closer to the Bangz Army territory, now he was on edge becoming extremely vigilant as they neared their favourite food spot. Finally, they got to the area where Bangz Army hang out and as expected, a bunch of Bangz Army were chilling on their block.

"Yoo ain't that Burst little brother?" Asked Splash, he was the first person to notice Kyron and Chunksta.

His older replied "Yeah I swear that's him, has he lost his mind? What's he doing round ere'?"

"I'm gonna back my Rambo and find out G... he's slipping!" Said Splash, as he approached Chunksta and Kyron.

Splash was one of Bangz Army main gang members, he was quite young compared to the others but he had a large menacing figure with a mean face! There was no Young Offenders Institution (YOI) he hadn't been held in! He was constantly in and out of Secure Units and then YOI's once he got older. Splash was active from young and always ready to put in work for his gang's namesake, he was wild and didn't fear anything... not the opposition, the Police... nobody! The only person he listened to was his older, Big Splash.

Splash charged at Kyron whilst searching his waistline for his knife "Oi! Little Burst what you doing round here!" Blurted out Splash.

Not fully respecting the danger, Kyron cheekily replied "Come to link your gyal' fam... WHAT!"

Chunksta immediately jumped in front of Kyron and told him to stop talking, then Chunksta said to Splash "Calm down bro, we just going shop what's wrong with you!?"

Splash was enraged by Kyron's response, he ignored Chunksta and focussed on Kyron then

"SHUT YOUR MOUTH RUDE BOY, don't make me back my ting on you and splash you!" Said Splash

The threat made Chunksta begin to see red too!

"BACK IT THEN, you think I'm shook?! Back your Kitchen and do your ting! Watch what happens!" Yelled Chunksta

Splash pulled out his knife and moved closer to Chunksta, Chunksta showed no fear and drew in closer to Splash at the same time. Things were tense! Then just as Splash was about to make the biggest mistake of his life and lunge towards Chunksta, Big Splash grabbed him and said

"What you doing, relax bro! That's Jerome, Raheem's little brother... no one ain't doing him nut'um... put that away and calm yourself down... sometimes you're too tapped fam."

On the command of his Older, Splash dressed back and put his blade away, "You're a lucky guy Jerome but you... Younger Burst... no one ain't saving you bro, you better dus' before I start splashing!"

Kyron was scared but being aware of his brothers reputation he was confident enough to say "Splash who bro, you know what my bro would do to you!?"

Both Splash and Big Splash started laughing, Big Splash eventually broke the laughter and said

"Your bro can't do nothing, man don't rate him round 'ere! Go ask him about me 'Big Splash'... furthermore tell your eediot' brother I'm looking for him!"

Then Splash interrupted and said "Fam forget that, give your brother this!"

Then Splash punched Kyron in his face making him fall to the floor with a bloody nose.

Chunksta immediately retaliated and punched Splash in his jaw side, knocking him out cold!

Big Splash said "Alright that's one all, Imma let that slide but you man better go before he wakes up cos I don't care who your brother is Jerome, after that violation I'm not stopping him again... if he backs his Rambo and starts chingin' that's your business!"

Knowing he just got one up on Splash, Chunksta decided to quit whilst they were ahead and leave. Kyron finally got back to his feet but instead of just doing the smart thing and walking away like Chunksta, he just had to get the last word. As he hot stepped to keep up with Chunksta he shouted

"You man ain't bout' nothing! Watch when man come back with my olders, mans gonna light up your dead block!"

Big Splash just laughed and began to wake up Splash.

Chunksta was angry with himself for getting involved but it was a natural reaction to defend his friend, the punch was literally a reflex. As he walked on he started cussing Kyron

"Why you always on a hype fam, Big Splash squashed it there and then... he gave man a pass but you had to say sut'um ennit! You couldn't just take a quick bad up from a older and keep moving? Now you've made mans face all bait... now I'm in beef with that dummy Splash".

Kyron didn't care, to be honest he wasn't even paying attention to Chunksta's rant. Even with a handful of tissue wiping his bloody nose, Kyron was still gassed!

"You just knocked him out fam! Bang youts' got Banged hahahahahaha one bang knock out you know, he ain't gonna' do nothing, it's done... why you upset? You should be gassed right now, man know you're the strongest on ends now hahaha, watch when everyone finds out... all the older Grabberz are gonna put me on now... Oiiiii let me say I did it"

Chunksta looked at him in disgust and said "You're some clout chaser" he couldn't believe what had just came out of Kyron's mouth.

Kyron was just interested in the reputation they will now have after winning a fight against a main member of the opposition. However, Chunksta saw things from a totally different angle, he knew there will be nothing but trouble ahead! He was angry and disappointed for the rest of the journey. Kyron and Chunksta went to a different shop and ordered their food, then got it and strolled home whilst eating their chicken and chips. Kyron carried on hyping about the fight but Chunksta ignored him and zoned out thinking about all the possible outcomes from this unnecessary altercation, he thought about how his father was going to react and also how Splash was going to seek his revenge! Chunksta wasn't scared or worried for himself, his been in much bigger fights than this before. In fact, the only real fear in his mind was what would happen to Kyron. Kyron ignorantly thought this was the end of it but Chunksta knew better, before Chunksta could even gather his thoughts together he saw Kyron with his phone in hand jumping around and shouting like an idiot for the benefit of social media.

"Yoooo my Grabberz dem, imagine man just cut through Op's block and put in on that yout' Splash... man left him sleeping hahahahaha, lucky I never had my flicky on me or they would've all got wrap up! It wouldn't have been injuries it would've been bodies! Man had them on toes, had to stick it on his older Big Splash too, he was shook! He weren't ready... he knows how my tings' set... them Bang youts' are irrelevant... they know what it is when Grabberz come round!"

Just as Kyron clicked the post button, Chunksta ran over and grabbed the phone out of his hand telling him "Turn that off fam, why you so tapped... you're a fool you know! You trying to get arrested or you just clout chasing again? Fammm, the worst thing is you didn't even do nothing! Why you ain't showing them how you got banged and sat on the floor like a little girl through the whole ting'"

However, it was too late, the post had already been sent out for everyone from the ends to see.

"Relax G, now everyone knows were on stuff d'you how lit this summer is gonna be now? Dem man are gonna put me on, so that's not only P's but chicks are gonna be on to me too fam" replied Kyron

"Is that what you think yeah?" said Chunksta

"Yep nothing but Gyallie' and Moneyyyyyy" said Kyron in a silly voice.

Kyron didn't comprehend the seriousness of the situation like Chunksta did.

Just as Chunksta was about to go in on him and make him delete the post, his phone started pinging.

"See G that's chicks, stop moving like a poop fam" said Kyron with the biggest smile, as he looked at his notifications.

Kyron wasn't wrong, his phone was going crazy with the majority of people sending him DM's being girls from the area who never paid him any real attention before but now hype surrounded his name, all of a sudden he was important. Still blind to the possible implications of the situation Kyron gloated to Chunksta feeling like a king.

As Kyron started to reply to the mass of DM's his phone rang, it was his big brother Burst!

"Yo what happen with the Op's, everyone dingin' off my line... you good?" Said a concerned Burst

"Man's coooool bro, them man ain't on nothing... they try run up their mouth and back a Rambo on me and Jerome"

"WHATTTT!!!" Shouted Burst down the phone.

"Yeah it's nothing tho' that Big Splash brudda' was shook, so he try call truce but his younger sucker punched me when I weren't looking... so I went mad and knocked him out then Big Splash was on ten toes running like Bolt fam!" As Kyron continued to lie and exaggerate his story, his brother interrupted and said "Hold on I got a private number calling my other line"

Kyron looked over a Chunksta as he held the line, Chunksta gave him the dirtiest look in reaction to the blatant lies, he just heard spill out of his mouth.

Kyron laughed and mimed out 'what?' As he eavesdropped on his brothers call.

The private number calling was Big Splash!

Kyron could hear an argument was taking place but could only hear his brother's responses.

"You man really think you can call me saying you're gonna' body my little brother and get away with it... you know what it is now! Come off my phone... I soon see all you pagans!" Said Burst

Kyron's post on social media made the disrespect too much for Big Splash to let it slide, his attempt to embarrass the opposition meant they had to react or people wouldn't take them seriously. Finally realising it wasn't a laughing matter, Kyron's body warmed up as it filled with fear.

After a heated discussion filled with threats and promises, Kyron's brother came back on the phone to him.

"Where are you?!" Said Burst

"Near top shops walking home from StackTo..." but before Kyron could finish his sentence his brother shouted, "I'M COMING NOW!" and hanged up the phone.

Chunksta read exactly what was going on and said "See... what I tell you bout' doing tings' for the gram! Now look it's all out war fam"

A much more humbled Kyron kept his mouth closed this time and rather than reply with his usual smart responses he just agreed with Chunksta, Kyron was scared witless! He finally realised he wasn't built for what was about to take place but before he could make sense of the situation his brother's car pulled up with the tyres screeching... Skkkkkrrrrrrrr!

"YOU MAN GET IN" commanded Burst, as his friend got out of the passenger side and pulled forward his chair to let the two youngsters into Burst's flashy three door coupe.

Kyron done as he was told but Chunksta peeped through the passenger door and saw the back seat was full of knives and balaclavas! He knew exactly what was about to take place.

"Narr I'm cool fam" said Chunksta and started to walk the other way.

Kyron called out to Chunksta "Jerome", Chunksta looked Kyron directly in his eyes and saw a terrified child. Kyron muttered out "Please Come Jerome"

Chunksta ignored Kyron's plea, shook his head and went on his way.

"He's shook, he ain't ready to do road... leave him and just get in the car Ky" instructed Burst whilst screwing up his face and looking at Chunksta.

Really it was Kyron who wasn't ready to do road, he wanted Chunksta to roll with him to give him the comfort and confidence he desperately needed. Things had escalated way too much for Kyron to handle but now he found himself in the back of a car behind tints pulling a balaclava over his face whilst picking up a knife, Kyron didn't want no part of it but he wasn't courageous enough to tell his brother he was in too deep!

Burst sped off and whilst driving erratically he shouted out every last thing he aimed to do to Big Splash and his crew whilst his friend just laughed his head off loving every moment of it. Kyron couldn't even hear his brother's rant as his fear put him in a trance, with his head all over the place he kept repeating in his mind "why did I send that snap... I'm so dum'!" He wanted to tell his brother to stop the car and turn around, but he couldn't get the words out.

Kyron's phone rang... it was Chunksta, unable to find the words he left the phone to ring out.

Then as Kyron went to put his phone down *DING DING* he received a notification from a girl that lives on the Bang block, when he saw her name pop up he knew it wasn't going to be good news or anything helpful. Kyron sat in the back of the sports car and just stared at the notification box on his phone, his brother looked at him through the rear-view mirror and could tell something weren't right

"Is that them messaging you?" Asked Burst "Unlock your phone and pass it" he demanded.

Kyron did as he was told and handed the phone over. Burst opened the notification to see Big Splash being secretly filmed sending a barrage of orders to his crew instructing them to attack Burst, Kyron and every other Grabber on site!

Big Splash was so mad that he could hardly get his sentences out! He couldn't believe that after giving Kyron a pass, Kyron would put out a video lying trying to chase clout of his name, there was no way he was going to let this blatant disrespect pass!

The video got Burst going!

"Are these guys mad, they think they can on sight me? Looks at the little amateurs he's with too... them youts' ain't done no drillings!"

Burst and his friend gave each other a look then looked back at the phone

"Oi, you see where they are right" said Burst's friend whilst pointing at the park in the background of the video.

"Oh yeah, how long ago she post that?" said Burst recognising the area as the park in the middle of what everyone called the Bang block estate.

"Not even three minutes ago bro... they must still be there" replied his friend

"Hear what you do, call them man and tell them to load up and link us there in five minutes tops!" Said Burst, he figure the best form of defence was attack and now he had the drop on the enemy's exact location!

"Say no more G" said Burst's friend with a face full of excitement.

Burst done the maddest U-turn right there in the middle of the main road and headed over to the Bang block whilst masking up and checking his weapon was loaded.

Kyron's heart dropped as he knew there was no turning back now. They finally reached the outskirts of Bang block. They parked off their cars as other Grabberz pulled up ready to ride!

Not sensing the fear in his little brother's heart, Burst put his arm around Kyron's shoulder and said

"You been wanting this for a while G, here's your moment to shine!"

Kyron put on a fake smile to impress his brother, even though he was really trembling with fear. As Kyron gripped a blade that was placed in his hand, the words from a conversation he had with Chunksta weeks back rang through his head

"Be careful what you wish for... cos' one day you might get it!"

Kyron never took heed to these words until this moment, now that he was really being initiated into the gang, he finally realised that this life wasn't for him but unfortunately it was too late.

Kyron finally plucked up the courage to tell his brother he wanted no part of this but as he walked over to his big brother, Splash and a few of other guys from Bangz Army came round the corner and saw the sea of Grabberz coming towards them.

One of the Grabberz saw them and shouted, "THERE THEY ARE!!!"

With not one ounce of hesitation, Burst and his crew sprinted towards Splash and his friends with serious intent, barging the inexperienced Kyron out of the way.

"BURSSTTT!" Shouted Kyron in attempt to get his brothers attention

"What you talking for? Come and ride" replied Burst instantly shutting down his scared little brother.

Thinking his crew's numbers were much stronger than Splash's, Kyron grew a false sense of security and quickly convinced himself to get involved in what seemed to be a fight they couldn't lose.

Noticing they were severely outnumbered, Splash and his friends retreated back towards the park to rejoin the rest of their gang and make the numbers more even.

Da Grabberz gave chase and managed to catch the majority of the fleeing opposition except Splash. As Da Grabberz laid into the Bangz Army members they caught, Splash managed to escape and get to Big Splash and the rest of his gang just in time!

Splash was out of breath, so he stopped for a second to get himself together as Bangz Army led by Big Splash ran towards the Grabberz all tooled up and ready to clash!

Bangz Army started coming from everywhere! Shouting "WOI WOI WOI WOI!" Some came from the park, some came from the shops and some literally came running out of their flats after hearing the commotion! Burst bringing the war directly to the Bang block wasn't smart at all, Da Grabberz came to ride and ended up being the ones who were getting rid on! The tables were now turned, Da Grabberz were outnumbered and out gunned!

Kyron looked ahead and saw all the opposition gang members running towards them and literally wet himself! The scared little Kyron was back, he came crashing back to he senses with just one look at the large intimidating figure of Big Splash and his crew coming directly at them.

Kyron stood there, masked up with weapon in hand looking like a seasoned villain ready to totally annihilate anything that comes his way! However, in all reality under that mask was the face of a lost and confused little boy, who was as terrified as a sheep caught in the middle of a pack of wolves!

The beef was truly on and with no Police or even one respectable adult figure in sight, a simple disagreement that could've been easily solved and diffused was now set to be blood bath!

Chapter 2 – Everybody Is Real... Until They Are Tested!

Chunksta made his way home after leaving Kyron with his big brother Burst. Whilst walking he felt a funny feeling grow inside of him, something wasn't right, and this made the rest of his day feel strange!

Chunksta felt unrested and on edge as if there was a dark cloud over him. He tried to call Kyron to see how he was after leaving him with his brother but the phone just rang out.

Chunksta got home and decided to get some tension of his chest the best way he knew how, he spent the whole afternoon and evening writing lyrics then recording them in the studio Gigantic built for him within their grounds.

Chunksta took some time to reflect on the altercation between him, Kyron, Splash and Big Splash. He knew knocking out Splash wasn't the right thing to do, he also knew things could've been resolved differently but his reactions and temper got the better of him.

Not going with the olders to ride on Bangz Army also left him conflicted, as no one hates Bang and anything to do with his so-called army more than Chunksta! But deep down inside, Chunksta was smart enough to know this battle was just a silly little road argument based on no foundation, he knew getting in the car would've been the wrong thing to do, but not going still played on his mind.

Just like any other teenager in the world... Chunksta began to second guess himself.

Obviously Chunksta made the correct and sensible decision by rejecting Burst's orders to ride but somewhere in his mind he kept tricking himself in to feeling that not only did he 'punk' out but he also left his best friend behind in his hour of need.

He went through a whole load of different emotions just trying to gain a full understanding of the situation.

Every time Chunksta went through a moment where he felt his pride was tested, or people would think that he was too scared ride against Bangz Army, he would jump up and erupt with an outburst of words.

"They really think I'm that guy.... I'm Chunksta you know! They must really think I'm just likkle' Jerome, I been riding on Bangz Army for how long now?! And not this little joke version of the army... the real deal, when they were really Bangz Army not these little wannabes trying to live off the name!"

His mind was spinning at one hundred miles per hour and that never has a good outcome. Thinking people would be laughing at him or label him a shook one, paranoia started to kick in but then he began to think

'If Kyron was really my homie, why would he wanna put me in a madness like that and why would he want me to go ride on his so-called Op's when he was shook himself?'

Chunksta now started to blame Kyron for the whole thing, deep down he didn't believe it was totally Kyron's fault, but passing over the blame made the weird feeling of guilt he was experiencing in the pits of his stomach feel a little better.

The conflicting thoughts continued to go back and fourth in his head for the whole evening, the whole family could see he was distant so they gave him his space knowing he would speak on the problem when he was ready.

It was getting late and Chunksta felt emotionally drained, he realised he wasn't able to record anything properly as his mind kept drifting away so he shut down the studio and went to grab a his left over chicken wings from the microwave.

As Chunksta locked the studio door he went in his pocket and grabbed his phone. Chunksta was surprised to see a barrage of missed calls, text messages and social media notifications. Confused to how he missed all these notifications, he realised his phone had been on silent all evening.

Chunksta felt a change in the air, his senses told him something weren't right, but he still showed no real urgency as he ignored his phone thinking it was just a backlash of hype from the video Kyron posted earlier. He slowly unlocked his phone with one hand as he used the other to take his half eaten box of wings out of the microwave, Chunksta eased on to a kitchen stool biting into his chicken wing as he decided which app to open first.

He glanced over his missed calls and noticed they were mainly calls from an unknown number and other numbers he didn't recognise. Suddenly his stomach began to knot even more than before, he took a sip on some Big J's Fruit Punch then opened his social media.

The first thing Chunksta saw was a photo of Kyron with the status quoting "Rest In Eternal Peace Kyron, the ends won't be the same without you!" Followed by heart and angel emojis.

Chunksta jumped up in shock making his glass drop and shatter all over the tiled floor!

His eyes started to fill with tears as he continued to scroll down his feed hoping it wasn't real but all he saw was more and more tributes to Kyron... and also Splash!

Chunksta was totally baffled now, but seeing R.I.P messages for both Kyron and Splash, gave him a slim glimmer of hope that it could all be a rumour.

'What's the odds of both of them dying, that's not realistic... it's gotta' be a mistake or a stupid prank or something, they probably just throwing shits at each other, doughnuts' thought Chunksta. He even selfishly hoped that his friends death had been mistaken for Splash's death, but his heart came crushing down as he scrolled further and came to Burst's page.

Burst profile pic had been changed to a photo of Kyron laughing on a summers day, he then posted it as a photo too, with a status saying 'This is how I'll always remember you, Rest In Eternal Power Lil' Bro... life won't be the same'.

Chunksta's tears came streaming down as he slapped his chicken box across the room and shouted "NOOOOOOOOOOOOO!!!" The power he released as he yelled shook the house and smashed a number of items in the room, this got his families attention.

Everyone except Pacer rushed to the kitchen to see what the commotion was, Pacer ignored the shout assuming his brother was just being dramatic over something petty, he closed his bedroom door and continued his phone conversation with Angel... still trying to persuade her to give him a chance.

Jay was the first to Chunksta's aid after hearing the crash and shout, Chunksta was going crazy! He battered everything in sight! Jay held him in an attempt to calm him down, but it was useless as Chunksta was blinded by tears, emotions and rage! Without a single thought Chunksta effortlessly threw Jay across the room. The others arrived and attempted to intervene, Tanya stepped towards Chunksta to comfort him but noticing it was something serious Jay shouted, "STAND BACK!" Then transformed in to Gigantic and summoned all his strength to put Chunksta into a bear hug! Their SG Gems began to glow as the two mighty Gigantian's powers intertwined. Then just as Gigantic was able to restrain his son, the Orange glow from Chunksta's Gem began to combine with Gigantic's Red Fire and shot out a flameless blast!

BOOOOOOOMMMMMM!!! The blast sent everyone flying back except Gigantic and Chunksta who miraculously found themselves at Chunksta's Bruck Down Section within the SG HQ!

Without even pertaining a thought on how they got to the SG HQ, a worried Gigantic calmly said to Chunksta "Let it out in here son... release all your tension".

Chunksta let it rip as the Mega D gave him object after object to smash, punch and let lose on.

As Chunksta released all his unwanted energy on the highest intensity level he ever performed on Gigantic stopped and took a moment to make sense of what had just happened.

'I just teleported' thought Gigantic. 'Literally, I just thought of the SG HQ and rahhh all of a sudden... I'm here'

Although Gigantic was overwhelmed he still let out a cheeky little smirk as it sunk in that he was able to teleport! Gigantic felt his capabilities rise daily, he was discovering new things about himself all the time. He noticed himself becoming stronger, smarter and all round more capable by the day as his ZuraGene was now activated within.

After a full ten minutes of destruction Chunksta dropped to his knees, red faced with his cheeks wet from tears, he bawled out "HE WAS MY BEST FRIEND!?"

Gigantic transformed back to Jay and hugged his son to comfort him.

Emotionally and physically drained, Chunksta near collapsed as he fell into his father's arms and sobbed on his chest.

"Jerome what happened?" Asked Jay

By now everyone was in the HQ, even though they were extremely concerned for the households youngest they stood back, allowing Jay to deal with the matter.

They've never seen Chunksta in such a state. Safarhi couldn't watch, Truth comforted her as she held her head in her hands with a lump in her throat.

Pacer couldn't make sense of it all, but he still managed to say the wrong thing as he laughed and asked Tanya "What's going on... is he going mad?" Tanya didn't need to reply, as the threatening look Truth gave him wiped the smile of his face!

"Everything ain't a joke you know bro, don't make me punch you in your face" said Truth

"Ooooo soorrrryyyy" said Pacer shaking his hands in sarcastic manner.

Before he even finished his motions, Tanya slapped Pacer in the back of his head and firmly said "Learn that if you ain't got nothing sensible to say... keep your mouth shut!"

Pacer accepted the bad up and apologised.

Chunksta had breathing spasms as he tried to pull himself together and answer his father, his chest shuddered as he sniffed and wiped away his tears, then like a child he looked into Jay's eyes and said "Kyron's dead! My best friend is gone!"

"I was with him like only a few hours ago, now I ain't gonna see him ever again! He was my closest homie! My only true friend that would never snake or anything! And now he's gone just like that! He's meant to be right by my side through everything! We said it... we were gonna go same college, we were gonna' make music and when we buss we were gonna go on tour together... EVERYTHING! We had so much plans... now I'm just here by myself with this pain in my stomach that I can't even explain! I don't know if I'm angry, upset or sad... I'm just... I can't even...." Then unable to finish his sentence he broke into tears again, Jay smothered him with the biggest hug as he held back his own tears.

Truth stood there showing no emotion but inside he really felt it for his little brother. Tanya now had to comfort Pacer as she could see the news hit him hard as well, Pacers the closest in age to Chunksta so he knew a lot of his friends too. Safarhi didn't know Kyron too well but she cried her eyes out as she couldn't bear to see her brother suffer like this. Safarhi started to feel overwhelmed with emotions that weren't hers, then she began to feel a knot in her stomach which was identical to the feeling Chunksta was experiencing. Unknowingly Safarhi accessed another one of her abilities that she didn't know existed, she was empathic which enabled her to feel others emotions and pains as well as some other cool things that she will one day discover!

Safarhi's love for her brother is so powerful that she activated this power and zoned into his emotional and physical feelings because she so wanted his pain to go away so much.

The comfort from Jay and Tanya helped calm Chunksta down but some how Safarhi was able to ease the pain Chunksta was feeling inside.

SQUAD GIGANTIC

The whole Gigantic household was shell shocked by the news of Kyron's death, there was a weird silence over the house as they all retired to their rooms.

Chunksta was more stable but still shaken and to make it worse, he still didn't know what actually happened. Hoping to get the full story of what took place, he went to his phone and checked the missed calls. Chunksta knew this bombardment of calls had to be the result of Kyron's death, he noticed there was one particular number that called him sixteen times! Chunksta saved the number under '???' so he could go in to WhatsApp and see their profile pic but the profile pic was blank, so the only way he was going to find out who it is was by calling the number.

Chunksta tapped call and waited as the phone rang about seven times, just as he was about to hang up, he heard a familiar voice on the other end of the phone, it was Burst... Kyron's big brother!

"Yooo" said Burst but something was different! Burst didn't have that larger than life confident tone to his speech, in fact he sounded weak!

Chunksta responded "Who's that Burst?"

"Yeah bro, you hear the madness?" Replied Burst

"Kinda... like I see some stuff on the gram and that, but I don't know the details and what really happened" said Chunksta inquisitively responding to Kyron's brother.

"My little bro and that Splash yout' are both dead... Big Splash got nicked and I swear jakes are looking for me too" said Burst

Chunksta's heart sunk even lower than before as he finally accepted that it was true.

Not only Kyron was dead but Splash too! Burst carried on speaking as Chunksta tried to get his head around it all.

"It all went nuts too quickly, I couldn't even deep what was going on... one minute we jumped in the whip to go ride on dem' pagans... then the next minute we was being rid on! Trust me bro you did the right thing by not getting in the whip, I wish I could turn back time and tell Ky to go with you!" Said a regretful Burst

"WHAT!" Replied Chunksta

"For real bro, as a matter of a fact I don't even know why I rolled it was just a stupid little argument that could've been solved man. People are always on a hype... especially youngers" said Burst, totally switching up his stance from earlier when he basically forced his little brother into the car.

Burst's word made Chunksta furious! "Nar nar nar bro... forget all that talk now, cos at the time you wanted to look at me like I'm nothing! Furthermore... you and your dawg was the ones on the hype! You lot was trying to make man go out there on the frontline and risk it all... don't act like you care now that things have gone wrong!"

Chunksta couldn't believe the audacity of Burst. Earlier that day Chunksta was made to feel worthless as if he didn't care for his friend or as if he was a coward, when all along he was the one who had his friends best interests at heart and was left feeling penalised for knowing to do the right thing.

"Yeah but things have changed it's all mad now bro, bro's dead and I'm looking at doing an L bro... twenty five years minimum!" Replied Burst

"You sound shook bro... I thought you man were bout it, remember it's you lot that said Kyron had to ride to join gang, where's all that talk now huh?" Replied Chunksta

Hearing the pathetic weakness in Burst's voice, Chunksta could tell he wasn't as bad as he portrayed, he was just another older from the area who took advantage of youngers, making them do things that they are scared to do themselves.

Each word from Burst began to irritate Chunksta more and more, so before he was able to say another word Chunksta spat out "Anyway stop the chattings' and say what happened!"

The roles had now reversed, Chunksta was in control and Burst sounded like a scared young buck.

Burst did what he was told with no complaints, then sounding like he was holding back tears, he took a deep breathe and went on to explain what took place earlier that afternoon.

"Imagine we got the drop on them Bang youts' from one chick's socials and pulled up on them. Everything was good, man dem' were on it and we had them outnumbered! Anyway cut a long story short we ran them down, grabbed a couple of them and done our ting. Then out of now where a bag of them started running towards us!" Then Burst went silent.

"Then what..." said Chunskta prompting Burst to say what he had to say.

"What you need to understand bro, there was nuff' of them" said Burst trying to manipulate Chunksta's thought process

"Yeah and, what's your point?" Said Chunksta clocking on to Burst's attempt to manipulate him.

"Bro... man had to run!" Admitted Burst contradicting one of the main street rules they imposed on the youngers in the area.

Chunksta was furious, he felt betrayed and lied to! Removing the phone speaker from his ear, he placed the mic near his mouth and shouted "ARE YOU MAD! What you mean run... I thought it was never run from Op's, never leave no one and always ride together? And to make it worse you had a ting on you... what, was that for show? YOU MUG! You lot ain't on nothing! Olders are always telling the youngers don't do that, blah blah blah, then as soon as you lot get into a situation... you man run! I can't believe how fake you man are! You know how much man my age have died following you lots rules that you don't even obey yourselves, you're out here pushing out illusions to us when you ain't willing to do nothing yourselves... you man are done out here!"

"I know I had the ting but I weren't expecting to use it I just had to scare them really, I know that sounds dumb but you weren't there... you don't understand bro" said Burst

"Shut up man, you're a fool bout scare man and I don't understand... just tell me what happen cos' you're getting me mad G" enforced Chunksta and with no more mouth Burst just obeyed and carried on explaining

"Bro everyone ran not just me, well not everyone... everyone except Kyron. I shouted out RUN BRO to him but he ignored man and stayed there with the Kitchen in his hand! First I thought he was on it but when Big Splash was in front of him... he didn't do nothing! I looked back and saw Big Splash punching him up and I'm not gonna lie... I carried on running... he's old enough to take a little beating, that's life but then one chick was like 'how you lot leaving him to get beat up like that, he's only a yout' and that kinda made me catch myself, so I came back and saw Big Splash took the weapon Ky had, then he held it to him, shouting 'come defend your brother then!' Everyone there was laughing at me, calling me names and all sorts... so I had no choice but to back the ting on him! But he weren't shook, fam Big splash is a mad man he did not care about the strap! He looked at the strap, laughed, then came at me and I can't lie... I froze... anyone would've! Fam I just like to make money and get gyal... I'm not on no smoke!"

"But it was cool to make your bro be on it tho... you man are frauds! All you do is cap! How can your name be Burst and you're scared to burst your ting?!? The worst thing is Kyron really looked up to you and you just took him for granted, he wanted to be just like you and come to find out you're wet, you sold him a fake dream that got him killed!" responded Chunksta

Burst still tried to gain back some glory with a feeble response

"I'm the only one who came back though, you should be rating me! Is it my fault Big Splash grabbed the strap out my hand?"

"Yes, one hundred your fault, cos' you're a eediot! Bout rate you... don't make me laugh, I don't rate frauds" said Chunksta he couldn't believe Burst was still trying to save face on the situation.

"Anyway as I was saying, Kyron was mash up on the floor but he saw that Big Splash had the ting pointing at me, and that's when it all went mad... Kyron got up and grabbed the shank off the floor, then ran up behind Big Splash and dipped him in his leg! Big Splash Shouted ARRGGGHH and dropped the mash, then fell to the floor, me and Ky finally had the upper hand on him and started to bruck him up"

"How does it feel knowing that your LITTLE brother had more heart than you, and even had to save you?" Mocked Chunksta.

Again Burst couldn't reply, instead he acted like he didn't hear Chunksta's cheeky comment and carried on explaining what took place.

"Everything was good, then out of now where that Splash yout ran up behind my brother, spun him around and stabbed him in his chest!!! It all happened mad quickly... in like a split second... I didn't even notice, I thought he just punched him... Kyron didn't even notice!

Then they started scuffing, then all of a sudden Kyron said 'I CAN'T BREATHE, I CAN'T BREATHE' then he just dropped! I looked at him and his top was soaked with blood, he just laid on the floor struggling to get air!

The whole world stopped for me, I zoned out for a second then all I remember was looking up and seeing more Op's coming at man, I saw the strap on the floor and grabbed it... then I closed my eyes and started squeezing! I let off all six shots I think... I just wanted to scare them and make them dust from me and brother, and it worked, I opened back my eyes and saw everyone running off... well everyone except Splash! He was on the floor next to my brother... he got hit... I didn't mean to fam, honestly I just wanted to scare them... but I SHOT HIM!"

Chunksta Replied with no sympathy whatsoever towards Burst.

"Well what did you think was gonna' happen, when you walk with a gun people get hurt... durrrr! And now because you're such a coward two teens are dead and one of them is your brother! Both of them had their whole life ahead of them but over a stupid argument they're both gone... both of their blood is on your hands!"

Burst had an emotional breakdown and started screaming down the phone whilst sobbing with tears as the severity of the matter hit him like a ton of bricks.

"DON'T SAY THAT... DON'T SAY THAT... IT'S NOT MY FAULT! I didn't ask to be on road this is the life that was given to me, I wish I had another option! I wish I never ever touched road, I don't wanna be apart of all this, I just wanna live a simple life and be a family man... now I'm on the run for murder and I've lost my little brother"

"COURSE IT'S YOUR FAULT... YOU DON'T WANT THAT LIFE FOR YOURSELF BUT YOU STILL PUSHED ON YOUR OWN BROTHER! WHAT KINDA MAN ARE YOU?! AND YOU KNOW WHAT... YOU'RE GONNA GO JAIL FOR IT TOO! AND THAT'S IF YOU'RE LUCKY, COS IF THEM CATCH YOU... THEY GONNA KILL YOU!" Taunted

Chunksta. He was disgusted by everything Burst said, he couldn't listen no more he had heard enough, Chunksta pressed the red button so aggressively that he crushed his phone to pieces! It was all too much for him, he was emotionally and physically drained. Chunksta laid his head on his pillow and literally cried himself to sleep.

Chunksta's words hit Burst hard which led him to fully understand he's life was over! Now more scared and paranoid as ever he ran to his window and looked outside to see if anyone was coming for him, seeing that the coast was clear he closed his curtains and double locked his doors. His mind was all over the place and after deliberating with himself for around twenty minutes, he decided his best option was to hand himself in to the LCP, as he knew the court room justice would be less severe than street justice!

Burst decided to tie up a few loose ends before handing himself in. He went to his son and daughter's house and left a rucksack with a note and the majority of the money he had stacked on their doorstep, then he knocked the door and drove off before anyone answered. Burst couldn't bear to see his children and their mother as he knew he would breakdown and possibly even try to run away with them, which would've selfishly put them all at risk.

Thinking about how much of his children's life he was about to miss out on, Burst got emotional and let his thoughts run away with him. He created crazy scenarios in his mind on how he thought his children's lives will pan out. At first the thoughts were all positive ones as he envisioned his son becoming a pioneering doctor and his daughter being the biggest footballer ever! Then his thoughts took a negative turn for the worst which made him start thinking what if they decide to take the path of crime, how he would feel if he heard they were on road being corrupted by an older just like him! These dreadful thoughts made him think back to how he misled Kyron and other youngers in the area, now thinking with a clearer mind he immediately wanted to repent and gain forgiveness for his wrongs. He picked up his phone and began to write a long message to Chunksta, he spilt his heart out as he highlighted his errors and apologised for how everything turned out but after going over the message he felt way to exposed and couldn't bring himself to actually send it, instead he deleted every last word and just sent "Don't ever do road bro... it's a joke ting! Do something big with you life and make the endz proud G #KyronsWorld"

Burst then drove to his mother's block where he sat in his car for a few minutes with his eyes full of tears. Knowing this area was hot he started to feel like a sitting target, so he wiped his face and got on with what he came to do. He grabbed an old fast food napkin from under his armrest then searched in his glove compartment and found a pen to write a short note to his mother, just as he wrote his last word a tear poetically dropped on to the napkin as he folded it. Burst placed the napkin at the top of a pouch filled with his remaining money then got out of his car. Rather than wait for the lift he decided to walk up the six flights of stairs that led to the floor of the flat that he grew up on. He reminisced on good and bad memories as he slowly walked along the landing having happy flashbacks of him and Kyron playing outside, but the happy flashbacks quickly switched to bad memories of the times when they would both sit in the exact same place for hours waiting for their no show Dad on weekends.

Finally he arrived at the door where he could hear the voices of family and close friends who had gathered at the house after hearing the news on Kyron. Burst was estranged, never before had he felt so alienated from his family. In his heart he knew he should be in there with his loved ones, so he contemplated knocking the door and giving his mum one last hug but in his heart he didn't feel he would be well received, so instead he just placed the pouch with the note and money on his mothers doormat then walked back up the landing. Burst's mum felt her mother's intuition telling her to go to the door and open it, she followed her instincts and went to investigate. Just as Burst turned the corner his mother opened the door, they literally missed each other by seconds! Seeing the strange pouch on the floor she looked left and right as she picked it up noticing the note on top, seen as no one was there she slowly closed the front door and read the note.

"I KNOW IF I PUT THIS MONEY IN YOUR HAND DIRECTLY YOU WOULDN'T ACCEPT IT BUT PLLEEAASSEE TAKE THIS FOR KY'S FUNERAL ARRANGEMENTS AND ANYTHING ELSE... I'M GONNA BE GOING AWAY FOR A LONG TIME AND I GUESS THIS IS THE LEAST I CAN DO... P.S I WISH I JUST LISTENED TO EVERYTHING YOU SAID... I LOVE YOU SOOO MUCH MUM AND I'M SORRY"

Realising the note was from her first born, she ran out her house and sprinted downstairs in the hope of seeing her son. Luckily Burst was strolling at a slow pace so she got to him just in time to see him opening his car door.

"BYRON" Shouted Burst's Mum using his real name.

Burst instantly recognised his Mum's voice, it reminded him of all the times she would shout over the balcony telling him to get in the house once the street lights came on, he smiled and thought 'I haven't heard no one use my real name in a while'.

As Burst spun round to answer his Mum, he was swamped by the biggest hug ever.

"I love you son, I always have... of course I forgive you, don't worry" said Burst's Mum as she held her son with the most loving hug that only a mother could give.

Sadly this beautiful moment was short lived, before Burst and his Mum could even separate from their hug, a convoy of armed LCP cars lead by Detective Superintendent (DSI) Officer KK SKKKRRRRRRR'D round the corner and jumped out on Byron and his Mum pointing their guns directly at them.

"BYRON GET YOUR HANDS BEHIND YOUR HEAD AND SLOWLY DROP TO YOUR KNEES!"

"Everyone's using my government today ennit" said Burst, as he did what he was instructed but his mother wouldn't let go of him, she couldn't bear the thought of losing two sons in one day... one to death and one to prison! But unfortunately these are the usual two outcomes of choosing a life of crime. Street life had finally caught up with Burst in the most harshest way, not only taking his brother's life but also destroying his mother and his children's life as well!

Seeing the area was secured Officer KK strutted towards Burst and his Mum as she tried to protect her son from the arm of the law.

"Sorry to break up this beautiful moment but you're coming with us Byron or shall I say Burst!" sarcastically said Officer KK in his usual smug and arrogant tone

"What's going on, why d'you want my son?" Asked Burst's mum as she was ripped off her son.

"Ain't he told you sweetheart, your sons been a naughty boy haven't ya?" Replied Officer KK whilst dragging Burst up to his feet and slamming his face onto the roof of his car.

"Tek' your hand off my son!" Demanded Burst's mum as Officer KK continued to use unnecessary force to apprehend her son.

This now created a stir in the block, so the family and friends from upstairs also came running down to see what was going on.

Burst's mum couldn't take watching the LCP continue to mistreat her son. She saw red then took off her slipper and started to slap Officer KK with it whilst shouting "HOW D'YOU LIKE THAT YOU COWARD!"

Burst's aunties and uncles held back his mum to avoid the LCP arresting her too.

"You're a feisty one aren't ya, you lot better hold her back or she's gonna get the same treatment as him" said Officer KK whilst nodding his head towards Burst.

"Anyway she ain't worth the paperwork, back to you... you little toe rag, you're under arrest on the suspicion of

Murder, you have the right to remain silent and refuse to answer any questions. Anything you say may be used against you in the court of law..." said Officer KK as he cuffed Burst.

"Blah blah blah" interrupted Burst as he was read his rights "I don't know why you're hitting me fam, I'm not resisting"

"I'm just using reasonable force pal" Replied Officer KK in a cocky manner.

"Can you at least let me say good bye to my mum, like... just a quick kiss or sut'um" pleaded Burst

To everyone's surprise Officer KK loosened his grip on Burst and said "Arr that's sweet, go on make it quick"

Burst couldn't believe his luck, still in cuffs he adjusted his body and moved towards his mother.

"Mum I'm soo...." Then WHAM!!! Burst was dragged back by Officer KK

"What d'you think I am, a bloody social worker... get in the car you twat" said Officer KK as he cut short Burst's goodbye and he literally threw him headfirst in to the back of his unmarked LCP car.

Then with no remorse he looked Burst's mum dead in her eyes and said "Your son is going away for a long time luv'... send him a letter!" Then he turned to his colleague and mockingly said "Say goodbye, do me a favour hahahaha this ain't the movies" they all laughed and got back in their LCP cars escorting Burst to the station. Burst felt empty and hopeless as he watched his mother

collapse and breakdown in the middle of the street
through Officer KK's rear view mirror.

Chapter 3 – A Dark Cloud Over A Bright Sun

Next morning Chunksta woke up in the same clothes he fell asleep in.

Truth checked on his little bro whilst he was sleeping last night and saw that he broke his phone to an unrepairable state... well unrepairable to most but not to Truth!

Sensing exactly what happened he gathered the pieces of the wrecked phone and repaired it for his little brother. Firstly, Truth recovered the operating system and then some how managed to retrieve the data and import all the stored information over to one of his spare phones. Once he was done, Truth went back into his brother's room and quietly placed the phone on Chunksta's Chest of drawers.

With yesterday being so intense, Tanya and Jay felt it was best not to wake him for school but Chunksta felt differently, he felt it would better to go school and keep his mind occupied rather than being locked up in his room moping about the situation, plus he wanted to be around the rest of his friends so they could get through this madness together.

Chunksta went into his bathroom and got himself ready for the day, it wasn't until he was fully dressed and creaming his face that he noticed the phone on top of his drawer. Automatically knowing the phone was from his tech savvy brother, he smiled and shouted "Thanks bro".

Truth's generosity set his day off nicely, his spirits were lifted even more as he looked at the phone and saw he had received a number of support messages from friends but unfortunately this positive feeling was short lived as he scrolled down a little further to see a message from Burst that made his anger resurface. All he could do was roll his eyes as he read the message, he decided not to respond straight away as he didn't want to let negativity ruin his day, instead he switched his focus back to the messages of love, then messaged his friends telling them to meet him at his house so they can all roll to school together.

Chunksta friends came to meet him, they gathered outside the Mansions gated entrance and rang the intercom, Chunksta quickly grabbed some breakfast on the go and answered the call "I'm coming now one second"

Just as he got to the door Tanya stopped him with a smile on her face and said

"What, no goodbye, no morning hug, no nothing... just grab toast and go yeah?"

"It's not like that, sorry morning Mum" said Chunksta as he walked over to Tanya and hugged her.

The teens really settled in London, the relationship was so strong with Tanya and Jay that they now called them Mum and Dad.

"Yesterday was a lot, you ok? You don't have to go school today you know" said Tanya in her usual loving and caring tone.

"Nar I'm good Mum, best way for me to deal with it is head on... I'm cool" Replied Chunksta assuring Tanya of his mental state.

"OK well if you're sure, have a good day... and If you're gonna' eat such a rubbish breakfast make sure you have a decent lunch OK" said Tanya in a much sterner voice.

"Yes Mum" said Chunksta as he rushed over to his friends who were waiting at the end of the drive. Chunksta was trying to leave before Jay came back from his morning training session, as he knew Jay would lecture him and his friends if he catches them.

Chunksta saw Jay coming in a distance and tried to act as if he didn't see him, he sped to his friends and attempted to make a run for it before Jay caught up with them. As the gates opened they all greeted each other with hugs and spuds each.

"Oi man dem let's dust quickly before my dad starts his preaching ting" said Chunksta, everyone caught the drift but just as they were about to move off, Chunksta's friend Kamari who's always in a world of his own, looked up, saw Jay and then totally missing Chunksta's point waved at Jay with the silliest look on his face shouting "Hello Jay" then tapped Chunksta on his chest saying "Jerome, look your dads there fam"

Chunksta gave him the dirtiest look as his other friend Jamal intervened and said "Kamari why you so dumb fam?!"

"Huh... what did I do" Replied Kamari still not cottoning on.

Jamal shook his head as he slapped Kamari in his freshly trimmed neck back.

The baldness from his fade made the sound of the slap so loud that they all started laughing whilst Kamari stood there still confused to what had just happened.

"Yoooo... wait a second, you lot come here... I wanna' talk to you quickly" shouted Jay, managing to catch them just as they were about to make their escape.

Chunksta turned his back so Jay couldn't see him kick the floor and huff in frustration, as he spun around he muttered to his friends "Watch the long ting now"

"Yep, good luck hahaha" laughed Jamal as Chunksta started walking back to Jay

"Coming" said Chunksta

"Ohhhhh" said Kamari as he finally realised what he was slapped for.

"You're a fool, just a big fool" responded Jamal to Kamari

"I wanna' talk to all of you, so all of you come here" instructed Jay as he wiped sweat of his face with a towel.

Jay always preached to their friends, because him and Tanya were relatively young parents, he felt the teen's peers would find him relatable. Jay really believed him and Tanya were seen as the cool parents and to be fair most of the teens friends actually thought they were too. A lot of times the teens friends would mention how much they loved Jay and Tanya, wishing they had young and fun parents too, sometimes they would even come to them for advice on things they felt they couldn't mention to their own families. However, there were many moments where Chunksta and his siblings felt Jay and Tanya could be a bit cringe, especially when Tanya tries to use certain slang or when Jay acts like he's up to date with the latest drill songs and even dances!

Chunksta knew Jay was going to give them one of his long annoying speeches, he spoke under his breath to his friends as they walked over to Jay.

"Broooo, he's going to give us the longest speech now! Alllll-ways preaching fam" said Chunskta stretching his words to get his point across.

Jamal started to find the situation funny, he tried to hold in his laugh so Jay couldn't see as he mumbled "Yep and he always tries to be sly about it, like he ain't gonna' preach... like he just wants to see how we are... then Boom, all of a sudden mans telling us a lesson about life and something he went through like twenty years ago hahaha"

"EXACTLY like things ain't changed fam" said Chunksta through his teeth

"I kinda like the stories he tells us... they're like TV" said Kamari

Everyone looked at Kamari then they all said, "SHUT UP!"

Jamal then predicted how the conversations was going to go "Watch, first he'll say... what's going on, everyone good?"

"Yep! That's just the jab, then straight after everyone answers he'll say... I ain't trying to preach or nothing but... then he'll start preaching fam hahaha its long" said Chunksta

They all straightened up as they approached Jay ensuring they were addressing him in a respectable manner

"Morning Jay" "Hello Mr Gigantic" "Hi Jay" said everyone at the same time.

"What's going on... everyone good?" Said Jay. Everyone burst out in laughter, they couldn't hold it in no more... Jay did exactly as predicted!

"What's so funny" said Jay with a serious face!

"Nothing, Nothing... just a joke we had from the other day" Replied Chunksta thinking on his feet.

Jay got a little vex as he felt they were mocking him, so instead of saying what he planned to say he just said "OK cool, I just wanted to know you lot were good after yesterday" and walk off.

"Rah, he louwed' it" said Jamal as he continued laughing.

"See you lot are wrong... I was looking forward to a story as well" said Kamari as everyone stood around in disbelief. Chunksta felt he acted disrespectful towards his father and began to feel a touch of guilt. He slightly squinted his eyes as he tried to process the situation fully and came to the conclusion that he insulted his father.

Chunksta went to apologise immediately but just as he was about to call out to Jay and act upon his guilt, Jay spun back round and said...

"You know what, forget that! You lot need to hear this!" Then he lined up the teens and forced them to listen to what he had to say!

"I ain't trying to preach or nothing but... I heard the stories on what happened yesterday and I been hearing about everything else that's been going on round here too, and what I'm about to say needs to be said cos' you lot need to realise that most of these so called olders are nothing but liars or washed up fools who are taking advantage of your young fearless hearts! I've seen it all before, it ain't nut'um new they been doing forever, from even before my days on road but it's escalated to new level with your generation! Little fassies are controlling the roads, there's no morals and no honour... everyone's scared to fight like a man and gain respect but quick to use weapons! Olders are even using you lot as weapons, forcing you lot to do horrible things! They want you lot to do things they're either too scared to do or not stupid enough to do! They'll let you risk your freedom and your life just to bring them gains... they don't care about you, they're just using you lot! Half these man you call olders wouldn't last a week if they had to really put in work and live the life they're trying to make your generation live! Majority of them couldn't last a day in your shoes and they definitely wouldn't even have lasted an hour in my times... we would've chewed them up! Little punks! A real older wants you lot to do better and will help you get there... not these little pathetic excuses of gangsters... they're frauds... YOU HEAR ME? FRAUDS!" Shouted Jay as his passion took over. Jay's raised voice grabbed their attention, if they weren't listening before now they was!

Jay calmed himself down and carried on talking

"You know what, may be I'm stereotyping and being a bit too harsh... cos' there's always exceptions, not every older is an idiot... just most of them! On the real tho' there's a few real ones out there that care enough to show youngens that five years of balling on road ain't worth twenty years in jail! And that's the ones you need to listen to and take note from.

You lot are Kings and Queens, but it's like you all been made to think that the only place you can be something special is on road... one day y'all see how wrong that assumption is! Road has nothing for none of you and the sooner you realise that the better! You lot are smart enough and talented enough to do anything you want in life!

YOU ARE THE STARS THAT ARE GONNA BRING LIGHT AND PROSPERITY TO THE FUTURE! THINGS MIGHT SEEM GRIM AND DULL RIGHT NOW BUT THERE'S ALWAYS SUNSHINE AFTER THE RAIN AND TRUST ME... YOU LOT ARE THAT SUNSHINE, YOU'RE DESTINE FOR SUCCESS AND GREATNESS... unfortunately right now there's a dark cloud over a bright sun but we'll get through this together!"

Surprisingly Jay's words had a big impact on Chunksta and his friends, the truth is they never really had anyone talk to them in such a way, most adults either put them down or as Jay said corrupt them! This was the first time someone communicated with them at a real level whilst letting them know they're not only loved and valued but are also the future of this planet.

Jamal's views on Jay's speeches took a one hundred and eighty degree turn, he even started thinking back to previous times Jay had words with them to see if he could decipher any other hidden jewels that he missed out on due to his ignorance. As they walked to school he kept saying "That was some real talk you know" gaining more and more clarity as he broke down key points of Jay's statement in his mind.

Chapter 4 – Old Faces... New Cases

School had finally broken up for the summer. As soon as the bell rang, Chunksta and a few friends linked up, grabbed a few bits and made their way to the spot where Kyron died to pay their respect and leave tributes.

Chunksta and his friends stood at the spot for hours whilst sharing memories and stories of Kyron. It's hard to explain but just chilling there made them feel closer to him, they played music from their phones as family and friends came and went, they also left Kyron's favourite sweets and drinks along with pictures of him attached to flowers with cards and notes expressing how much they were going to miss him.

The most beautifulest thing was that Splash's friends and family was also there doing the same thing and instead of fighting with one another everyone saw the bigger picture and mourned together as one, there was no conflict or negativity whatsoever... well that was until a little later when the LCP pulled up and Officer KK once again decided he wanted to abuse his power!

"What do we have here then, social distancing is looking poor" said Officer KK trying to find an excuse to harass the public as he slowed down his unmarked LCP car and cruised by at no more than five miles per hour, ensuring everyone on the kerb was fully aware of his presence.

"It's where those lads got killed boss, just looks like a bunch of kids showing respect to their friends... nothing going on we might as well keep moving" said his partner – Officer Payne who immediately came to the defence of the young people.

"Don't know about that, you say kids but I see a bunch of gang members standing around an active area where gang members have previously been killed... it's not nice for the taxpayer to be made to feel so intimidated plus a crime could be about to take place right now! We better check it out" Replied Officer KK as he slapped on his sirens and frantically done the most exaggerated U-turn before pulling up on to the kerb where Chunksta and a few others were congregating.

"What's wrong with this guy" said Chunksta! As Officer KK jumped out his car and aggressively walked up to the teens.

"What's going on here then lads" cheekily said Officer KK, as Payne adjusted his clothes and caught up to him

"What d'you thinks going on bro" responded Jamal

"Oi Less of the lip boy and trust me I'm not you're brother, you really think we could have the same mum"

"And I'm not you're boy either! But you're right about one thing tho... my mum would never give birth to something so butters" said Jamal.

Everyone started laughing! Even Payne had a little smirk on his face.

"Officer Payne I hope you're not endorsing this kind of behaviour" said a red faced Officer KK

"Nar but you gotta admit that was a good one" replied Payne. Payne was a good Officer who always dealt with people fair and just, it was just unfortunate that he was partnered with his senior Officer KK who didn't share his code of practice.

"Yeah well now let's see how funny you find it now that I gotta search him" said Officer KK as he grabbed Jamal and slammed him against a wall.

"WHAT YOU DOING, on what grounds are you searching me... I ain't done no crime!" Said Jamal

"That's illegal you can't search without any just cause" said Chunksta

"Shut up you midget! I make the law round ere" said Officer KK as he conducted the illegal search on Jamal.

Both sides of the mourners reacted and started going crazy on the officers. This just riled up Officer KK even more, he gave Jamal a few sly punches in his ribs until he realised someone began filming on their phone, then he changed his approach and shouted

"STOP RESISTING" even though Jamal was clearly being cooperative.

Officer Payne snatched the phone from the hand of the person who was recording as his colleague continued to assault Jamal. Officer KK was now on a rampage and not even Officer Payne could calm him down, he lined the teens up one by one then began searching or shall I say roughing them up!

The teens were too scared to defend themselves as they feared they would receive a beating too! Chunksta clinched his fist in frustration as he watched Officer KK violate his friends but Chunksta knew that if he reacted he will expose his hidden identity.

Chunksta did well to control his temper but eventually Officer KK got round to him! He got right up in Chunksta's face then shoved him in the chest in an attempt to force him against the wall, this didn't work! Not realising who he's dealing with, Officer KK thought his push didn't connect properly so he gripped Chunksta by his hoodie and used all his might to throw Chunksta to the floor, once again this didn't work... Chunksta barely moved, he was way to strong. Officer KK felt Chunksta's strength and didn't know what to do, every one started cheering Chunksta on "That's it Jerome" "Don't have it fam".

Now Officer KK was embarrassed! Refusing to lose face he decided to take things to a next level.

"Oh you're a tuff nut yeah" said Officer KK

Chunksta didn't reply.

Officer KK reached for his baton and flicked it out.

"You got nothing to say now have you little man" taunted Officer KK still trying to gain a reaction from Chunksta.

By now a crowd had grown and many people were recording the altercation whilst shouting words of disgust at Officer KK.

"I don't think that's necessary K" said Officer Payne to his partner in the hope of calming the situation down.

Then Officer Payne looked around and said "Look at all these people... lets not do something we'll regret"

But Officer KK's stubbornness had him in too deep, refusing to back down he replied

"No he is resisting and I'm about to use the appropriate amount of force to restrain him" as he stared in Chunksta's eyes trying his hardest to intimidate him.

"You never know... if we're lucky, I might hit him in the right place and we'll get one more dirty little gang member off the streets" said the corrupt officer.

Chunksta looked him back in his eyes and said "Do what your doing big man!"

Officer KK raised his baton and launched towards Chunksta as he said "Oh I will mate"

Chunksta braced himself to take the blow... but the blow never came!

"NO YOU WON'T!"

IT WAS GIGANTIC! He snatched the baton out of Officer KK's hands and effortlessly pushed him to the ground. The crowd laughed and cheered for Gigantic's arrival as they were fed up of watching Officer KK violate the young people.

Luckily, Truth sensed an altercation was taking place with Chunksta and informed Gigantic right away! Without any hesitation Gigantic transitioned then jumped on his SG Quad and sped down to the area, followed by Truth and Safarhi on Truth's SG1000. When Gigantic arrived and saw the altercation involved Officer KK, he knew some sort of foul play was being administered, as he too went through many situations like this with Officer KK whilst growing up.

Finally Officer KK was forced to take on someone his own size and predictably just like any other bully he folded.

"Big mistake you oversized Cat!" Said Officer KK as he got back to his feet

"You think I'm scared of you?" Said Officer KK... who was clearly scared of him.

Gigantic laughed and said "Yep, the way you're shaking shows me you definitely are"

"Well... well... well that's assaulting an officer... you're nicked!" Stuttered Officer KK

"Well arrest me then, make my day so I can have you charged for assault on all these kids too!" Replied Gigantic.

Officer KK was bricking it, he was well aware of how silly he was being made to look but each time he took a look at Gigantic's tall, hench and commanding figure he knew there was nothing he could do about the situation he now found himself in.

Cowardly trying to deflect the hype away from himself, Officer KK told Officer Payne to make the arrest "Payne grab him!"

"That's your arrest mate" said Officer Payne as he stepped behind Officer KK. Whether it was out of fear or simply not defending KK's terrible behaviour, Officer Payne wanted nothing to do with the altercation.

"I'll do it myself then you wussie!" Said Officer KK.

He drew his gun from his holster and pointed it at Gigantic whilst shouting "GET ON THE FLOOR YOU BIG BLACK C... CAT!!!"

Everyone froze as their laughter turned to gasps of fear, well everyone except Gigantic, Truth and Safarhi.

They all started bussing up and without one ounce of fear they drew closer to Officer KK giving him the total opposite response he hoped for.

Now Officer KK found himself in a stand off with the older half of the Squad.

"Do you think I'm joking with you, stand still or I'LL SHOOT" said Officer KK as he got into stance.

"What wrong with this doughnut?!" Said Safarhi, whilst making a confused hand gesture to Truth.

Just as serious as always, Truth didn't respond! Stoned faced he just locked his eyes on Officer KK and read his mind!

"Can you feel his fear sis?" Said Truth telepathically to Safarhi

"Yes he's shook" Replied Safarhi

"Imagine, he's gonna put all these innocent people at risk and actually buss his gun cos he's soooo shook... this eediot is actually gonna shoot!" responded Truth in total disgust.

Chunksta stood in background with his fist clenched, he had no choice but to stand back and watch everything take place because he wasn't suited up, so he couldn't risk making any sort of move that would give away his identity.

Officer KK hands began to shake even more as he gripped the pistol and aimed it at Gigantic.

"Stop posing with it and use it you prat" said Gigantic, even with a loaded Gun in his hand he still had no respect for Officer KK

Gigantic took a step closer to KK and continued to taunt him!

Officer KK closed his eyes and squeezed the trigger, letting off a total of four shots at Gigantic.

Officer KK was so scared that his wobbly hands made all shots go off in different directions!

Gigantic and Safarhi tensed up and prepared themselves to take the flurry of shots as Truth stood fearless whilst focussing on the bullets.

Officer KK opened his eyes hoping that Gigantic would be on the floor in a pool of blood... but Truth had other ideas!

As the bullets flew out of the gun, Truth used his new developed telekinetic powers and stopped the bullets mid-air, literally centimetres away from making contact with Gigantic and two innocent bystanders.

Truth finally broke his silence saying "That ain't gonna work fam".

With the previous bullets still mid-air, Officer KK opened fire again this time continuing to until his clip was empty but Truth just done the same thing and again stopped each bullet in transit!

With all the bullets now floating in mid-air, Truth used his powers to spin them around and rapidly fly back at Officer KK as he reloaded.

Officer KK looked up to find each bullet no more than six inches away from his forehead.

"Behave yourself" said Truth as each bullet hovered in front of Officer KK

"What type of superheroes would kill an Officer?" Said Officer KK as he feared for his life.

Officer Payne intervened and said "He's right... you're better than that, plus they'll lock you up forever... is it really worth it?"

Chunksta shouted out "They can't hold man... DO IT!"

But as much as Truth wanted to punish KK, he knew killing him would be the wrong decision to make in every way.

Instead Truth telepathically communicated to his sister "Let's give em' a show... crush em sis!"

"On it" replied Safarhi, then as the bullets hovered in front of the ever so still Officer KK, Safarhi used her hands to draw air from the atmosphere, then with one quick clinch of her fist she compressed the air and crushed each bullet into shapes resembling pennies. Then Truth released the coin like bullets which dropped in front of Officer KK after conking him on his head with one.

As soon as the bullets fell, Officer KK raised his gun to shoot at the heroes again... but he wasn't quick enough! Gigantic gave him a swift right hook that left him sparked out on the floor.

Gigantic stood over KK and said "Don't ever draw your ting on me, are you mad!?!"

Gigantic knew Officer KK's back up must be on the way, he looked around and realised that nearly everyone had their phone out recording the stand off, so rather than stick around and have a full blown battle with KK's back up when they arrive, he calmly said

"Time to go" to Truth and Safarhi.

Truth and Gigantic hopped on their vehicles immediately and put them in to stealth mode as they made an invisible getaway with Safarhi following in the sky.

Chapter 5 – The Throne Is Mine!

Everyone was going crazy over Squad Gigantic's altercation with The LCP, London was in complete pandemonium. There were so many different versions of the story floating around, some that had Squad Gigantic as Heroes and of course some that had them as villains. However the ends knew the true story and stood by SG's actions, the videos people posted went viral and it clearly showed Squad Gigantic defending a bunch of kids from a corrupt officer.

Eventually Sandra Patty caught a whiff of the the story and of course she decided to report it in a totally different light through the mainstream media!

Sandra had her team strategically crop the recordings to only show the last piece of the conflict where Gigantic knocked out Officer KK! She wanted to paint Squad Gigantic out to be reckless renegades with no respect for the law and in some places, this was working!

Headlines read "Super Heroes or Villains???", "Lawless Thugs with Powers", "Enough Is Enough!" there were even click baits mocking Gigantic's appearance whilst slandering the Squad's name.

Squad Gigantic were front page news for days and on social media, this was the main story in the feed.

"OHHHHHH Lights out mate! Oi Mechanics, come have a butchers at this" shouted Bang to Mechanics as he chilled in a luxurious outdoor hot tub in a discreet location in the north of England.

"Arr go-a away, I'm-a watching something man, if it's not Steve the mad-a-man, it's Funny Marco, it's Imjustbait, it's Shade borough... I've-a had enough" replied Mechanics fed up of Bang constantly bothering him to watch silly videos online.

Bang and Mechanics had been on the run for a while, laying low frustrated Mechanics as his operations were still up and running with no issues whatsoever, but Mechanics displayed his loyalty to Bang and skipped town with him when everything came on top with Dealer, Thug Rock and Squad Gigantic.

Mechanics told Bang "You always-a calling me for-a stupid things... assentarsi" he had enough of being on the run.

"You'll like this you soppy little so and so, this is exactly what we needed to happen so we go back to London and grab back my throne" said Bang with a half smile, apart from scrolling through social media all day, one of the only other pleasures he had in life was winding up Mechanics.

Hearing there was a chance of going to back to his normal life made Mechanics all ears, Bang now had his attention.

"What-a you got there?" enquired Mechanics

"Oi now you're on it ennit hahahaha, here you are... take this and click the link you cry baby" said Bang as he threw his wet phone over to Mechanics"

"Mama Mia! Lo stupido idiota" Shouted Mechanics as he caught the soaked phone and clocked the link.

"ENOUGH IS ENOUGH! This is Sandra Patty reporting directly from the crime ridden area known as The Bang Block, where infamous gangs such as 'Bangz Army' and Unknown Hittaz' terrorise with constant lawless activity and senseless violence! However, today we are not here for them... we are here for a much bigger threat! The so called good guys... Squad Gigantic, Yep you heard me SQUAD GIGANTIC! The group of vigilantes dangerously armed with superpowers, who claim to protect London from the evils of the world... but how true is this?

Earlier this afternoon, LCP was doing a routine gang prevention check on the area before highly decorated Officer Knavish Klandestine was brutally attacked and knocked unconscious by The Squad Gigantic leader whose identity was hidden in the terrible disguise of a Black Lion! He delivered a near fatal blow to the Officer in an unprovoked attack. Luckily, this vicious assault was caught on the phones of local residents who stood in fear whilst this act of violence took place, sensitive viewers please be advised of extremely violent scenes to follow"

The altered footage went on to play, conveniently only showing from where Gigantic punched Officer KK.

"Hahahahaha no-a wonder why-a your hiding pal... you scared-a he-a gonna beat you like-a that again hahahaha who's-a the baby now man" mocked Mechanics as the footage came to an abrupt end.

Bang could dish out the banter but he hated to be on the receiving end of it, he blurted out

"Shut up you doughnut! You think I'm scared of a big pussy Cat! Behave yourself mate"

Mechanics just laughed then said "Whatsa this got to-a do with us-a going back?" Confused to how this helps their cause.

"Don't you see it, they're becoming the bad guys... everybody who's anybody knows that Officer KK is under the Mayor. So for KK to go at them, he must have a direct order for the Mayor... that means that those Squad Gigantic rodents are now the enemy of the city hahahaha, now is the perfect time for me to reappear and build alliances with the Mayor and provide the muscle to not only take down Squad Gigantic, but to also get the rest of my Gems back from that softy Dealer... then kill him and anyone else that gets in my way!"

"Ok ok ok ok-a I see now" said Mechanics, he thought the plan was weak but he didn't care as long as it was a chance to go back to normal living, so he just humoured Bang and went along with it.

"Get your stuff together mate we're going home! And not a moment to soon either, this bloody country living got me turning soft... pedicures and massages all day, it's a joke! Time to get my hands dirty again!" Said Bang as he jumped out of the hot tub and walked toward his property.

In less than five hours Bang and Mechanics we're back in London.

"Arrrr feels good to be home" said Bang as they pulled up near the Bang Block and went to grab a bite of food.

"Nothing beats two piece of chicken and chips with a Big J's fruit punch mate" said Bang as he walked to that one chicken shop that no one from the ends goes to.

"Disgusting mate... it's-a nothing but old oil, cheap meat and-a fat mate" said Mechanics

"That's what gives it the flavour" laughed Bang as he walked off eating the chips without paying.

"Excuse me mate..." shouted the chicken shop worker.

"Shut up Bossman or I'll take the till too" responded Bang as he went back to his car to enjoy the food.

Bang and Mechanics sat behind the tints of his 4x4 and discussed what the next steps were.

Bang decided that he was going to march down to the Mayor's office first thing and get the ball rolling. After finishing his food he scrolled through the internet on his phone, until he found the number for the LCP head office, he gave them a call to let Officer KK know he was back and that things were about to change but little did Bang know, Officer KK and the Mayor had different plans!

As soon as Officer KK came off the phone to Bang he called the Mayor and arranged an early morning meeting to figure out a way to deal with Bang and shut him up forever!

Officer KK wasn't the only phone call Bang made, feeling chuffed with his progress he made contact with a few of his loyal soldiers from Bangz Army, who he left in charge of operations whilst he went incognito, however Bang's soldiers didn't tell him the things he wanted to hear!

Bang was furious to hear the changes that had taken place, his business had slipped and so did his hold over a London! Bangz Army was no longer a feared criminal organisation, it was now merely a petty street gang filled with amateur gang members in their teens and early twenties who were just about scraping by!

Bang decided to put an immediate stop to Bangz Army's pathetic operation, he ordered his captains to round up all these so-called gang members and meet at the old spot tomorrow night!

Bang decided it was time to destroy and rebuild! He made it clear that in his eyes Bangz Army only consisted of his last twenty five trained soldiers and if anybody else disagrees or tries to rep the Army they will be disposed of accordingly... no matter what work they've put in! The street gang era of Bangz Army was now over!

Bang's mood spun upside down, he was enraged! Just as he slammed his phone in anger, it began to ring again. Bang looked at his caller ID and saw it was his associate Crazy Dave.

As soon as Bang answered Crazy Dave bellowed "OI OIIIIII! I heard they let the trash back in town hahaha" greeting Bang in his usual lunatic manner.

"Dave what's happening stranger, tell me something good I've had a crappy day mate, you better not be calling to make it worse!" Answered Bang whilst shaking his head.

"Arrrr mate, I'm about to make your night!" Replied Crazy Dave

"Oh yeah, spit it out then" said Bang

"Easy easy mate, no how are you's or what you been upto's, just straight to business... bloody hell you know how to make a man feel special ennit, probably why your bird left ya hahahahahaha" responded Crazy Dave in a sarcastic tone.

"You call me to insult me and laugh at my L's or you really got something that's gonna make my night?" Said Bang

"Alright alright, calm down Marlene..." said Crazy Dave winding up Bang by calling him Marlene instead of Marlo.

Crazy Dave and Bang knew each other for years and he was one of the only people on the world who could take the mick out of Bang and get away with it, not only because they were friends but also because he was just as dangerous as Bang, so Bang knew not to mess with him unless he really had to! They respected each other highly and done a lot of moves together in the underworld which gave them a special bond.

"I would tell you to keep your hair on but we all know that's to late hahahaha" said Crazy Dave continuing to mock Bang

"Today's not the day for banter mate!" Said a frustrated Bang, he was just about to cut the conversation short then Crazy Dave said

"You still after that softy Dealer?" Said Crazy Dave

"Always mate, why?" Replied Bang as his excitement made him position himself higher in his luxury car seat

"Listen, listen, listen I'm here collecting payment in one of those funny clubs I protect and guess who's in here letting his hair down... your mate Dealer!" Said Crazy Dave

"Yeah... how many guys he got with him" enquired Bang

"That's the thing, he's here alone... well with just one mate who he's on the dance floor doing the bloody salsa with" said Crazy Dave

"That's too good to be true" replied Bang

"Nar mate I asked around, the owner said he comes here regular, he slips the bouncers a few hundred to let him in round the back so no one sees him" explained Crazy Dave

"He's always been a flashy one" kidded Bang

"It's not that mate, he's living a double life, and something tells me Elisha wouldn't be happy to find out he's having nights out with his bit on the side" said Crazy Dave

Bang grinned from ear to ear as he received the drop on Dealer! This was perfect for Bang, he was able to find him on his own with no back up and crew. This was Bang's first piece of good news since coming back to London, he finally felt things were going his way.

"So what d'you want me to do mate? I got a few of the lads with me we can drag the two of them out and make em' go missing?" Offered Crazy Dave

"Nar Nar Nar this is personal, I wanna get my hands dirty on this one... plus it's been a while" said Bang as he sent Mechanics to grab his remaining Soul Freezer from the boot.

"You sure, I still owe you from that situation round the back of Peckham that time" said Crazy Dave

"I told you don't worry about that... I still owe from that time in Tooting Broadway hahaha" laughed Bang as they both reminisced on times they got each other out of sticky situations.

"All I need you to do is give me the club name and location, then get Dealer away from his chick and bring him out back, then I'll do the rest... but Dave whatever you do don't kill his lady friend, I know how you do business and I'm trying to be low key... I don't want no extra heat!" Instructed Bang

"Who said it's a lady mate, he's bit on the side is more Daniel than Danielle if you get my drift, the clubs a spot called Colours, round the back of Vauxhall"

Bang was taken back for a second, that information surprised him but at the same time it gave him clarity.

'It all makes sense, all those times Dealer was sneaking around and coming back with those stupid weak excuses, he wasn't linking up with the opposition and plotting against me, he was just scared to come out. Why didn't that fool just say something... things could've been different" thought Bang.

Dealer's sneaky behaviour is what led to him and Bang's relationship falling apart. Bang lost all trust in Dealer because he believed he was working with his enemies and plotting against him, Bang had no idea

Dealer's double life was based on his preferences and not on betrayal towards him.

Bang stalled his reply to Crazy Dave for a moment as he got his head together, Bang felt that he may have got it all wrong with Dealer, and if only they had just spoke on the matter, they would have been able to clear up a lot of the mistrust and continued to have a strong friendship.

However, things had now gone way too far for Bang to forgive Dealer, Dealer not only took the love of Bang's life, he also took one of his Soul Freezers, his Assets and even his Soldiers! This was now unforgivable, Bang wanted Dealer's blood!

Bang snapped back into action as Mechanics dropped the Soul Freezer on his lap then simply said to Crazy Dave "Whatever floats his boat, I'm on my way now... I'll call you when I'm out back". Then he made his way to Colours to end his feud with Dealer once and for all!

Chapter 5.5 – Death To My Enemies!

Bang pulled up round the back of the club and saw a white coupe in the alley with the registration plate D34LER

"I always said his arrogance will be the death of him" laughed Bang to Mechanics then he called Crazy Dave and said "I'm here mate, right next to this Bousjie toe rags car"

"Give us two seconds" replied Crazy Dave as he signalled four of his henchmen to grab Dealer.

Dealer was on the dance floor enjoying the music whilst his friend went to get drinks from the bar. Crazy Dave's guys played it cool, they calmly told Dealer there was an issue where he parked his car and that he'll need to move it.

Dealer questioned the henchmen "I always park my car there, why is there a problem today?"

"We don't wanna create a scene mate, please just come this way and move it sir" replied Crazy Dave's men as they escorted him towards the back of the club.

Dealer could feel something wasn't right, he looked at the henchmen who were all at least six feet tall and stacked with muscles, he realised they had no security badges... they didn't even have uniform that matched the club's security.

"You lot think I'm stupid" said Dealer, as he attempted to reach for his cards, but Dealer had been drinking alcohol, so his reactions and reflexes were slow!

"HE'S REACHING FOR HIS POCKETS!" said one of Crazy Dave's guys just before punching Dealer in his stomach.

Dealer was winded! As he tried to recover, Crazy Dave's guys grabbed him by his limbs and carried him out the club. They tossed him into the alley then shut the door and carried in as if nothing ever happened.

Dealer got up off the floor, brushed down his designer outfit and then barbarically began to bang on the door shouting "I'MMA BODY EVERY LAST ONE OF YOU FOR THIS... D'YOU KNOW WHO I AM!" With all his attention being focussed on the door, he didn't realise the real danger at hand!

Bang slowly came out of the shadows and said "Hello Mate".

Dealer froze as if he saw a ghost! "Bang?!? You're back" said Dealer

"Yep and I think we got a score to settle, don't you?" Asked Bang

"You're done out here mate, one phone call and Spade Gang will come and finish you" threatened a confident Dealer

"Yeah maybe, but then you're gonna have to explain why their boss is in Colours and I'm sure Elisha will have questions too" said Bang playing on Dealers insecurities, Dealer froze again.

"We gonna play the blackmail game yeah? What do you want from me? Money, Soul Freezer or those Gems?" Said Dealer proposing an offering to Bang

"I'm a take all that anyway mate hahahah... but I'm gonna take it from you in blood!" Replied Bang.

Dealer took a big gulp in fear as he looked at Bang and saw nothing but bad intent in his eyes.

"You know what I'm gonna give you a chance" said Bang as he laid his Soul Freezer on the ground.

"Let's have a one on one like men, I wanna feel every blow when I destroy you... I'll put my Soul Freezer down and you don't use them fancy cards of yours... just a good old school tear up between two men"

In Dealer's heart he knew he couldn't take Bang alone but with the alcohol running through his system his judgement was blurred, which filled him with a false sense of strength and bravery.

"You know what, no one ain't scared of you, come on then... let's do it!" Blurted out, Dealer as he ran towards Bang and punched him in his face.

Dealer followed up his punch with a multiple hooks and elbows aimed directly at Bang's dome.

Each one connected but Bang shrugged them off laughed saying "Finally you showed some balls hahahaha... come on give me more" then he picked up Dealer as if he was an annoying child and effortlessly threw him against the wall

"Come On is that all you got luv" taunted Bang mocking Dealers lack of strength.

Then Bang launched his brutal attack on Dealer! He delivered a cross uppercut to Dealer's jaw leaving him startled then he followed up with at least five belly busting blows to Dealers abdominal area. Dealer was already defeated but Bang carried on battering the living daylight out of him! Crazy Dave watched the onslaught through the CCTV camera link in the Club's office, he was as excited as a child watching their favourite episode of wrestling... his crazy mind loved it!

Bang released every last bit of his tension on Dealer, then as Dealer laid on the floor barely conscious Bang walked over to Mechanics and told him to bring the car to the alley.

Mechanics did as he was told then jumped out the car shaking his head in laughter at the mess Bang had made of Dealer.

Bang stood with his back to Dealer and lit a cigarette saying "Arrrr that felt good, do me a favour and throw him in the boot"

Mechanics looked down at the beaten man and noticed that a glow was coming from the pocket Dealer's hand was in. Mechanics made the mistake of looking into Dealer's eyes as his arm began to diamond up. Dealer was down and out but managed to connect to his cards and hypnotise Mechanics!

Bang had his back to both Dealer and Mechanics, he continued to babble on about how good he felt not noticing his accomplice was now under Dealer's control but luckily for Bang, Crazy Dave could see Mechanics and

Dealer's transformation through the CCTV stream, so he came running down with his henchmen.

Eventually realising Mechanics wasn't responding to his command, Bang spun around to see the reason for the silent treatment only to be greeted by a forearm smash! Bang fell to the ground baffled and confused as Mechanics jumped on him! As Bang defended himself against Mechanics one-man ambush he realised Mechanics was under Dealer's spell, but Bang couldn't do nothing about it! Mechanics was possessed and had a force unlike no other, he throw blow after blow bashing Bang's face in, Bang was about to lose consciousness then... SMMMAAAAAAACCCKKKK!!!

Crazy Dave bussed a bottle over Mechanics head but still this did nothing!

Mechanics released Bang from his grip and now placed his focus on Crazy Dave.

"LETS AVE ITTTT!" Shouted Crazy Dave as he cocked back a sawn-off shotgun and aimed it a Mechanics

A groggy Bang then shouted to Crazy Dave "DON'T SHOOT... he's not himself"

"He better find himself real soon mate or they're gonna find him all over the place in pieces" replied Crazy Dave refusing to lower his aim.

Bang had to think quickly or Crazy Dave was going to kill Mechanics. Bang picked up a brick that was next to him and threw it in the back of Mechanics head to divert his attention from Crazy Dave, it worked, now Mechanics was on to Bang again!

Bang reached for more items to throw at Mechanics hoping he could knock him out of the spell, he threw brick after bottle and bottle after stone until there was nothing left but Dealer was back on his feet too, so his hold over Mechanics was now at full strength!

Still on the ground with Mechanics coming at him, Bang pushed himself backwards trying to get to his feet.

"Just say the word and I'll blow him away" said Crazy Dave but Bang couldn't do that to his best friend Mechanics.

Bang continued to feel around the area he was in, and finally the Gods shun down on him as he clutched on to the familiar feeling of his Soul Freezer.

With Mechanics now less than two metres away, Bang gripped the Soul Freezer trigger and aimed but then he hesitated

"SHOOT OR I'M SHOOTING" Belted out Crazy Dave giving Bang one last chance to defend himself.

With no choice left Bang squeezed his trigger and let off a Freeze Shot!

The Freeze Shot raced out of the barrel and narrowly flew pass Mechanics and hit the right side of Dealer's body freezing his hand, arms and cards!

"SHOOT HIS ARM NOW!!!" Shouted Bang to Crazy Dave as Mechanics grabbed him and began to choke him out.

"BOOOOOMMMM!!!" Crazy Dave didn't dilly dally at all, he let off a shot which connected and shattered Dealer's whole arm to pieces!

Mechanics dropped Bang as the spell was lifted.

"Oh-a my days, I'm so sorry matey... I don't know-a what came over me" apologised Mechanics

Bang coughed and said "Don't worry, happens to the best of us"

As Bang caught his breath Crazy Dave stood over Dealer with his Gun resting on his head and said

"I've got one more shot in here, you want me to finish him?"

"Nar he's still got a few things I need" replied Bang referring to the Dark Gems Dealer stole from him.

"Tie him up and throw him in the boot" instructed Bang

"Urrrgh, and-a how we gonna do that mate he's-a only got one arm" Asked Mechanics

"I always said he was 'armless hahahahaha get it... armless... harmless" joked Crazy Dave.

"Just think of something and Dave, do me a favour when you stop being a comedian can you get in the back and make sure he tells us where the Gems are" said Bang as Crazy Dave and Mechanics kicked Dealer on to his back like a captured Pig and tied his left hand to his right foot, whilst laughing at how silly he looked.

"Ohhh no probs, I love a gentle bit of interrogation" said Crazy Dave as they hopped in the tinted 4X4 and drove off with Crazy Dave's guys following behind.

As requested, Crazy Dave got every last piece of information out of Dealer which led them to his hideout on the outskirts of London.

Dealer handed over all the Dark Gems he stole from Bang along with his second Soul Freezer. Still not completely satisfied, Bang also helped himself to the two million pounds in cash that he found in the safe

"That should cover what you took plus interest" gloated Bang then he roughly split one million between Mechanics and Crazy Dave then kept the rest for himself.

"Nice doing business with ya" said Crazy Dave "I'm assuming you no longer need my services today, so I'm gonna get my guys to drop me somewhere that I can enjoy spending this money tonight"

"That's no probs mate, I'll finish up here... as I said this is personal" said Bang

"See ya later alligator, well maybe not you Dealer the squealer hahahahaha" said Crazy Dave as he swung his duffer bag full of cash over his shoulder and strolled over to his henchmen.

Mechanics and Bang placed Dealer on a chair as he pleaded for his life! Bang wasn't hearing any of it, Dealer was doomed!

"I've got more money" offered Dealer

"Keep it" said a nonchalant Bang

"You can have back Elisha" appealed Dealer

"Don't want her" Replied Bang

"I'll bring you Squad Gigantic" lied Dealer

"That's just desperate now" laughed Bang "At least take your death like a man" said Bang as he grabbed Dealer by the cheeks

"Anyway, I done all that talking stuff earlier mate, I even gave you a chance to have a one on one... no weapons... no powers... no nothing! But you still couldn't even honour that... so it's done, all I'm thinking now is how should I kill ya, Fire or Ice" said Bang

"Pleasssseeeeee Bang spare me" begged Dealer

"Ummmmmmm.... Nar" Replied Bang

"I've got it, since you like to Diamond up and all that. I think it it's only right to ice you up hahahaha" decided Bang then he placed a Soul Freezer in each arm and pointed them both at Dealer...

"Any last words?"

Then just as Dealer was about to speak Bang said "Sike" and Blasted him for ten seconds straight with Freeze Shots!

This still wasn't enough for Bang, he picked up Dealer's phone and took a picture of him!

Bang sent the pics over to Elisha with a location link saying, 'Come get your man!'

Elisha was woken up by the sound of her phone going off. As she reached for her phone, she noticed Dealer wasn't back yet, half-awake she rubbed the sleep out of her eyes and smiled as she read the phone stating "Message from Dealer". Elisha got out of bed and walked towards the bathroom as she opened the message...

"AAAAAAAAAAAAHHHHHHH!" Screamed Elisha, she fell to the ground... DEALER WAS DEAD!

Elisha was in disbelief, she thought it was a sick joke, so she called Dealer's phone immediately. It rang three times then it was answered

"Phewwww, don't ever play games like that again babes" said Elisha thinking that Dealer was on the other end of the phone.

"I think we've gone pass the days of calling each other babes" Replied Bang

Elisha felt a chill in the room as the scary familiar voice sent a shiver down her spine!

Crippled with fear all she could do was whisper "BANG"

"That's my name don't wear it out!" Said an ever so cocky Bang

"Your mans dead but I'm feeling kind of sentimental, so I've sent you a location for where you and your goons can pick him up from, I'll be most appreciative if you can let the world know what I've done... and Oi Leesh, take this as warning... no one messes with Bang and gets away with it!"

Elisha didn't even manage to hang up the phone, she just dropped it as she began to wallow in fear. Eventually she got herself together enough to round up a few members of the Spade Gang and make their way to the location. Upon arrival they walked in and saw Dealer on the chair frozen to death but rather than crumble and cry, Elisha kissed his cold face and simply said "I will get your revenge!"

Bang sent out a major message to the entire underworld... he was back and as heartless as ever, ready to begin his new reign of terror on London!

Chapter 6 – Who's really Bangin!?

It was the morning after the madness and as promised Bang marched down to the Mayor's office with serious intent.

On arrival he pushed pass security and barged straight into the office not caring who or what was going on in there! However, as Bang burst into the office he was greeted by Officer KK and the Mayor who anticipated Bang's abrupt arrival and already had an early morning meeting regarding what they aimed to do with him.

"Morning Marlo, as elegant as ever" said Officer KK sarcastically insulting Bang and calling him by his government name.

"That's Bang to you mate" responded Bang not accepting any of Officer KK's cheeky lip!

"Ohhhhh soorrryyy" said Officer KK continuing to mock Bang

Bang was livid! "You think it's a joke don't ya, you better put a lock on your north and south or I'm a jump over that table and shut it for ya!" Threatened Bang but Officer KK wasn't scared,

Officer KK move towards Bang and squared up saying "Do It!"

"Ok ok let's all calm down" intervened the Mayor as he tried to bring peace to the room.

"I'm sure you didn't come here for a fight Bang... how can I help you?" Asked the Mayor

"Help me? You couldn't help me if you tried mate" replied Bang

"So what is it you want?" Asked the Mayor

"I've come to tell you what's gonna happen now I'm back! I want clear passage from you and the LCP, so I can take back these streets that you guys have allowed to become such a mess! And I'm no longer given you a twenty percent kick back that's being reduced to five for the mean time and when I'm happy that you guys are playing you're role correctly, I'll push it up to ten!" Stated Bang

Remembering how easily Bang took his daughter in the past, the Mayor was ready to accept Bang's demands there and then, but Officer KK had different plans. Just as The Mayor was about to agree to the new terms, until Officer KK butted in.

"Is that it mate, anything else you want?" Said Officer KK humouring Bang's ridiculous demands

Not realising he was being mocked, Bang looked at Officer KK and said "Glad you've come to your senses mate, I honestly thought you were gonna be a problem in all this"

"No not at all, I think you're being totally reasonable... is there anything else we can do to accommodate you even more... d'you want some cash, some property, keys to the town anything like that, now is the time to say... please continue" mocked Officer KK as he stalled Bang and discreetly sent a stress signal to his task force.

Bang was slightly shocked that things were going his way and being the greedy man he was, he decided to push his luck and go for more

"Yeah that actually sounds good, I could do with a few new hideouts... my spots at the docks are a mess! But it better not be any crappy locations, like... they gotta be the dog's bollocks" requested Bang

"Sure mate, just do me one favour first mate" asked Officer KK

"What's that?" Said a reluctant Bang

"Go over there, open that window, look in the sky and tell me if you can see any Horses, Cows or bloody Pigs flying! Cos that's the day I'll bow to your demands you pathetic little man!" Responded Officer KK

Bang was fuming! "Are you dumb! D'you know what I can do to you?!" Said Bang and he rushed towards Officer KK and grabbed him by his neck!

"Yeah absolutely nothing or I'll deal with you just like how we dealt with your parents!" Said Officer KK as his LCP Special Taskforce stormed into the room and threw a shellshocked Bang to the ground.

"WHAT D'YOU MEAN MY PARENTS?" Screamed Bang as he tried to leap towards Officer KK, but his attempt had no success as the LCP caught him in motion and gave him a good beating just for his audacity. The LCP lifted Bang to his feet so Officer KK could tell him what was really going to happen!

"I've dealt with criminals much bigger and badder than you mate and guess what... not one of them are around no more!" Said Officer KK then he went on to say

"Let me tell you a little story mate, this may take a while but you ain't going nowhere for now so I'm sure you can make the time" cheekily said Officer KK as his man held Bang against his will.

"Many years ago I started my career at the LCP as a bright eyed and some would even say naïve rookie, they didn't even call me KK then, I was just little Officer Knavish Klandestine, the son of Eastern European immigrants, who foolishly wanted to make a difference and thank the UK for giving my family a better life.

I ran around on my best behaviour for a few years trying to climb the ladder and become the super, but every time I tried to do the right thing... I was pushed back by some corrupted Officer, which some stupid gangster family would have in their pockets. Eventually I got smart enough to realise if you can't beat them join them! So I decided to get my hands dirty and you know what, things started happening for me and mine but there was only one problem... a scummy good for nothing family that had control over London's criminal world called The Bangs!" Explained Officer KK

Hearing his family surname made Bang angrier! He tried to break loose and attack Officer KK but again was unsuccessful as he was overpowered once again.

"Thought this story might rattle your cage a little hahahaha" laughed Officer KK as he continued to tell his tale.

SQUAD GIGANTIC

"Now although I was next in line, your father Big Bang had my super under his thumb, so one day when he took his family on a camping trip up north, I had to make sure he didn't make it back! Then I became super. The first part of my plan was in place but there was still one more stupid lump of a problem... your Dad! He was a know it all idiot who couldn't take instructions, he could fight like a Bear and was as strong as a Mountain, but he was as dumb as a box of rocks... a complete twat! All muscle no brains, he couldn't run a bath! There was no way he could be my partner."

Bang's eyes began to well up as he was restrained by Officer KK's best men, not sure whether it was emotional tears of upset or anger and frustration. Officer KK taunted Bang and said "Yep that's the cry baby I remember from that night, grabbing on to Mummy G begging for her to keep him, don't cry yet mate the story gets better and better! Can I continue or do you need a tissue?" Said Officer KK as he picked up two sheets of tissue from the Mayor's desk, then walked over to Bang and wiped his eyes like a mother does her baby. Bang spat directly into Officer KK's face.

Officer KK laughed as he slowly took the same tissues and wiped Bang's saliva from his face.

"Guess that's a yes" said Officer KK then he gave Bang a menacing right hook for filling his face with phlegm.

"As I was saying, your loser of a Dad could never be my partner, he ruled with an iron fist and no logic, just straight force! Things were changing and everyone was fed up of this style of... 'management', so it was time the Bang era was put to a stop! There was a new set of kids on the block led by a guy called Swarvez, you know him don't ya, I'm sure you lot killed him not to long ago... I guess in a weird way it was poetic justice but anyway I digress, bad habit of mine, my mother said it'll be the end off me... see I'm doing it again hahahaha.

Basically, Swarvez was innovative, he understood how things could work going forward and even though he was still pretty young he showed a level of leadership that was years beyond his age. I decided he was to be my partner and together we could bring London's underworld into the future but that left one problem... the Bangs, we needed to get rid of these disobedient fools! So I made a nice little proposition to Swarvez and his crew who at that time was relatively small, it was literally just him and a few guys that he grew up with... it was so organic and beautiful. I gave Swarvez the opportunity to be a boss and take over these streets, all he had to do was get rid of Big Bang and his annoying wife! She never knew how to play her role either, she had the kind of attitude that made you not wanna press your brakes when she's crossing the street! She was pretty as a penny but my gosh she had the biggest mouth ever, I always said you're the beautifulest thing ever... until you start to talk and I use to always tell your Dad she was wasted in crime, her chops should be down at Tooting Broadway market shouting that she's got fruit and veg on the cheap... would've made a killing" said Officer KK as he strayed of the topic again

"I keep going off the point, sorry lads hahahaha" said Officer KK as he put himself back on track.

"Basically Swarvez was a smart lad and knew a good deal when he saw one, so of course he took my offer and on that same night him and a few pals went into you house and then... well you know the rest hahahaha you were there hahahaha" laughed Officer KK totally disrespecting Bang and his families memory.

"I'LL KILL YOU!" Shouted Bang still trying to wriggle out of the LCP's grip, he flipped! All these years he never knew who killed his parents, he searched so hard trying to find the hit men who cold bloodily murdered them, to find out all along it was a young aged Swarvez under the command of Officer KK!

"Easy tiger, whooooaaaa seems I've touched a nerve, be happy you already got your revenge technically hahaha" joked Officer KK

"Plus, you should be happy, you were meant to die too! The mission was to eradicate the whole bloodline so the little Bang offspring didn't pop up one day, lucky for you Swarvez was still a little wet behind the ears and of course with you being the little slippery piece of work you are, you managed to escape and run next door didn't ya... you forgot that I was the officer who came to your house that night and put you in care, I can't lie, it took all I had, not to just put one in your head as you sat in the back of the panda but you would've been too much paperwork, plus there was witnesses by then... would've been too messy, would've given the whole game up! If you only ever knew, after your mum and old man were disposed of we spent months and years deliberating on whether we should kill you or not and luckily for you we voted against it... even though seeing you charge in here today like you're something special made me wish we decided otherwise" stated Officer KK.

SQUAD GIGANTIC

After wrapping up his story, Officer KK shoved the Mayor out of his seat and threw his feet on his desk, as he sat down knocking the Mayor's photo of Angel off the desk making it clear that he was the man in charge.

"I know that was a bit long winded and you probably heard a number of things that you either didn't like or point blank didn't want to hear, however I hope it didn't go over your head because there was a direct moral to the story if you like" said Officer KK

"Yeah and what's that" said Bang with a firm face

"DON'T MESS WITH ME! I run London and if you ever forget that, I'll get rid of you and your team in less than an hour... just like I did your parents!" Said Officer KK in a now serious manner.

"Here's what's gonna happen, I'll let you run the streets... for now, but you'll give me thirty percent of everything you bring in, and I mean everything! If you make one pound... thirty pence is mine mate! You'll also make sure you put firm pressure in the correct places to ensure the Mayor's word is fully respected and enforced... and one more thing, you won't step on toes or mess with anything held by the Unknown Hittaz, as they're directly under my wing... is that clear mate" commanded Officer KK

Bang stalled in his response, then reluctantly replied "Yes" as Officer KK's guys beat the agreement out of him.

"Let him go lads, I don't wanna see his stupid face no more" instructed Officer KK.

"How d'you want to leave, through the window or the door? And please know that if you go against the boss's

agreement in any way the only option will be the window...
now get out there and make him his money" said one of
Officer KK's men as they released him and just to add
insult to injury the same man kicked Bang in his bum as he
scrambled out of the Mayor's office to safety.

Bang ran straight out the building to Mechanics who
was waiting with the engine on

"Ayyee aayyya where the fire matey, you walked in like
a big man and now-a you walk like little girl hahahaha...
guess it went well aye" joked Mechanics

"Shut up and drive mate" said Bang, he wasn't in the
mood for any banter.

"Make the call and gather up the lads and all those
little fake Bangz Army soldiers... the foolishness comes to
an end tonight! It's time for war, anybody who's ever gone
against us is dead! No more games" promised Bang, he
was now a man on a mission.

Mechanics arranged a meet later that evening, Bang
was ready to do a clean-up and attack the streets of
London once and for all!

Chapter 6.5 – You ain't Gang!

It was now the evening and as requested Bang's main twenty-five soldiers rounded up all the so called members of Bangz Army, everyone was there from old to young.

They all came up with different theories as they waited around speculating on what they thought was about to happen, some were gassed, some were scared and some where even star struck as they waited like fans to finally see Bang in real life.

"He's come back to make us all rich"

"He's come to give us straps so we can shut down everyone's block"

"I heard he's got Peds' and whips for all of us"

They were so wrong! Bang's whole intention was to kick every last one of them out of Bangz Army! All except his original twenty-five soldiers, his aim was to destroy and rebuild. His creation had become a mess, what was once the most feared unit in London had become a laughingstock, a small-time gang scraping to get by whilst begging for a place in London's underworld.

Now that Bang was back with serious plans of domination and revenge, he knew fully well he had to get rid of the dead weight.

Bangz Army met up at the ruins on the docks where the battle with Squad Gigantic took place, Bang made this the meeting point so everyone involved could see how real it gets.

Bang purposely made them all wait around for over an hour just to demonstrate his power and position.

Finally, he arrived and jumped out of his 4x4, the whole area went into a dead silence as they all laid eyes on their boss – Bang.

"Shut your mouth and make space" commanded Bang's elite men as Bang and Mechanics walked through the parted crowd.

"D'you lot know who I am?" Said Bang to his assembly

Everyone immediately said "Yes"

"Well from this day forget who I am... NOW GET LOST!" Said Bang

They all looked around not knowing what to do, some thought he was joking and others began to do as they were told.

"See bunch of pansies, little wet mummy boys...GET BACK HERE!" Said Bang as they held their heads down and returned to the congregation.

"This is exactly why I called all you little wannabes here today! To clean up and get rid of all you soppy weaklings. You're a bunch of snowflakes who run around with dish rags on your heads, playing gangsters whilst trying to live off the Bangz Army name! An army that's given blood, sweat and tears to control the streets of London and beyond... I've lost soldiers who put their lives on the line just for the Bang name and you Nancys have the cheek to think you can live up to the Bangz Army standards!"

Everybody stood in silence as they were insulted and disrespected by Bang.

"Since I've been gone, you've all run this Army down to a petty street gang who scrambles around doing petty crimes, not making no real money or anything! Just clout chasing for no reason, wasting time running up on so called Op's with shanks just to try and look hard... you disgust me, not one of you are man enough to go one on one and have a good old tear up! You've got no morals, no code, no honour, no sense and no nothing!" Said Bang, he was disgusted at how things had changed.

"From this day NONE of you are Bangz Army... not a single one of you little yellow belly softies! I'm actually disrespected that you were cheeky enough to think you were at the level of this Army"

"Man shut up... I'm banging for life, you can't tell me nothing!" Shouted someone in the crowd

"Who said that? Grab him and bring him to me" ordered Bang

Two of Bang's men walked into the sea of now former Bangz Army members, who all pointed at the loud-mouthed gang member and stepped back as Bang's men dragged the perpetrator to the front of the congregation.

"Finally, someone with a bit of balls but you decided to show them at the wrong time mate" said Bang

"Repeat what you just said... that bit right after you told me to shut my mouth" Politely asked Bang as he leaned into the teenager's face

Now riddled with fear, the teenager tried to be brave and stuttered his words out "I'm I'm... I'm b-b-banging for life"

"Fair enough mate, glad you showed some incentive... let him go lads" commanded Bang

Feeling that his bold move gained him some respect, the teen began to ease a little.

Bang slowly walked behind the teenager and put his arm around his shoulder.

"So you're banging for life yeah?" Asked Bang

The teenager now stood strong and confident, he pushed out his chest then nodded saying "Yeah g I'm banging for life... No cappin' I'm on job!"

Then Bang Replied "I believe you pal" as he tightened his grip around the teens shoulder and put him into a submission hold... then SNAP!!!

Bang twisted the teen's neck and instantly killed him!

"Banging for life, right till the end... at least he weren't lying hahahaha" joked Bang.

This stunned everyone! A loud gasp swallowed the air as Bang went on to speak,

"Let this be a lesson to you all, as I said from today none of you are Bangz Army and if you don't adhere to this simple request, you'll end up slumped like little loud mouth over here who really did bang to the end... is that clear?"

Everyone agreed right away.

"Now get lost! I'm sure those Unknown Hittaz are hiring" mocked Bang

Everyone ran off... they couldn't get away quick enough!

As they left Bang felt a spell of illness come over him, his Dark Gem powers were running low and he needed a top up.

Bang quickly gave his Army of now twenty-five soldiers their instructions

"And you guys, send this little prat for a swim in the Thames then meet me tomorrow, we got business to get on to" then Bang leaned on to Mechanics and said "Get me back to the HQ, I need to top up".

Mechanics walked Bang to the car without any questions, he helped him into the passenger seat, pulled his seat belt over him, then jumped in and sped to Bang's HQ.

"Bloody hell it's been hard using only half the Gems, can't wait to get back and have a full top up now we recovered the rest of them from Dealer... I'll be unstoppable again" said Bang as they drove to his mansion.

They finally arrived at Bang's HQ and he was in a bad way! Mechanics threw Bang's arm over his shoulder literally dragging him into the HQ, smashing ornaments and décor as they made their way to Bang's safe to grab the Dark Gems.

Mechanics helped Bang put on his suit to ensure his safety whilst drawing power from the Dark Gems.

Mechanics sat Bang down and asked him "Whats-a your safe combination mate?" As he went to get the Dark Gems for Bang

"Do one mate, I'm not telling you that so you can rob me one day" seemingly joked Bang but many true things are said in jest. Mechanics may be Bang's best friend, but in this world, things can change any day, so rather than give over his safe combination, Bang just told Mechanics to pull him over to the safe so he could unlock it himself.

Mechanics just shook his head and said "Mama mia" as he helped Bang over to the safe.

Moving slower than ever as he battled through the pain, Bang eventually unlocked the safe and took out the Dark Gems, he finally had all the special Gems from around the planet except the SG Gems that were in Squad Gigantic's possession.

Mechanics eyes lit up as Bang placed the Dark Gems on his desk and got ready to draw its powers.

Just as the dark glow began to omit from the Gems, Mechanics stood behind Bang and Shouted "WAITTTT!"

This startled Bang! He accidentally used his last piece of energy and jumped up out of his seat saying "What?" Thinking Mechanics saw something that put him at risk.

Mechanics didn't respond, so Bang turned around to ask him again, as Bang spun around Mechanics lifted his hand and sprayed a gas into Bangs face which instantly knocked Bang out!

"Sorry I had to do this to you buddy, but duty calls" said Mechanics as he locked cable ties around Bang's hands and feet before gathering up the Dark Gems and dragging Bang out to the land behind the HQ.

"This-a should do" said Mechanics to himself, as he found the perfect spot out back.

Bang's consciousness came back round just in time for him to see Mechanics line up all the Dark Gems on the ground. Mechanics fiddled with them until they all aligned and began to glow in a way Bang had never seen before. Bang tried to escape from captivity, but he was still weak, so his efforts were in vein, all he could do was sit and witness what was taking place.

The Dark Gems levitated off the ground, then the glow created beamed into Mechanics eyes, as his pupils turned red. It was as if the Dark Gems had possessed him! He zoned out, then began to speak as clear as day without his usual accent.

"Master it's me, I come to you with the honour of being the first in my line to deliver our destiny. I have acquired all the Gems that are not in the Chosen Ones possession... it's time for you to come and take what's yours!"

Bang laid on the floor powerless and speechless, he couldn't believe his eyes!

Just as he finally began to get his head around what was happening, his mind was blown again!

Mechanics stood with the Dark Gems glowing and ascending a few metres in front of him, then for a few unreal seconds there was a lack of gravity in the proximity surrounding Bang, Mechanics and the Dark Gems. The glow beaming into Mechanics eyes shot back at the Dark Gems and passed through them like light does a prism, this omitted a much larger second beam into the area behind the Dark Gems.

Bang sat there paralysed from fear, shock and amazement as the second beam solidified the oxygen particles surrounding it then ripped a hole into the Earth's atmosphere, creating a portal which connected the Earth to Planet Zurakaya... which was now known as Supreme Earth!

The portal let off a blazing bright light, then suddenly a massive shadow was casted by a frightening figure! It had a body built from a robust but flexible jet-black metallic substance with touches of red chrome, you could take one look at the entity and see it was built from something light years ahead of anything from this world. The cyborg figure had arms built like houses and the body shape of a well carved robot! Bang tried to identify the being but all he could see was its red piercing eyes as its face was covered by a helmet like contraption.

The portal was fully open and as soon as the monstrous figure entered Earth's atmosphere Mechanics bowed his head and said, "Welcome Master".

The contraption covering the intergalactic travellers face swiftly retracted and revealed its identity... it was the true sworn enemy of Gigantians and The Source... Zeitan Supreme!

"And who are you when you're at home?" Said Bang

Zeitan slowly turned his head to Bang and replied, "Shut up you menial Earth bumpkin, who are you to address me?"

Zeitan looked at the glowing Dark Gems and tapped Mechanics on his shoulder

"Well done EOTS you fully delivered, now all we need is the SG Gems from the Chosen Ones then we can destroy The Source and its protectors once and for all"

Mechanics was an EOTS! All these years he hid his identity and posed as a human in order to execute his life's one true mission of recovering all the SG Gems and delivering them to his master – Zeitan Supreme!

Mechanics was from a long line of EOTS called the Collectors, who were planted on Earth by Zeitan millions of years ago! Mechanics lineage was sent solely to infiltrate Zurakayans on Earth and find all the SG Gems, then return them to Zeitan so he could take the power and destroy The Source or control the Universe. Until now every allocated Collector had been unsuccessful as they tried to do the job on their own, however Mechanics decided to take a new approach once he became a Collector. Rather than exhaust all his resources on a wild goose chase, Mechanics decided to play it smart, he manipulated Bang and sat back whilst Bang took all the risk. Mechanics even made millions of pounds from Bang, when he supplied him with weapons and armour to unknowingly get the job done for him, it was a fool proof plan which worked perfectly and would have been executed quicker if Bang hadn't lost half his Dark Gems to Dealer.

"What the hell is an EOTS?" Said Bang as he sat there confused.

"I'm an EOTS" said Mechanics then he said "My bloodline isn't from this planet! I'm what you would call an alien I guess, I would explain things in more complexity, but you wouldn't even understand anyway".

Bang looked around in disbelief and started laughing "I'm being pranked ain't I... where's the camera man mate this is a joke surely... hold on you ain't even got your stupid accent no more" said Bang

"No mate I only use that to fit in with humans. Even tho I was born here my lineage was created on a planet on the other side of the Universe, how do you think I got you all this alien weaponry and tech? And why do you think I supported you on all these missions? I used you to gather the Gems so I could give them to Zeitan... I'm sorry, I really like you I do but you're just collateral damage in this cause mate" said Mechanics who had slight sense of guilt for his betrayal of Bang, as weirdly he still genuinely saw him as his best friend.

Then Zeitan interrupted Mechanics "Don't you ever let me hear you apologise to these low-level species again, he should be bowing to your feet... you are superior to him!" Said Zeitan, then he had a realisation and went on to say "Furthermore why is he tied up? Don't give him that level of respect... what can he do to you? RELEASE HIM!" Demanded Zeitan.

Mechanics did as he was told and cut the cable ties off Bang's hands and feet.

Bang was still in a bad way but he could see his Soul Freezers inches away from where he was being held captive, he waited for his opportunity then grabbed them both and shouted "BIG MISTAKE" as he blasted Zeitan with Fire Shots from both Soul Freezers.

Bang was chuffed with his attack but that feeling of glee didn't last long! When Bang removed his fingers from the trigger, he saw Zeitan standing there without one piece of harm on his solid body armour.

"You pathetic fool, you still use primitive combustion weapons and tools... did you really think I would send you weapons that could harm me? I suppose you still got one of those old suits that gives you adrenaline boosts too hahahaha" as he laughed off Bang's attack.

Zeitan walked over to Bang and slapped the Soul Freezers out of his hands, then effortlessly lifted him by the scruff of his neck

"I can crush you like an Ant, you're nothing to me!" Said Zeitan as he dangled Bang around like a baby.

"Earlier you asked me who I am, the funniest thing is that you should already know... does this sound familiar? I can give you this dream but not only will you need to find all the other gems associated with my power, you'll also need to understand the risk and sacrifice you will personally need to take"

"You're the spirit of the Dark Gems!" Said Bang as he recognised the voice

"The Dark Gems have no spirit you fool, I tricked you all along! And it wasn't hard, I even gave you a choice to walk away but your greed and thirst for power led you right into my arms. Mechanics marinated you nicely then shoved you in the oven! The Dark Gems weren't even dark until your dirty hands got hold of them, The Source extract that runs through all the Gems converts them to the energy of the holder... your evil energy turned them to Dark Gems and allowed me to communicate through them via my extract of The Source that I have! The Gems didn't do this to you, I did... it was me who told you what to do... it was me that implanted pain and agony in to you then hit you with sharp devastating reminders to knock you down and put you back on track every time you got complacent... it was me who spoke to you through the Gems and sent you to find them all along! I connected to the Gems and used my abilities to control you and break you down" stated Zeitan

Bang tried his hardest to escape Zeitan's grip, but it was useless... he was simply out powered!

"It's pointless resisting but don't worry I plan to let you live longer just so you can show me around your habitat. However, keep irritating me and I'll take pleasure in killing you now!" Expressed Zeitan.

Bang spat in Zeitan's face and said "Do your worse!"

"Urgghh you disgust me" said Zeitan as he pulled Bang closer and literally used him to wipe the spit of his face.

Zeitan was now done playing! He held Bang high above the ground with one hand as he raised his other and slowly began to clinch it into a fist. As Zeitan's fist closed, Bang felt his insides crushing piece by piece, then his bones snapped and his organs began to fail as he passed out from the pain!

Zeitan threw Bang's lifeless body on the ground with no remorse and continued to crush him from within but Mechanics couldn't just stand by and watch Zeitan kill him.

"Master wait, don't kill him" yelled Mechanics

Zeitan stopped and with a stern look on his face he said "You better not be choosing these animals over your boss"

"No master, never" quickly replied Mechanics. "It's just I think he will be more use to us alive! He is a loyal man who has managed to gather all the Gems apart from the Chosen Ones and even then, he was the first man to find their precious Paradise Mountains and destroy it!"

Zeitan's eyes lit up when he heard Paradise Mountains, because when Zeitan managed to download the Earth file from The Source and upload it to create Supreme Earth, the only piece of the file he couldn't retrieve was Paradise Mountains, as The Source managed to send a bug to wipe it from his files in order to protect itself from a future attack. Zeitan realised that he would need assistance in getting to Paradise Mountains as he was convinced this was where The Source was planted.

Unknowingly, Bang managing to locate Paradise Mountains saved his life, as Zeitan now found value in keeping him around.

"You might be right but if he is to join our team, he needs to be modified and improved, he will not be conquering planets with me using old weapons and silly childish suits" said Zeitan

"I totally agree master" replied Mechanics who was willing to do anything to save Bang's life.

"He seems to like these insignificant weapons" said Zeitan referring to the Soul Freezers

"How about I implant them into him permanently, I can place Plasma in his veins that will flow alongside his blood, this will solidify and discharge high pressured Plasma Burst Punches whenever close contact is made! This substance is useable on this Earth and will amass much more power than these weapons"

"Well his name is Bang... now he really will be banging" said Mechanics

Zeitan smashed the Soul Freezers to smithereens then resuscitated Bang and began working on him there and then.

Bang screamed with pain as Zeitan altered his body and DNA with Mechanics assistance, Zeitan bypassed the screaming reassuring Bang by stating "The gain will be stronger than the pain, now shut up".

Bang's body began to go through a crazy transformation! His arms were now weapons of mass destruction, Zeitan was almost complete then he stepped back whilst looking at Bang as if he had forgot something then said

"Oh yeah that's it, this suits got to go! With a touch more bio hacking his body will be able to do everything this suit does plus more allowing cellular regeneration to take place naturally... well kind of".

Zeitan drew power from within the Dark Gems and blasted it into Bang, this brought back Bang and had him feeling as strong as an Ox, it was as if nothing happened. Bang looked himself up and down and noticed he had a tattoo like 'B' stamped on his torso.

"That is the central hub of all your power, you now have a power within you like never before" said Zeitan

"I know you can feel the strength of the Plasma running through your veins but let me tell you one thing... you work for me now! I'm your master, your boss or anything else you want to call it... agreed?" Stated Zeitan

Feeling extremely confident with his new abilities Bang hesitated with his reply!

Zeitan looked him dead in his eyes and said, "Don't test me, you may be stronger but you're still nothing to me!" Then he aimed his hand at Bang once again and started to clinch his fist.

Bang yelled in pain and quickly agreed to Zeitan's terms "Yes, Yes... YEESSSSS!"

Bang and his army had officially gone under Zeitan's umbrella, Mechanics smiled with a face full of happiness as he managed to save Bang's life and get his friend back.

After forcing Bang to pledge his allegiance to his cause, Zeitan went over to the Dark Gems as they hoovered and continued to glow. He picked the Gems out of the air one by one disrupting its cosmic like balance, then smashed them all into his chest creating a massive explosion which blew Mechanics and Bang backwards. They got off the floor and dusted themselves down just in time to see Zeitan grow even bigger as he absorbed the energy from the Dark Gems.

Zeitan grew into an even bigger horrifying unit!

Zeitan looked at Mechanics and Bang saying

"Whenever I got close to launching my attack on the Gigantians and The Source, they would purify the land on Earth and hit me hard"

"But why would them destroying Earth harm you?" Asked Bang

"Because on my planet – The Supreme Earth, our environment is a direct live stream of your Earth which replicates every last section in real time, even tho we have a much more superior level of beings and technology, we still have your atmosphere, landscape and environment... so basically if a tree disappears on your Earth, it disappears on Supreme Earth too!

So every time they saw I had them under pressure they would purify the land and launch an attack which tore me down bit by bit, many times I built back and got stronger then they would purify and attack again... shutting me down over and over!

But after a while I realised the attacks stopped, so I did a little research and established that every time they launched attacks or purified the planet, it weakened The Source! The frequent high level of activity made The Source unstable, so eventually they had to stop their attacks or risk exploding it all together! However, the Dark Gems and extract in my possession were separated from The Source, so although they can connect with The Source, they've technically become their own entities. This meant they were not affected by the purifications and attacks which took place, so the law of balance now allowed my extract to become a stronger piece of the puzzle so to speak and the same goes for the Dark Gems. Now all I need is the SG Gems from the Chosen Ones to bring me to my full capacity of power which I have never seen before"

That evening, Zeitan sat with Mechanics and Bang to discuss the plans he had! Zeitan instructed them both to carry on as normal, which meant Mechanics was to keep his earthly identity and even that loopy accent as that is how he is known on Earth.

Zeitan wasn't happy to hear Bang's hold over London was at jeopardy after his altercation with Officer KK, he told Bang "Well I guess tomorrow will be the perfect time to try out your new gifts"

Bang smirked as his looked down at his loaded arms!

Zeitan was happy to hear that Bang was also a direct enemy of Squad Gigantic, who he referred to as the Chosen Ones! Zeitan instructed Bang to bring him to Jay Gigantic and the rest of the Squad. He also told him they will soon travel to Paradise Mountains to destroy The Source once and for all. However, he stressed that this will only be possible once he is in full possession of the last remaining SG Gems from the Chosen Ones.

Things were seriously about to change in London and the rest of the World!

Chapter 7 – Zeitan Patterns Up!

It was the day after the night before and Bang was raring to go!

He had the whole night to think about the new position he found himself in and came to the conclusion that it was the best thing that had ever happened to him. Not only did he have powers, but he also had the most powerful being he's ever met in his corner, he felt unstoppable!

Bang was done with pretending to be the respectable businessman, he was ready to be an all-out villain!

With Bang feeling ready to take London back, it was time to pay Officer KK and the Mayor a second visit, to let them know what time it really was!

Bang grabbed his phone and put a call out and within minutes his army was at his HQ in a convoy of blacked out 4x4's, loaded up with weapons and soldiers.

Bang and Mechanics jumped in the 4x4 at the front of the fleet expecting Zeitan to follow, noticing Zeitan was not entering the vehicle Bang stepped back and said "Sorry where's my manners… after you Zeitan"

Zeitan looked at both Bang and Mechanics in disgust and said "Do you really think I'm getting in that piece of junk"

Bang and Mechanics looked at each other in shock, this 4x4 was the top of the range… highest spec with all the extras and a bulletproof matte finish. However, the technology from Zeitan's world was light years ahead of Earth in this day and age... cars were even lower than the equivalent of horse and carts to us!

"You go ahead, I'll make my own way" arrogantly stated Zeitan

Bang didn't need to be told twice, with his modified blood pumping and adrenaline rushing, he jumped in the whip and bleeewwww down to the mayor's offices with his gruesome battalion following behind! They caused maximum havoc on route as they lawlessly ignored every red light and ripped through the traffic.

Luckily for the Mayor, Bang's lawless behaviour created a scene which alerted the LCP, Officer KK's team reported the disturbance to him and Officer KK instantly reacted commanding them to create road blocks and diversions to stop Bang in his tracks... but that didn't work!

Officer KK knew exactly what Bang was up to, so he also loaded up and deployed a team to defend the Mayor's office.

Officer KK and he's elite team managed to get to the Mayor's building just before Bangz Army arrived. They secured the entrance with reinforced steel and gave extra protection in the form of LCP officers standing guard in a strategic formation.

Bangz Army pulled up and whipped out their weapons... so the LCP did the same!

Seeing guns being drawn on both sides, all the civilians on the area dispersed to avoid getting caught in the crossfire! With all the pandemonium taking place outside, Officer KK and his armed elite team escorted the Mayor to his office surrounding him from all angles to ensure his safety.

Bang hopped out the 4x4 and slowly walked up to the line of LCP officers as they stood guard at the entrance. Bang looked each one of them in their eyes then asked

"What you little Prats gonna do?" As he laughed.

One brave Officer raised his Gun!

"Big mistake mate" said Bang, then he grabbed the nozzle and with a short squeeze, he incinerated the gun's barrel leaving nothing but the magazine and handle in the officer's hand!

Everyone stood amazed, Bang just laughed as he continued to give London a display of his new power.

"OK you wanna play do ya?" Asked Bang as he grew more confident by the second "WELL LETS PLAY!" Screamed Bang, then he totally annihilated the line of LCP officers who stood guard of the door!

A big brawl broke out between Bangz Army and the LCP right outside the City Hall, Bang left them to it as he used his explosive punches to break through the reinforced entrance and get to the Mayor and Officer KK.

"What you doing here Bang!" Shouted Officer KK from the Mayor's office window

Bang yelled back "I'm coming to kill ya, that's what!"

"It's useless, you won't even get through that with a tank mate hahahaha" laughed Officer KK

"Come down here and fight me like a man, instead of hiding in your ivory tower princess" Replied Bang trying to provoke Officer KK into a fight.

"Blah Blah Blah mate, keep talking... Squad Gigantic will arrive and batter you again before I come down to you" Stated Officer KK

"Bang calm down, I'm sure we can discuss this" Shouted the Mayor over the madness, the Mayor wanted to find a neutral solution to resolve this, but Bang wasn't having none of it!

"Calm down! Are you crazy... you guys have changed your tone haven't ya! Keep that same previous energy!" Said Bang

"No, you better keep your energy mate, I've just sent for more men to deal with you and your pathetic little army" shouted back Officer KK.

Meanwhile, Tanya got report of the commotion through the SG System. She immediately informed Jay Gigantic and briefed him on the situation. Not knowing the risk Bang now posed, Jay decided to handle this one alone without the Squad, he transformed into Gigantic, hopped on his SG Quad and headed over to the battle.

Bang continued to go to work on the entrance, delivering explosive blow after blow as his Army engaged with the LCP.

"You're in trouble now mate" Shouted Officer KK from the window with a newfound smug confidence, "Look who's decided to join the party"

As he was located on higher ground, Officer KK had a broad view of everything and he could see Gigantic whizzing towards them on his Quad Bike.

"Gigantic's about to tear you to pieces!" Gloated Officer KK

But Bang had a few new tricks up his sleeve, last time they fought, Bang was a mere mortal! Just a man with his Soul Freezer Gun but now he had powers! Bang was relishing the opportunity to take on Gigantic with his new attributes!

Bang looked over his shoulder and he too saw Gigantic drawing nearer.

"This just gets better and better, not only two birds with one stone... but three! Hahaha"

With not one bit of hesitation Bang ran towards Gigantic to initiate battle, still in motion Gigantic jumped of his SG Quad and dived right at Bang!

Whilst mid-air he said "Park then Engine Off" The SG Quad did as commanded and whipped itself into a nice space and shutdown.

There was no love lost between Bang and Gigantic, it was on sight! No talking, no insults, no nothing... just straight to war!

As Bang and Gigantic collided mid-air, Gigantic grabbed Bang and threw him on to the steel reinforced doors!

Bang got up straight away and laughed saying "Is that all you got?"

Gigantic replied back saying "I ain't even started yet fam".

Then Bang charged at Gigantic and threw three punches that all missed!

"Still slow as ever" mocked Gigantic, then he gave Bang two body blows and a right hook across his jaw!

Officer KK laughed and shouted from the window "Hahahahahahaha I told ya, you're done mate!" Then he prematurely instructed his LCP team to retreat, as he was so confident that Gigantic had this under control.

Bang was dazed for a few seconds, but he wasn't down and out! He didn't even go down, instead a blue and orange serum ran through his veins and sprung him right back.

"I ain't the same Bang as before mate" said Bang.

Gigantic was in slight shock to what he just witnessed.

Bang took advantage of Gigantic's lack of concentration and delivered two explosive blows to his face BOOOOMMMMM... BAANNNNNGGGGG!

Each blow sounded and looked like a grenade going off when they connected, Gigantic went flying back and was laid out on the floor!

"That was easy" said Bang thinking he had defeated Gigantic with his new explosive punches that he named the 'One Bang'.

Officer KK watched in horror, he couldn't believe what was taking place. Bang had a power he's never seen before... punches that explode on contact!

"We need to just give him what he wants" said the Mayor, begging Officer KK to surrender.

Officer KK shook himself out of his state of bewilderment and shouted back "OVER MY DEAD BODY!"

Then out of nowhere a flame appeared in the middle of the room, then in a clockwise motion it literally burnt a circle at least eight feet high and four feet wide!

Then a tall broad shadowy figure began walking through the circle!

"WHAT THE....." Shouted Officer KK, as some of his men rushed in front of the Mayor to protect him from whatever was coming.

The rest of his men took guard in front of the portal and some went behind it to do the same only to realise there was nothing there!

Within seconds the mighty Zeitan Supreme walked out of the portal and said

"Over your dead body... well that can easily be arranged!"

The whole room stood speechless as they stared at Zeitan's intimidating figure.

"Why do you look so startled? Have you never seen molecular transportation before? This planet is such a joke" Genuinely asked Zeitan

Officer KK was the first to come round, he gasped in fear then half-hearted blurted out to his Elite team "Don't just stand there... SHOOOOOOOOTTTT!"

BACK OUTSIDE THE CITY HALL

Meanwhile, Bang was in for a shock of his own!

Thinking he had defeated Gigantic was a big mistake, the sheer power of Bang's explosive 'One Bangs' was able to drop Gigantic, but it wasn't able to have no lasting effect on him as the Red Fire on Gigantic's Diamond just absorbed the plasmas force and transferred the energy around Gigantic's anatomy. Bang actually did the total opposite to what he hoped for, rather than weakening Gigantic... he technically made him stronger!

Bang made the arrogant mistake of stupidly turning his back on his opponent as he walked off without checking to see if he was truly down.

"Hahahahaha you think your little modifications can done me so easily" said Gigantic

Bang couldn't believe it! He stopped in his tracks with his eyes wide open thinking, 'how did he survive that!?!'

Just as Bang managed to turn around, he was met by one of Gigantic's brutal onslaughts!

Gigantic was now as mad as ever, Bang had no chance as Gigantic smacked him all over the place!

Bangz Army tried to join in and defend their boss as he took such a beating, but their assistance was useless as Gigantic went through them too.

BACK IN THE MAYOR'S OFFICE

Officer KK and his men opened fire on Zeitan, however this was just a waste of bullets as the majority of them just bounced off Zeitan's remarkable armour and ricocheted around the room making the shooters have to take cover, the rest of the bullets were caught by Zeitan and thrown back at them with the same speed!

"Alright you've had your fun now" said Zeitan Supreme once Officer KK's men ran out of ammunition, "Now it's my turn!"

Within five seconds flat, Zeitan gruesomely dropped everyone in the room only sparring Officer KK and the Mayor, then Zeitan leaned over the two and said

"You will now run London under my command, with your first point of contact being my new worker – Bang, I heard you and Bang recently had a minor dispute and as he put it you in particular Officer KK gave... 'nuff chattings' I'm hoping this 'chattings' will now stop and you'll see that it is imperative that you both listen to and agree with anything that myself or Bang tells you to do."

For once Officer KK had no mouth, "Of course you do have the option to say no but then I will have to viciously kill you and replace you with someone from my constituency... now I don't think that'll be helpful for neither of us, as I don't want to have to train up people to learn your roles, etcetera, etcetera and I'm sure you don't want to end up like everyone else in this room, do you? But as I said the choice is yours... what will it be?"

Officer KK and the Mayor took a quick look around the office and saw the bloodbath Zeitan effortlessly created, then they collectively agreed to his demands.

Zeitan went on to introduce himself, "Great, my name's Zeitan Supreme. I'm the last Enemy Of The Source and the true destined leader of the Universe! You already know Bang, who is currently my designated boss of this city who I have upgraded with new powers and strength which now places him higher up the hierarchy in comparison to you basic punitive humans" as Zeitan mentioned Bang he went over to the window to gloat and show them Bangs new powers first hand but unfortunately he glanced out the window only to see Bang getting destroyed by Gigantic!

"You stupid humans can't do anything correctly can you?!" Said a frustrated Zeitan.

Zeitan then grabbed Officer KK and the Mayor and said "Come On" then he teleported them all outside, where Gigantic was battering Bang.

"What no pretty flame thing this time" said Officer KK as he found his cheeky mouth again

"No, the distance is short so basic teleportation is more than sufficient... actually why am I explaining myself to you... SHUT UP you little flea!"

"Oh sorrrryyy" said Officer KK.

When Zeitan appeared Gigantic was slapping about at least five of Bang's men, as Bang laid on the floor recuperating his strength.

"Hahahaha you're finished now" said Bang to Gigantic as he saw his boss arrive at the scene.

Gigantic quickly disposed of Bang's men and cautiously approached Zeitan

"Tanya are you seeing this?" Said Gigantic through his comms

"Yeah babes, but I don't know what it is! I'm trying to identify him but nothings coming up, it's as if he's not from this world" responded Tanya

"He's a big lad, can you identify any weaknesses to take advantage of?" Asked Gigantic hoping to come up with a strategy.

"Sorry hun, no weaknesses unfortunately just strength and power, he's omitting a crazy amount of energy. I think you should call the rest of the Squad if you're aiming to take him on" stated Tanya

"Nar, let me see what I'm dealing with first" replied Gigantic not wanting to put his children in harms way.

"Be careful babes, this ain't the usual enemy!" Said a fearful Tanya

By time Gigantic replied "Cool" he found himself in front of Zeitan's colossal figure.

"You must be the one that carries the Gigantic name, the Chosen One" said Zeitan

"Yeah something like that, and who are you?" Replied Gigantic

"He's Zeitan Supreme and he's gonna smash your head in mate hahahaha" Shouted Bang from the floor.

"Is that right yeah?" Said Gigantic to Zeitan

"I guess so" Replied Zeitan

Thinking attack is the best form of defence Gigantic jumped up and smashed Zeitan across his face SMAAACCCCKKKK!!! For the first time Zeitan stumbled backwards, Gigantic then charged into him and followed up his attack with a number of punches, kicks and elbows! But Zeitan just laughed as Gigantic threw his all at him!

"Stop, stop, stop you're tickling me" mocked Zeitan then he delivered a blow directly to Gigantic's stomach that immediately dropped him!

"I like you, you got that fighters spirit in you! I can tell you have Zurakayan blood, you're a clear descendent of the Gigantian bloodline but you ain't demonstrating the real power of a Chosen One, I'm almost upset that it's going to be this easy to destroy you and The Source" said Zeitan as he gave Gigantic a beating he had never experienced before.

Gigantic was getting battered and he couldn't do a thing about it, he tried to fight back but all his efforts were brushed aside by Zeitan who was too powerful and skilful for Gigantic.

Bang was loving it! Him and Mechanics also joined in as they horribly rushed Gigantic with Zeitan leading the attack.

Tanya saw enough, with Gigantic's vitals extremely low she was just about to send in the rest of the Squad, then a voice whispered into Gigantic's mind "You are the leader of the Chosen One's, the most favoured and honourable. The Source walks within you all... especially you!"

Then.........
BAAAAABBBOOOOOOOOOOOOOOOMMMMMMM!!!!

A MASSIVE Red Flame combusted out of Gigantic's Red Fire Diamond blasting Zeitan, Bang and Mechanics at least twenty metres away! Gigantic had a new surge of energy but rather than waste it fighting a fight where he was hurt and outnumbered, he called for his SG Quad to make an escape.

The SG Quad made its ways to him and he hopped on to getaway but just before he left, he heard Zeitan shouting something to him

"OI, the Prodigal One... I'm the soon to be leader of the Universe – Zeitan Supreme! I'm the BIG MAN! Not you or your Gigantian leaders...you were given your choice since birth and YOU SHOULD'VE BEEN WITH ME! RIGHT BY MY SIDE... WE COULD'VE RULED TOGETHER, YOU COULD HAVE SAT WITH ME AS A GOD BUT INSTEAD YOU SHOW YOUR WEAKNESS AND EMPATHY! RATHER THAN CONTROL AND DESTRUCT YOU'VE CHOSEN TO BE BORING, TRYING TO HEAL AND GROW! YOU'VE CHOSE TO GIVE BIRTH TO A RACE OF ZURAHUMANS RATHER THAN OWN THE UNIVERSE! BUT I WILL NOT LET YOU LIVE LONG ENOUGH TO FORFIL THAT DESTINY... MARK MY WORDS, I WILL KILL YOU AND DESTROY THE SOURCE LONG BEFORE!!!"

Zeitan had previously unlocked digital scriptures from The Source extract which highlighted Jay Gigantic's possible paths of destiny, Zeitan assumed Gigantic knew all these things and unknowingly exposed all this to him.

Gigantic sped off back to the SG HQ with Zeitan's words played on his mind.

'What did he mean by I should've been with him and about we could have ruled together, who is this guy? How does he even know me? What's he talking about I give birth to ZuraHumans, what even is ZuraHumans? Bout we could've ruled together... and what's all this Source talk and he's gonna kill who?! He must be mad, I'm about to go into next level training for him... WATCH!' Thought Gigantic.

Gigantic's mind kept on spinning, he decided he was going to see the one person who could possibly tell him what's going on – Mummy G.

"Yo Tan" said Gigantic into comms

"What's up babes, you ok that was a close one" said his concerned wife

"Yeah I'm good, but it was a madness, you wouldn't believe what happened!" Replied Jay Gigantic

"Trust me nothing shocks me anymore haha" laughed Tanya

"I'm about to come in but I'm not stopping, I just gotta transform and change then I gotta go see my Mum ASAP... there's a few things I need to discuss" said Gigantic

"Cool, opening secret entrance now" said Tanya

Jay Gigantic got in, got ready then sent for his driver 'Whipz' and headed straight over to Mummy G's to find some answers on Zeitan and exactly who he is!

Chapter 7.5 – Home Truths!

Jay Gigantic arrived at Mummy G's house within minutes, he jumped out of the moving car and said

"I'll be thirty minutes max bro"

Whipz just nodded and continued to park the car.

Jay ran to the door, just as he went to press the doorbell he heard his mother's voice through the intercom "Come in son, the doors open", Jay walked in to see Mummy G coming out of the kitchen.

Mummy G was expecting him, she already knew of his altercation with Zeitan and knew he would have questions.

This new threat was set to be a serious problem so Mummy G contacted Paradise Mountains to get advice and instructions, upon hearing the name Zeitan Supreme Paradise Mountains immediately sent Santago!

"We need to talk" said Mummy G, as Jay followed her through the hallway, Jay realised they were not alone as his mother was carrying a tray with three crystal tumblers, a small ice bucket and three bottles of Big J's Fruit Punch.

"Who's here mum?" Asked Jay

Then as they both stepped into the lounge he looked over his mother's shoulder and saw Santago.

"BIG MAN SANTAGO! Wha gwarnnnn, you good?" Said Jay happy to see Santago, they hadn't seen each other since their last battle against Bangz Army.

Santago gave Jay the biggest hug and was just about to respond when Mummy G replied to Jay's previous question... "Your fathers here, that's who"

"MY WHATTTTT?!?" Shouted Jay.

"Your father son, there's a few things we need to discuss ASAP" said Santago

"Jay looked around the room confused, then he placed one hand on his head as he sat down on Mummy G's luxurious sofa.

"My father, you're my dad..." said Jay

Jay took a few seconds to get his head around everything. All his life he grew up not knowing who his father is, whenever Jay would ask Mummy G about him, she always told him 'it's complicated, just know you are loved'.

Eventually Jay just stopped asking as he never got a detailed response.

"Yes, he's your father... the love of my life" said Mummy G confessing her love

"Just as she's the love of mine too" said Santago

"I've always wanted to tell you, but the time was never right but with Zeitan popping up now's the perfect time for you to know exactly who you are!"

"What d'you mean who I am Mum, I'm baffled" said Jay

Santago sat next to Jay and began to speak...

"This goes back to the beginning of time son, it's prophecy..." then Mummy G interrupted Santago saying "It'll be better coming from me" then she sat on the other side of her son and was about to explain but Jay interrupted

"I knew sut'um weren't right you know, after I rocked that Zeitan guy he Shouted out I should've been by his side, what does he mean?" Asked Jay, his mind was now running overtime as he wound himself up more and more.

Jay jumped up and aggressively shouted "SOMEONE TELL ME WHATS GOING ON?"

Mummy G responded in a calm but even firmer manner "You better remember who you're talking to!" Jay quickly humbled himself!

"Stop acting like pickney and sid' down so we can talk like big people, what I'm about to tell you is gonna be a lot to take in but know seh' the whole world literally depends on it" said Mummy G

Reading the seriousness in his mother's tone, Jay sat down and began to listen.

"First let's start with that Zeitan Supreme, remember I told you stories of our bloodline and Zurakaya?" Said Mummy G

"Yeah" said Jay

"Well in a nutshell he's a Cyborg from them ancient times, the days of the Gigantians and Lords... we don't even know his actual age but he's literally millions of years old!

Zeitan in the last known surviving EOTS and he won't rest until he's killed or successful in his mission to destroy The Source... and obviously we can't let the latter happen"

"Yeah I remember all the stories about the ancient times, my Gigantian ancestors leaving Zurakaya and coming to Earth... all of that but I don't understand how I was never told about this Zeitan brudda' and I'm still confused to how he directly affects me" questioned Jay

"Maybe it'll become clearer if you explain Jay's direct history and the prophecy attached to him" said Santago

Mummy G agreed then continued to explain

"There a few things I had to hide from you regarding the full prophecy" said Mummy G

"Like what?" Said Jay as he cut his mother off once again.

"Stop interrupting and listen then you will find out" replied Mummy G, putting her son in his place.

Jay apologised and allowed his mother to speak.

"As you know prophecy told us that the child born with the Fire Red Diamond will lead the Chosen Ones but here's what you didn't know! The Chosen One with the Fire Red Diamond had the choice to choose from two paths... one of Good and one of Evil!

The Chosen one would have the ability to protect The Source and eventually bring Zurakayans and Humans together creating the final superior being... The ZuraHumans.

The other path is an outcome that's unthinkable where the Chosen One will side with the Major force of evil - Zeitan Supreme and destroy The Source, ending the life of all Zurakayans and humans!

"No pressure then" joked Jay as he sat there mind blown.

"This meant there was a fifty-fifty chance that you would leave the Zurakayan teachings behind to side with the EOTS! So drastic measures had to be taken when you were born" explained Mummy G, a tear fell down her face as she relived everything she went through because her child was born as the Chosen One.

"Mum why you crying?" Asked Jay as he comforted his mother

"It was a hard time for us all son, we had to make some harsh decisions and sacrifices. It had Paradise Mountains torn in two! Even Chief Danjuma and Lady Jenay were at loggerheads, it was crazy!" Said Santago, carrying on for Mummy G as she pulled herself together.

"Why what happened?" Said Jay

"It's why you ended up here" replied Mummy G as she wiped a tear from her face

"Ohhh" said Jay

Mummy G was still pretty upset, so Santago went on to say

"There's a reason for the fire in your Diamond, fire burns and destroys, or fire purifies and creates new beginnings. There was no way of knowing which path you would choose at such an early age, so a decision had to be made to protect Paradise Mountains.

One morning, we woke up to see Chief Danjuma standing over us with you in his hands and lady Jenay behind him crying, I jumped up and asked what's going on? You were no more than a couple weeks old. Me jumping up woke your mum, she said 'Gimme' my son!' She knew exactly what was happening whilst I was still trying to figure it out.

Chief Danjuma looked us dead in the eyes and said that you can't stay on Paradise Mountains! They said you needed to be put in exile for the safety of the world! We went crazy! Lady Jenay was on our side, but it wasn't enough, Chief Danjuma made the decision that his own grandchild was to be banished and no one weren't gonna change his mind!"

Jay couldn't believe what he was hearing, as he was sure that he was born in London at St George's Hospital but the truth is he was born on Paradise Mountain and just like the other Chosen Ones, a precious stone appeared under him but not just any Gem it was the most special Gem of them all – The Fire Red Diamond.

Mummy G took over the conversation as Jay sat there shellshocked

"They decided that you will be sent to London and made to live as a orphan... my baby was going to be dumped some where in a strange land by himself, to be found by some random people who will raise him... I weren't having none of that! Not from my father or The Source itself! I didn't care about prophecy or anything... you're my son and to me that comes before anything else!

I was ready and willing to go to war against my own people! Me and your Dad snatched you back when a few men stood guard, whilst Mum and Dad went into negotiations. I told them straight... I would kill us both before I let them take you! They know I don't play so they had to take it serious.

There was a stand-off for days, it was horrible families fighting families and friends fighting friends! It felt like the prophecy was being for filled right there and then, Paradise Mountains had never seen civil war before, it was as if you were influencing people to choose good or evil and to make it worse... no one could tell which side was which! Eventually Mum and Dad came back saying they've come to an agreement. There was an immediate ceasefire and they explained that there was no stopping you from being banished and nullified as you were deemed to be too risky, the only option was that they would allow me to go to London with you.

I accepted the offer without hesitation and prepared for travel, Santago said he would come too but he was the best fighter on Paradise Mountains, so realistically he was never gonna be allowed to leave his post, it would've left The Source and everything else at a disadvantage.

Before leaving, the Fire Red Diamond was separated from you and placed under Chief Danjuma's direct protection. A special serum was created to nullify your ZuraGene and special abilities, so if you did choose the path of the EOTS you'll be easier to stop! I argued against the serum as you were so young, and there was still a big chance that you would be good and need your powers to protect our worlds. I was assured that if you choose the path of the righteous, you will be called back to Paradise Mountains where you will go through the Falls of Purity which will cleanse you and eradicate the serum allowing your ZuraGene to reactivate and restore your full abilities"

"Falls of Purity!? What's that?" Said Jay

"The waterfall you were scared to walk through" mocked Santago

"Ohhhh" replied Jay "...and I weren't shook, don't try it"

"Whatever you two, let me carry on saying what I'm trying to say" said Mummy G

They both laughed and continued to listen to Mummy G

"I accepted the terms and went to London with you, we were set up in a humble abode to ensure you found your own way with minimal external influences.

Paradise Mountains constantly looked over us! Santago personally made sure of your safety throughout your whole life. I had to be careful not to influence your choices in anyway or make decisions for you, all I could do was be the best mum for you and I can't lie, that was harddd! There were certain times you had us worried, especially when you started doing road!

I thought we were done for, you were constantly tested and somehow that EOTS Zeitan was able to send things to your path, loads of battles took place to protect you... without you having the slightest clue to what was going on! And that bad little pickney Marlo Bang was one of Zeitan's best infiltrators he managed to manipulate him at just the right time, just after he grew up and got to know so many stories about Paradise Mountains! My biggest regret was ignoring my instincts and telling him those stories too but those times he was just an innocent child... but now look! Look what he grew to be and all the trouble he's caused us! I was vex when you continued hanging around with him as a teen, there were times I was like yep he's going the sheggery path... I've lost him!

But somewhere deep down inside I always had hope for you and let's be real you're my son... you must do good." Joked Mummy G.

"That's nuts" said Jay

"Once we saw you separated from Bang and started living a legit life, we knew it was just a matter of time before you would be called back the Mountains and take your place amongst your people" said Santago

Mummy G's face finally had her big beautiful smile on it as she said

"It was the happiest day of my life when Santago popped up out of nowhere and said they were ready to bring you home. I was getting ready to go home too, everything was in place. The plan was to let you go back on your first journey so you could reactivate your ZuraGene and meet your true people then I would comeback with you on a second trip, reveal all the secrets and I'll stay whilst you were to be free to live between London and Paradise Mountains. It was a perfect plan until what happened happened!"

Everyone's head bowed as they thought about the near destruction of Paradise Mountains and all the family and friends they lost from Bang's attack.

Santago quickly lifted the mood

"Anyway, whether we like it or not, everything happens for a reason... The Source knows best and we're back stronger than ever! The Chosen Ones are thriving, you chose the right path and thanks to that attack you got that extra addition to your powers"

"What extra addition?" Asked Jay

"Never in Zurakayan history has anyone ever been able to transform to a Lion or any other animal. That's from that Black Lion scratch merging with the regeneration of you ZuraGene, it would never have happened if that battle didn't"

"Truuuuue" said Jay, seeing the brighter side of things.

"Anyway, I can't afford to sit here in self-pity and big and serious why should I? Everything that happened had to happen and I'm probably stronger because of it. I'm just happy to know I got a dad hahahaha" laughed Jay

"You owe me quite a few bday presents big man, but we got nuff' time to catch up and all that, right now we got bigger issues... Zeitan Supreme! This brudda's a level of strong that I've never seen before... he's like a cyborg or sutum'... I couldn't find a weak spot!" Said Jay

"I ain't gonna lie to you son, this is gonna be the biggest battle we've ever faced! Zeitan ain't no joke, he's been doing this ting' for millions of years! We've managed to hold him back many times, but each time has weakened The Source, that's how powerful he is! This has made The Source to unstable, one wrong move could make it explode and end us all... both here and Supreme Earth!"

"I hate calling Zurakaya that" said Mummy G in disgust to the newly labelled Supreme Earth

Santago continued "This time we're gonna have to stop him once and for all... the basic way!"

"What's the basic way?" Asked Jay

"We gotta bruck' him up and body him!" Said a straight faced Santago

"Oh the oldskool' way yeah" replied Jay

"If you really knew how advance the true oldskool' was you wouldn't say that hahaha" said Santago

"What d'you need me to do from here" asked Mummy G

"From here!?" Replied Santago "Nar my love, I've spied on Zeitan for years, he's something else... a whole new beast! Powerful, intelligent and ruthless! It's too risky to leave Chief Danjuma's daughter here. I'm taking you home right away and I don't want to hear one argument from you"

"Oh Ok" said Mummy G, slightly excited by Santago's firm words

"Wow, first time I've seen her take instruction with no talk" joked Jay

"You too Jay, I need you to round up the Squad and prepare them for travel to Paradise Mountains, it's time for some intense training and development, everyone's gonna need to be on a whole new level to stand any chance against Zeitan and his Zupremes! I'll give you a week to get all your affairs in order and come" said Santago

"We got a top-notch training centre at the HQ you know" replied Jay

"Yeah top notch for London is nothing compared to Paradise Mountains son" said Santago

Jay shut his mouth and agreed.

Mummy G grabbed a few important bits and hugged Jay. She was so happy to be going home to Paradise Mountains, she didn't think twice about anything and anyone she was leaving behind as the only important beings were following in a week's time.

"Hurry and come you hear me" said Mummy G to Jay

"I will Mum, I'll be ready soon as" replied Jay

"Make sure" said Mummy G as she left in a haste "Make sure you lock up everything and leave my house tidy" instructed Mummy G, Santago took her things from her then she wrapped her arms around him.... BOOOOOOMMMMMMM a multi-coloured portal opened around Santago and Mummy G which they disappeared into.

"Rahhh who's that guy your mum disappeared with bro" said Whipz as he sat on his car bonnet eating a packet of crisps

"Long story bro, I'll tell you on the way... you ready?" said Jay as he made sure Mummy G's front door was locked tight.

"Yeah let's go" replied Whipz as he ate his last crisps and threw the packet on the floor

"Oiii pick that up man" said Jay disgusted by Whipz littering

"Sorry sorry bro" said Whipz then they jumped in the car and drove over to the SG HQ.

Chapter 8 – We Run The Block!

A few days had past since Mummy G went home to Paradise Mountains, Jay explained to the Squad what took place and they prepared to follow.

The teens were excited to be returning to Paradise Mountains but no one was more excited than Tanya, she thought about all the advanced technology she was about to be exposed to and she loved that she was going to meet the rest of their family.

Although Jay was looking forward to the return too, he tried to play it down and explained to everyone that the Mountains won't be how they remembered it and it's very likely they have lost a lot of loved ones to the battle against Bangz Army. This brought the teens back to a cold and harsh reality but nevertheless they all remained enthusiastic.

As promised Jay got all his affairs in order and was basically ready to go, then one evening he sat in his room with Tanya with the news playing in the background.

"This is Sandra Patty with a live exclusive interview for London News with respected businessman and Mayor's personal friend Marlo Bang"

"Turn that up babes" said Jay, the TV now had his full attention!

"Arrrr he we go, what rubbish is chatty patty gonna put out there now" said Tanya as she picked up the TV remote an increased the volume

"So Marlo, I hear you and the Mayor have agreed on some big plans to improve this now run down area which is coincidentally referred to as Bangz Block?" Said Sandra Patty

"Yes that's correct" said Bang using his professional voice.

"Listen to how he's talking, sounds like he's got a plum in his mout'" said Jay as he became irritated by Bang's fake behaviour.

"Shush man, it may all be lies but I still wanna hear what he's got to say" said Tanya

"As you know this areas gained a terrible reputation of gangs and violent crime, without even mentioning the drug dealing that takes place right here! But the other day was my final straw, in like one week, three young lives were taken! Two of them in a gang fight and another one randomly found in the bins like a piece of trash... this is terrible! As soon as I heard about this I got straight on the blower to the Mayor and said it's time to make a change" said Bang

"Amazing, this is what we need real members of the community taking action. Not rogue criminals who act like heroes whilst disrespecting our law enforcement and destroying our area" said Sandra Patty taking the opportunity to send indirects at Squad Gigantic.

"The cheek of this chick!" Shouted Jay, he was livid! Tanya had to calm him down.

"This sounds great but unfortunately we frequently hear these promises of change and then we never see any action... what change are you proposing?" Asked Sandra Patty

"I'm glad you asked, we decided it's time for a complete regeneration of this area. We're going to renovate every last apartment block by block. We'll also add new businesses such coffee shops, high end furniture shops, a quality supermarket, instead of these local authority gyms we'll bring in a spa and wellness centre, this will all bring a new lease of life to the area. We'll also be getting rid of what I call the chicken shop culture and start bringing a better clientele of customers" said Bang

"This sounds unbelievably marvellous to me I can't wait, when are these plans going to be put into action?" Asked Sandra Patty

"ASAP, the Mayor has been given the go ahead by the government for area regeneration and were the lead to deliver it, the cost will be approximately sixty million pounds and we have half the funding already, now were just fundraising for the rest" said Bang with the smuggest look on his face.

"They think their smart you know" said Jay "They know what they're doing! Bang's got the Mayor in his pocket, he'll get to take over the block officially and have it looking like a nice posh area where rich people can come and socialise etcetera, etcetera, whilst he's running an untouchable underground organised crime system in the same area!"

"I've seen how these so called regenerations work, they make the locals build it up with blood sweat and tears, whilst having to live through the most wickedest times, then they pretty up the area and decided it's too good for the residents, and push them out of their own home back into another poverty stricken area, whilst they reap the benefits of the newly build area… it's disgusting!" Said Tanya

"Exactly I'm not having it! That blocks basically behind our yard… that's our people! No way I'm sitting back and watching that… what they say it cost sixty million, I'm buying it!" Said Jay Gigantic

"Whoa whoa whoa, slow down, this ain't monopoly you know… bout I'm buying it" said Tanya trying to bring Jay back to reality

"Nar serious, we got more than quadruple that amount of cash… and you know my motto 'only buy it if you can buy it three times!' we can change lives. Instead of bringing in all them bousjie outside businesses, we can build the block to a high standard and allow the residents to own the businesses in the area giving as well as giving them subsidised rent… not only will we see the money being spread and circulated around the community, we'll eventually see our money returned too and even if we don't who cares, it's bout time we gave back properly" stated Jay

Tanya totally agreed "let's do it!"

"You know what, I beg you locate Miss Chatty Patty's News team's systems so we can ask them a few questions" said Jay with a cunning smile on his face

Tanya located the systems and phones, then intercepted the service allowing Jay's to appear live on air.

"Ohh it appears that we have a live caller on air, hi who's this I'm speaking with?" Enquired Sandra Patty

"My name's irrelevant but my questions aren't" replied Jay

"Mr Bang, I heard all the promises you just made on air and something ain't adding up to me. Tell me how do you expect the local residents of that block to afford to live in this place you described, and furthermore how d'you even expect them to pay for these expensive sounding new amenities?"

"It's simple really, get a job and stop looking for handouts! Change your ways or change your address!" Said Bang

"Wow" said Jay, Jay knew who Bang really was, so he knew exactly how to draw him out, he stayed quiet and allowed Bang to dig himself a grave

"Majority of these people are the offspring's of immigrants, who were welcomed into this country and have done nothing positive for it, these are the people who are not only costing the tax payer loads of money with no return but are also causing the problems in the area, I think it'll will be best for everyone if these uncivilised people are given the clear message to either change their ways or go elsewhere... simple!" Said Bang in a condescending borderline racist manner!

"It's a bit rich coming from you ain't it, I'm sure your parents were also migrants and even though you're here acting as if you're Sh!t don't stink, we all know that block is named after you because of you reign of crime and terror in that area"

"He swore... cut him off" begged Bang realised his cover could be blown

The news team tried to disconnect Jay Gigantic, but Tanya's hack was too strong, so Jay went on

"That touch a nerve yeah, truth hurts don't it!? Your family background and you especially is one of the main reasons the area has all these issues and you got the nerve to come on the news talking about kicking out the locals, who are actually the victims of your badness, so you can spin a profit and likely continue to have the area poisoned with crime backed by that corrupted Mayor! Not on my watch mate... let's get this straight there will be changes on that block, but I guarantee you won't be the one making them! Firstly I'm gonna personally contact the main Gang leaders to call a truce between the gangs and something tells me that Bangz Army and the Unknown Hittaz won't play ball but everyone else will, then we'll personally develop the block and instead of strategically pushing out the residents, we'll empower them and only remove your scummy gang members, then you'll see a whole new lease of life in the area... I'll put my life on it!" Promised Jay

Sandra Patty and Bang were gobsmacked!

"Now we can end this call" said Jay as Tanya gave back access to the News team.

Bang was vex! He ripped his mic off and demanded they stopped filming. He immediately left the set and went to his car where he insisted Mechanics finds out where that interception came from, so they could retaliate straight away.

"Aaaah I tried matey, but-a-they were to strong... I couldn't even get a IP address... you-a gonna have to-a take-a that on the chin pal" said Mechanics

Bangs block erupted in cheers as he drove out, a few local residents noticed him and began throwing bottles and any other rubbish they could find at his car.

On the other side of the ends, Thug Rock sat and watched a rerun of the interview on YouTube. Thug Rock weren't the sharpest tool in the box, but he knew what was being said by the anonymous caller was the right thing for the area, a truce would be best for everyone in every way possible. As he watched the video back, he felt he knew the voice and this was bugging his mind, after rewinding the clip several times he eventually clocked it was Jay Gigantic.

Thug rock decided that if Jay is to reach out to him, he will accept a truce as long as it was within reason, plus he now hated Bang so much that he'll gladly make he's enemies enemy his best friend.

Word got back to Zeitan of Bang's embarrassing moment on live TV. Zeitan wasn't happy at all, he wasn't willing to let anything jeopardise his London takeover because as far as Zeitan was concerned if he took over London, he would be in control of Squad Gigantic's home.

Zeitan told Bang that he's becoming a laughing stock and that he needed to make a bold statement to all the other gangs in the area!

"You need to show the entire country Who Runs The Block! Who are the main gangs in your way?" Asked Zeitan

"There's only a few left... there's Unknown Hittaz but we have an underwritten allegiance, I would say the other main one is Thug Rock's Guys... what they call Rock Ard Thugs aka RATs, there's also Da Grabberz and those Spade Gang prat's but I got rid of their leader already so their a mess right now, and I don't see Grabberz as no threat at all" replied Bang

"Well there's your answer! Before the day is up, I want those RATS or whatever you call them exterminated!" Demanded Zeitan.

"I'll get on it right away boss!" Said Bang then he rounded up the army and prepared for war, the ends was about to go nuts!

Thug Rock was completely unaware of the beef that was coming at him but luckily for him he called a meeting with all his crew to discuss the possibility of a truce, so at that precise moment his numbers were strong.

Just as all the Rock Ard Thugs congregated outside of their hideout, Bang and his Army pulled up!

CHAPTER 9 – Old Enemies... New Friends?

"WHATS GOING ON HERE" said Thug Rock as Bangz Army pulled up and jumped out with all sorts of tools.

Bang slowly walked through his Army of men till he got to the front of the crowd and with Mechanics by his side holding a Mac-10 machine gun he said

"You know what it is bro, either bow to us or get rubbed out!" Proposed Bang

Thug Rock and his crew laughed their heads off, he looked at Bangs numbers and realised how weak they now were

"How the mighty have dropped" said Thug Rock, messing up the classic saying

"How the mighty have fallen" whispered one of Thug Rock's guys into his ear.

"Oh, well you know what I mean anyway" said Thug Rock, as Bang's men sniggered at him

"Still as smart as ever aye" mocked Bang

"Still as cocky and stupid as ever yeah" replied Thug Rock

"You can see what it is mate, you're not only outnumbered you're out gunned too... we can do this the easy of the hard way" stated Bang

Thug Rock gave a cheeky laugh then looked around and said

"The ROCK ARRDD way!" Then out of nowhere, at least fifty more of Thug Rock's men came out of the shadows tooled up and raring to go!

Bang step back and for the first time since arriving showed fear.

Thug Rock noticed Bang was on his back foot and launched his attack!

Thug Rock sent a flurry of Rock Shots at Bang, Bang smashed the first three with his One Bang's but there were too many at least five more connected and dropped him!

"DON'T JUST STAND THERE... GET EM!!!" Shouted Bang

Mechanics held the Mac-10 and started letting off shots! The two gangs ran at each other and began to rumble!

It was crazy, one of the biggest gang fights you'll ever see! Both sides we're getting it, they all gave as good as they got but Thug Rock's men began to get the upper hand, they were solid! Every last RAT was hench and an expert in either MMA or Jujitsu! Bangz Army couldn't keep up, every time they got close, they were disarmed and greeted by bone crunching grabs, throws and blows!

All Bangz Army's tough talk was gone, they were doing more running than fighting but the Rock Ard Thugs showed no remorse! They sent shots at their fleeing oppositions, hitting them in the back with shells so powerful it went in their backs and flew out their stomachs... it was a blood bath!

All out of bullets, Mechanics read the play and knew this was a losing battle and shouted

"Ayya ayya-mama-mia I'mma outta here" as he ran away.

Mechanics was a bit of a coward, but in his defence he always stated he was a lover not a fighter.

Seeing that they were being torn to pieces Mechanics made a contact with Zeitan who was currently on Supreme Earth.

"Boss-a-Boss we need your help, this-a plan... ain't going to plan!" Begged Mechanics

"You idiots can't do nothing right, what is it?" Asked Zeitan

"They killing us... like-a really they are killing us, I-a got-a dead man next to me right now... we need help!" Responded Mechanics

Zeitan sighed and said "Fair enough, I'm sending in back up now"

Then all of a sudden, a portal opened and a small army of Zupremes came through to defend Bang.

"WHAT THE HELL IS THAT!?!" Shouted Thug Rock, then he commanded all his men to shoot at the portal.

Thug Rock sent big Boulder Shots as his men fired their Guns, it dropped a few Zupremes but still a major amount got through!

SQUAD GIGANTIC

The Zupremes had advanced so far that they now looked just like humans, the only difference was a hint of red in their eyeballs. The bullets and rocks hit the Zupremes and ripped through their artificial flesh but just ricocheted off their metallic interior. Thug Rock didn't know what to do, he wasn't smart enough to recognise their weak spots and find a way to defeat them.

Now the tables had turned, and it was Thug Rock's Guys who were being ripped to shreds! They tried as hard as they could to fight the Zupremes and even managed to drop a few but it wasn't enough. The portal and the arrival of the Zupremes began to get attention, random conspiracy theorists arrived at the scene, risking their lives just to capture footage and expose the alien life forms.

One conspiracy theorist got right in the middle of the action and started broadcasting on his social media's live section

"I told you I weren't cappin' look live and direct here's alien entering Earth and fighting mankind... all these years you wanted to tell me the Earths not flat and were alone in this universe, I told..."

"...GIMME THAT!" Said Thug Rock as he snatched the phone out of the guy's hand and kicked him over

"Squad Gigantic if you're out there... we need your help! Rock Ard Thugs are down for the truce and we need you now or Bangz Army will take over the ends!! They got alien help fam... come now PLEASSSEEE!"

Luckily for Thug Rock, his SOS call flagged up on the SG System as it possesses a special feature that alerts Tanya anytime Squad Gigantic is mentioned online, the SG system then assesses the potential risk of the mention and notifies Tanya if deemed necessary.

The SG System's face recognition identified Thug Rock and alerted Tanya straight away.

"Jay, I just got a crazy call for help come through from Thug Rock!?!" Said Tanya

"Thug Rock... you sure?" Replied Jay

"Yep he's under pressure! They're beefing with Bang right now on the ends and hear this... he claims Bang's got some sort of aliens helping him!" Said Tanya

"That's gotta be that Zeitan guys doing!" Said Jay

"Thug Rock said he is down with the truce and wants you to ride with them on Bang and these alien things now" said Tanya

"We ain't gotta a choice... aliens on ends can't run!" Said Jay as he transformed to Gigantic and gathered the Squad

"So we really do this Yeah... we definitely going cos' I'm not suiting up for no reason, I've just straightened and style my hair, you know it's going into Afro puffs once I suit up!" Said Safarhi, she weren't in the mood to waste time, because no matter what hairstyle she has, once she suits up her hair goes into beautiful Afro puffs to draw extra energy from the sun to combine with her SG Gem.

"Yessss Rhiarn we're going" responded Gigantic as he rolled his eyes.

Then teens suited up and rolled out with Gigantic, Chunksta hopped on the back of Truth's SG1000, whilst Gigantic grabbed the SG Quad with Safarhi flying alongside them. Pacer as cocky as ever went into the kitchen and made a sandwich as the rest travelled to where the battle was taking place

"It's cool man, I'll eat this then pull up. I'm fed up of always getting there first... I give you man a head start" said Pacer as he took a massive bite of his sandwich.

Pacer waited until his comms showed him they were about twenty seconds away then.... Zoooooooooommmmm he was off!

They all pulled up at the same time to see Thug Rock's men getting handled wickedly!

"As much as I like watching this... we can't just sit back and watch these things rip up our ends!" Said Chunksta. There was no love lost between Chunksta and Thug Rock they had real bitter rivalry but Chunksta knew this fight was bigger than his pride.

"Well let's stop talking and put in some work" said Truth then he effortlessly swiped his hand in to the air using he's telekinetic power to lift four Zupremes up off the ground, then Safarhi flew in and kick them all back down!

Squad Gigantic were now part of the action!

Chunksta was smashing them one by one and Gigantic was doing the same, Pacer's speed was too much for them to keep up with, he was unleashing hundred hit combos on each Zupreme in a matter of seconds! Safarhi was now able to summon multiple elements and animals at the same time, she used the speed and agility of a Cheetah alongside the strength of a Bear, as her and Truth tagged teamed and tore up the Zupremes.

SQUAD GIGANTIC

Squad Gigantic now turned the tide in the battle and the Zupremes were being dropped but there was one major issue... even though they fell down, they would not stay down! It was as if the pain was temporary, they took the beating then in a matter of seconds they stood back up!

Safarhi realised that she could barely feel their emotions and Truth couldn't read their minds, there was a simple reason why... because they are not human beings or beings at all! They're AI's.

Clocking the play Gigantic decided to investigate, he grabbed the Zupreme closest to him and punched his face in then brutally ripped it in half.

"Just as I expected, they're robots... they're not human... they're mimicking humans" Shouted Gigantic to his Squad.

Realising they were AI's replicating humans Gigantic told his team

"Aim for their Heads or where their artificial Hearts should be... I guarantee you their power source will be located in one of them places"

Gigantic was right! Ascertaining that information was a game changer, once again Bang was on the back foot as he witnessed the Zupremes who were sent to save him be shut down and destroyed!

"NO.. NOOO...NOOOOOOOO!!!! I'm not getting defeated by this oversized pussy again!" Shouted Bang in frustration.

Then he felt a massive presence come from behind him and tap his shoulder saying

"Don't worry I got this!" It was Nefarious - Zeitan's right hand Zupreme, who killed the very first Gigantic and Lordisha millions of years ago!

Nefarious was updated and ready to go, he came through a portal with whole new fleet of Zupremes. Nefarious led the new batch of Zupremes and went straight to battle, his arms transformed into blasters sending powerful shots at Gigantic who was lacking! Before he could tell what was going on, Nefarious's two shots slapped him right in his chest blasting him to the ground.

Chunksta saw this and shouted "IT'S ONNN!!!!" and the teens alongside Thug Rock and his team charged at Nefarious and attacked! It was crazy, bodies were dropping from both sides but now Squad Gigantic and the Rock Ard Thugs were on the back foot!

The Zupreme's numbers were too strong, more and more just kept coming!

"This is a madness! There's too much of them... we need some assistance" said Truth

"You're right" agreed Gigantic "Tanya send for the Hit Squad... this is nuts!" Said Gigantic into his comms.

"I'm on it" responded Tanya

Then within seconds another portal opened but this time it was a colourful one and SG Hit Squad came rampaging through, led by Santago with a few new recruits!

"Trapz send these Zupreme losers somewhere and 2's serve these fools a double serving of everything, SG Hit Squad... GO GET EM!!!" Commanded Santago

Trapz and 2's were brothers who came of age and now played a major role in the SG Hit Squad, as well as being the immediate protectors of The Source.

"I'm on it" said Trapz as he attacked the Zupremes with an expert level of martial arts that no one on Earth had ever witnessed before! He punched, kicked, grappled and tossed the Zupremes left to right without being touched once and at end of every combo he disposed of each Zupreme by trapping them in mini portals that he literally created by punching the air.

2's obeyed his captains command too,

"Dun kno, dun kno" replied 2's, for some reason he always repeated the last words of his sentences twice... maybe this was why they called him 2's or maybe it's because he always leads with his two Force Swords, which he used to cut through the Zupremes like a hot knife through butter!

He took them out in twos, going fist to fist with the opposition whilst he sent out his Force Swords to deal with the others. It was as if the Force Swords had a mind of their own, they scoured the area then killed and destroyed anything identified as a threat and when they were done they went right back to their owners hands and continued to put in work... they were amazing!

Oddly, Trapz and 2's instantly linked up well with Thug Rock. They worked together to take out a number of Zupremes and Bangz Army members, Thug Rock sent

SQUAD GIGANTIC

Rock shots and Trapz opened mini portals behind enemies, catching them off guard whilst 2's used his Force Swords to chop Boulder Shots in two and double up the attack.

Bangz Army and The Zupremes were getting slaughtered! The addition of the SG Hit Squad was too much for them to manage, Zeitan watched from a opening and decided to pull his Zupremes out, he was losing way too much of them in what was meant to be a simple battle. Knowing he had a real war ahead of him, Zeitan opened portals and commanded his AI's to retreat and return to Supreme Earth.

Bangz Army now stood alone and outnumbered. The Rock Ard Thugs, Squad Gigantic and the SG Hit Squad realised they had won, so they stopped fighting and started laughing.

"Looks like your done Bang, do the sensible thing... run off and live another day" said Gigantic

"Shut your north and south mate! We can still have you fools... come on Thug Rock your guys versus my guys, gang for gang no Superhero squads coming to any ones rescue... just you against us"

Thug Rock and Bang started throwing insults at each other but really and truly Bang knew he was defeated.

As the cussing match continued, someone spoke into Santago's ear through his comms

"It's time to come home, this is gang versus gang now... a petty squabble, we got much bigger fish to fry! Zeitan would never retreat unless he had something big planned!"

"I agree boss, imma open a portal now" replied Santago

"Tell Squad Gigantic they must also come now! Forget waiting til the end of the week, we don't seem to have the luxury of time to waste, they need to come immediately and begin intense training and enhancement as I can feel a major war ahead... we can't afford to get caught slipping!" Said the voice

"Hold on, who is that man next with arms of rocks?" Asked the voice in Santago's ear

"They call him Thug Rock, I actually want to kill him! I'm sure he was apart of the crew that destroyed Paradise Mountains... gimme the go ahead and I'll do it now!" Replied Santago

"No you can't" said the voice

"Why not?" Replied Santago

"I can't believe it... because he's family!!!" realised the voice

"What d'you mean? I'm confused" said Santago

"I'm coming through now all will be explained" said the voice

"Are you sure that's wise, I thought we had a plan" responded Santago

"If that's who I think it is, I must" responded the voice

Then the most beautiful and elaborate portal you'd ever see appeared and the body belonging to the voice walked through and set foot in London.

"Who's that now" said Pacer

"For real man I'm bored, I just wanna go home and play computer now" replied Truth

They thought it was more troops being sent by Zeitan but they couldn't be more wrong!

Even Bang and his men had enough, knowing that it could be more people to fight he gathered his remaining soldiers and dispersed.

"NO WAYYYY, it can't be fam... no way! Are you lot seeing this" said Gigantic

Gigantic rushed over to the portal and shouted

"IT'S CHIEF DANJUMA.....GRANDDAD!!!"

The voice was Chief Danjuma... he's alive!

Gigantic couldn't believe his eyes, he thought Chief Danjuma was dead!

He thought his grandfather died a bitter death in the battle on Paradise Mountains... but no! Chief Danjuma survived and after years of healing and rebuilding Paradise Mountains here he was standing as tall and as strong as ever!

They all ran over to him, Gigantic hugged him so hard he took him of his feet

"Chief Danjuma" screamed Safarhi as she hugged him

"Arrrr Rhiarn, as beautiful as ever" said Chief Danjuma

"Do I call you Chief or Great Granddad now" said a confused Pacer

"Arrrr Danny as sharp as ever, Chief will do, don't make me sound old" said Chief Danjuma with his usual charming humour.

Truth walked over and shook the Chiefs hand and Chunksta followed

"Raheem still a man of little words" said Chief Danjuma "And Jerome that grips got even stronger!"

"I was hoping for a much better reunion on Paradise Mountains, but I've seen something... well someone that made me have to come directly to investigate!" Said Chief Danjuma

"Tanya, please shut down all cameras and comms within a ten-mile radius... I don't want no one to hear what I'm about to say" instructed the Chief

A star struck Tanya obeyed and did as she was told, she couldn't believe she was being instructed by Chief Danjuma himself

"You, man with hands of rock... come here" said Chief Danjuma, summoning Thug Rock.

Thug Rock screwed up his face and said "Who's this guy talking to" ignoring the Chiefs request

"Are you mad?! You better respect the big man" said Chunksta, as he grabbed Thug Rock and threw him in front of Chief Danjuma

"Calm down, there's no way he'll remember who I am" said Chief Danjuma to Chunksta and the rest of the Squad who were also angered by Thug Rock's lack of respect.

"You are one of us, you were born on Paradise Mountains" stated Chief Danjuma

Everyone looked around in shock, even Thug Rock!

"Yes Chunksta he's actually from your tribe" said the Chief

Pacer started bussing up "He's your family blood, that's why you man love each other so much hahaha"

"Shut up Pacer!" Said Safarhi shutting Pacer down as he once again made a joke at an inappropriate time

"You are from the mixed bloodline of the Lords and the Umvikeli... your family have been the chosen protectors of Paradise Mountains for generations" said Chief Danjuma

"You're talking rubbish, I don't even know who my parents are" replied Thug Rock

"Well I knew them very well and believe me when I say you are from Paradise Mountains, your name is Umbukhali Umvikeli the second... named after your father meaning strong protector, your mother's name was Kuhle Amanda Lord, meaning powers and beauty. Your family was the first response frontline of defence for Paradise Mountains based in Tanzania" said Chief Danjuma

"That could all be lies!" Said Thug Rock

Chief Danjuma interrupted him remembering an old saying Thug Rock's father use to say to him as a toddler "To defend is to protect..."

Then somehow Thug Rock knew how to complete the sentence "and with honour... comes... res...pect"

"See you remember, your father use to repeat that to you daily! Here look, I have a photo of you that I walk around with, as I promised him that one day, I would find you."

Thug Rock looked at the photo Chief Danjuma projected out and instantly recognised himself as a toddler... now he finally believed!

"That's me, you really do know my parents, tell me more... what did you say my name was again?"

Now Thug Rock was attentive, he wanted to know all about his history and Chief Danjuma was the one person in the world who could tell him.

"Your name is Ubukhali Umvikeli the second, your mother and father was posted in Tanzania defending any possible attack to Paradise Mountains, then one dreadful day their private base was invaded by an enemy trying to invade Paradise Mountains... similar to like Bang did!

Your father battled with full honour til the end as far as we could tell, he defeated the opposition leader and managed to create enough of a diversion to allow you and your mother to flee but this came at a heavy cost and eventually he died from the wounds he received in the battle.

When we heard the invasion was taking place, we rushed to help but by time we got there it was too late, we arrived just in time to hear your Ubukhali's last words!

He told me personally 'Find my wife and son' then he transferred a photo of you to me and I vowed to find you as he died in my arms.

We searched the whole area and unfortunately found your mother dead by the river, but still there was no sign of you, all we found was a washed up boat, so everyone assumed you were dead but in my heart I always felt you were alive somewhere. We left that decoy base as its cover was blown, however, the enemy situated their platoon there as they believed they were close to finding Paradise Mountains. This was perfect for us, so we left them to settle in that decoy area however many years later they were destroyed anyway... karma I guess" explained Chief Danjuma.

Thug Rock was mind blown, but he found a warmth in knowing this. Not only did he finally receive closure but he was also able to make sense of a strange feeling he was recently having, an overwhelming feeling where he now wanted to do good. A life of crime began to feel unnatural to him and deep down he knew he was meant to be more than a criminal. So weirdly finding out Paradise Mountains was his home made complete sense to him.

"But Paradise Mountains... my home! I was a part of destroying it" said an apologetic and remorseful Thug Rock.

"The child who is not embraced by the village will burn it down to feel its warmth" replied Chief Danjuma

"You knew no better, your mind was corrupted by an evil man and you were suffering! Paradise Mountains is your home, but you must earn you way back in through righteousness and correcting your wrongs and that is something you can do right here in London. Genuinely make a change and your world will change for you too! Unfortunately, I can't stay here with you much longer as we are at war but know that you are one of us and whenever you need us you can call upon us." Confirmed the Chief.

"I appreciate that" said Thug Rock

"When this all calms down we will meet again and discuss a way forward, hopefully that discussion can take place on Paradise Mountains... it all depends on your choices from here on!" Said Chief Danjuma.

Then Chief Danjuma took his attention off Thug Rock and placed it on Gigantic

"Things have changed, we can no longer afford to wait! You and the teens must come tonight! Get your bits together and also bring Tanya, I'm dying to meet her"

"Yes sir" responded Gigantic

Then the Chief and the SG Hit Squad went back to Paradise Mountains through Chief Danjuma's amazing portal.

The enlightening that take took place left Thug Rock thinking, he decided to make a change that same night. He decided the gang truce must take place and one of his new main purposes in life will be to ensure the growth and safety of his community... especially the children. Thug Rock went to bed peacefully, finally feeling a true sense of belonging, he was at peace with himself and could feel things were about to change for the positive.

Just before he went to sleep, he made one very important phone call to get the ball rolling.

Later that same night Gigantic, Tanya and the teens were all escorted to Paradise Mountains by Santago where they were greeted by family and friends in a massive welcome home ceremony. It was an amazing occasion full of joy and happiness, but this was the calm before the storm, a mere interlude to the intense training that was about to take place.

SQUAD GIGANTIC

Squad Gigantic and Zeitan Supreme were officially at war! This was about to be their biggest test ever!

CHAPTER 10 – Welcome home!

"We're here for real ennit" said Pacer

"Where you think they were taking us bro... Balham?! You're so dunce" replied Chunksta

Squad Gigantic had arrived at Paradise Mountains. It was years since they set eyes on their magical home, but things weren't the same, Chief Danjuma was forced to make some major changes since Bang's attack.

The Squad was met at the entrance to Paradise Mountains by Chief Danjuma, Trapz, 2's and a few other warriors.

As Jay realised he was near the entrance, he started to get all giddy and began to act childish. He was so excited to show Tanya his birthplace, ahead of him was a Waterfall full of multi coloured diamonds and gems. Jay couldn't resist the opportunity to show off and be 'Mr Know-it-all'

"Tanya just follow me I'll show you wha' gwarn, trust me this is my ends" said Jay as he held Tanya's hand and led her towards what he thought was the same Waterfall of Purification he went through when he first entered Paradise Mountains many years ago.

As they got closer to the Waterfall Chief Danjuma smiled and slyly signalled Tanya to abort leaving Jay to enter the Waterfall alone.

"What you stopping for? Trust me don't be scared. When I first came I was shook too, but it's not really a Waterfall, it's a purification ting'... I didn't even get wet" said Jay trying to convince Tanya to take leap with him. However, Tanya is no fool! Chief Danjuma told her not to go... so she weren't going!

Then the Chief interrupted and said "Well, action speaks louder than words, if you want her to follow lead by example... you go first"

"Once again wise words Chief" said Jay as he turned around and confidently stepped right into the Waterfall

"WHAT THE....." shouted Jay as he lost his footing and fell right into what happen to just be a Waterfall.

Fearing for her husband's life Tanya screamed "JAAAYYYYYY"

Chief Danjuma erupted into laughter after successfully tricking Jay

"Trapz get that fool" instructed the Chief

"Cool" said Trapz

"Don't worry Tanya he'll be fine" said Chief Danjuma, as Trapz teleported into the Waterfall grabbed Jay and teleported right back.

"HELP ME, HELLLP MEEEE" screamed Jay like a little girl, he didn't even realise he was back on dry land. Everyone started bussing up at Jay

"Oh, you lot find that funny yeah... watch! Rhiarn stop creasing up and dry me" said Jay

Safarhi eventually stopped herself from laughing, then she gathered the surrounding air and forcefully dispersed it at Jay drying him and his clothes in seconds.

"First lesson of the day, don't assume because you just make an ASS out of U and ME" said Chief Danjuma playing on the letters in the word assume.

Everyone joked about the prank Chief Danjuma played as they walked through Paradise Mountains.

It was as if celebrities had arrived, there was a welcoming party that played music as people carried little gifts to them as they walked through. Random people were also coming up to them recalling stories of when the teens and even Jay were little babies and toddlers, it was beautiful but overwhelming, the Squad didn't know how to respond.

Chief Danjuma took back control of the situation and told them there would be plenty of time to catch up with people and celebrate their homecoming, but right now there was things they needed to do!

"As you can see everyone is happy to have the Chosen Ones home but by no way is this a party or a holiday... you all got some serious training and development to get through, so serious that it'll be one on one with The Source directly!" Said Chief Danjuma bringing a sense of reality back to the situation.

"As you can probably tell, there's been a lot of changes. As you discovered Jay, The Waterfall Of Purification is no more! After it was smashed in the attack we took the pieces and made it a The Purification Cube what beings now enter for purification, a lot has changed here but I'm happy to say for the better" said Chief Danjuma.

"Changes like what Chief?" Asked Truth

"Well firstly we no longer live in separate tribes, now all tribes live together. This has allowed everyone to develop at a much higher level and with the tribes blending we now have children born with multiple powers and skills.

Although we lost many, we also gained a lot more! We trained and developed the SG Hit Squad to a whole new level and thanks to the mix of tribes powers our new age warriors can do things the oldskool' could only dream of doing!

The Source is still housed in the Forbidden Area on the Soul Disc but unfortunately it has become extremely unstable since the last attack! So we now have a section of the SG Hit Squad led by Trapz & 2's, dedicated to guarding it twenty for seven under Santago's guidance... a lot of strange things have been happening with The Source recently and we feel this is due to Zeitan! We discovered he's been powering himself and his Zupremes with an extract of The Source, which he attained millions of years ago, we need to retrieve it in order to help stabilise The Source and hopefully defeat Zeitan once and for all but we'll get into all that later!

The main thing to take from all this info is that the attack didn't defeat us... it actually made us stronger! It could even be the best thing that has happened to us... everything happens for a reason" ended Chief Danjuma.

Just as Chief Danjuma ended his explanation, a small cute fat kid came running over

SQUAD GIGANTIC

"Hi Chief, is this them?" Asked the excited little boy

The Chief laughed and said "Yes Jahsie, this is them"

"He's been running around excited all day knowing you were all coming" said Chief Danjuma to the Squad

"He looks like he needs to run a little more" muttered Pacer under his breath, mocking Jahsie's weight

"Shut up he's cute" said Safarhi

"It's cool, I'll punch him up if I was actually offended and honestly not catting to see all of you... well I mean you're all cool... but Chunksta's my guy!" Said Jahsie then he ran straight over to Chunksta and said "My names Jahsie but everyone calls me Stompy, I know everything about you! I even know most of your lyrics too, I'm gonna put in work just like you when I'm older... like I'm ready now! I'm mad strong G but the olders keep telling me to chill, well... they say my time soon come though!" Said Jahsie as he babbled on.

"Arrrr he rates you Chunksta, look at he's sweet little chubby face... can I get a hug?" Said Safarhi

"Corse babes" said Stompy as he confidently leaned in and hugged Safarhi then walked right back to Chunksta

"Narrrr he looks like a little version of you Chunksta but you don't wanna be like him lil' man, he don't get no gyal or nut'um" said Pacer as he laughed his head off

"Shut up bro, I get more gyal than you... you're just hating cos' ain't no one here rating you" replied Chunksta

"I'll move to him if you say so you know" said Stompy ready to ride for Chunksta

"Nar he's only playing G, plus he's family unfortunately" said Chunksta

Chunksta's liked Stompy, he loved his spirit and for some reason his soul drew to him like a little brother.

Chief Danjuma shook his head at Stompy and said "You gonna get yourself hurt one day, your strong but big boys will still give you a beating"

"Nar I'm on job Chief, I'll slap up big man or little man" replied Stompy in his usual cheeky manner

the Chief just laughed "Chunksta he's actually very similar to you, he's also of strength and has power just like you but he also has one more trick up he's sleeve"

"Yeah, what's that?" Asked Chunksta

"Show him Jahsie" said the Chief

"Well when the attack happened, my Mum was pregnant with me in her belly and the Ops attacked her, she survived but the doctors said the attack stopped the growth of my arm, so I was born with one shorter than the other" said Stompy

Safarhi smiled as Stompy explained, she could feel that Stompy had no sadness about his arm and was extremely proud of it.

"You're a lil' G for real ennit" said Safarhi

"You dun' kno', plus it's cool anyway… watch what I can do!" Said Stompy

"Yep, he's half strength and half creativity, best of both worlds he can turn his arm into anything he wants!" Stated Chief Danjuma

Then Stompy took a step back and his arm began to extend into a Sword

"Yooo that's a Mazzzaaa" said Chunksta

Noticing he had the audience locked in, Stompy decided to show off and put on a show, he changed his arm into Baseball Bat and said "Fancy a game" then started laughing, then he changed his arm to a cup and said pour me a drink fam and started laughing again.

"You're just showing off now" said Pacer

"Narrr this is showing off fam" said Stompy

Then his arm slowly turned into a Blaster and said "watch this" then he buss a shot into the sky, then he got over excited!

"I'm showing you I'm on stuff, any man come at me it's BLOAAA BLOAAAWW BLOOOAAAWWWW" Said Stompy as he jumped around irresponsibly letting of random shots! Everyone took cover

"What's wrong with this gassed yout'" said Truth

"Yeah this is why he isn't ready yet! He gets too excited and puts himself and everyone else at risk" said Chief Danjuma, as he slapped Stompy in the back of his head and said "Calm down"

"Sorry big man, sorry... I'm just gassed right now" replied Stompy

"I can tell, anyway get out of here we got things we need to do" said Chief Danjuma sending Stompy on his way

"Cool but Chunksta we'll link later bro" said Stompy as he walked off in the opposite direction talking to himself "Big man Chunksta you know"

"I like that yout', he's funny" said Chunksta

Chief Danjuma continued walking the Squad through Paradise Mountains. Jay, Tanya and the teens strolled in awe as they admired the beauty of the land.

"Jay you always told me how amazing it is here but seeing is really believing... this is next level" said Tanya.

"Tanya, this is just the beginning! I heard of your intelligence and capabilities... I've got a few things to work on with you" said Chief Danjuma

Tanya gleamed with excitement, but she held it in and calmly responded "I look forward to it"

Our numbers maybe low but our warriors are strong and unbeatable! Right now it's definitely quality over quantity but eventually we will have quality and quantity and the world will be in a much better place.

Establishing this new wave of warriors is the exact reason why we have called you here for development. We now know that your ZuraGenes have the ability to do more than just the one or two abilities you already display! We're going to completely unlock your ZuraGenes and have you all performing at your full capabilities! You're all going into training right this second... no delay!"

Then the sweetest voice interrupted "Oh no they're not!" It was Jenay!

"Grannnnyyyy" Shouted Jay as he ran over gave his grandma the biggest hug ever!

SQUAD GIGANTIC

The teens followed and also bombarded their now Great Grandmother with hugs and kisses, they all really missed her and her firm but loving ways.

"Before they go anywhere they're coming with me to eat some food that me and their Mummy G has spent the last how much hours preparing"

Chief Danjuma knew better than to argue or disagree, instead he just rolled his eyes and said

"Cha, do your thing, I'll go get everything ready" then he went off with his warriors to prepare for the most physically and mentally intense training session the Squad have ever had to endure!

The Squad arrived at the Chief and Jenay's quarters where they were not only greeted by Mummy G but also by the smell of fresh cooked food. They all ran up to Mummy G and hugged her

"Mmmmmm, that's what I'm talking about" said Chunksta as the whiff of Mummy G's Stew Chicken and Rice 'n' Peas hit his nose

"Granny, I didn't even know how hungry I was till I smelt that" said Chunksta

"I would've preferred a Stack and fries from StackTown... not feeling all that rice and them tings' man" said Pacer

"You're so rubbish" said Truth to Pacer, then he asked Mummy G "Is there any Jollof too?"

"Yes Raheem and Curry Goat, Pepper Prawns, Stew Beef, Ribeye Steak, Jerk Chicken... Jerk Lamb... Red Bream... Festival... Potato Salad, Tuna Pasta and all you

215

guys other favourites... even some REAL Fried Chicken"
said Mummy G as she fixed her face and aimed the last bit
of her sentence at Pacer

"Fried Chicken... you should've led with that" said
Pacer, then he paced into the house and was round the
table ready to eat in less than a few seconds

"What's the long ting, let's eat" said Pacer with a plate
full of Fried Chicken.

They all looked at him and laughed "Relax Danny,
we're still waiting for others to arrive" said Jenay

"And don't worry Rhiarn, I haven't forgotten you're
vegan... we got at least five salads, some BBQ Jackfruit
Wings, Vegan burgers, Vegan Hotdogs, Vegan Pepper
steak... Vegan everything!" said Jenay

"Ayyeeeeee we all eating good today" said Safarhi in
Joy.

As the evening went on more family and friends
arrived, they travelled far and wide from all areas of
Paradise Mountains. Once everyone arrived, they all sat
together and enjoyed the feast Jenay and Mummy G laid
out.

The festivities went on all night, they sang, they
danced, they laughed, they joked... they fully celebrated
the return of the Chosen Ones.

As the night went on, they met new and old family
members as well as being reunited with childhood friends
who were now fully grown, they reminisced and
exchanged stories from when they were kids. The teens

loved every last minute of it, even Chief Danjuma let his hair down and simply enjoyed the night.

However, the Chief noticed Safarhi seemed a little upset so once the opportunity arose, he pulled her to a side and asked what was bothering her.

"Rhiarn what's wrong? You seem sad" asked the Chief

"Just a little" replied Safarhi

"Why?" Asked the Chief

"Sounds silly but remember before I left I had two pets... Chalky the white Wolf and Greazy my Grizzly Bear... I thought I would've seen them by now, I know they're just animals, but they were like family to me" said Safarhi

"I wondered when you ask for them, there's no easy way to say it... their dead, they weren't fortunate enough to survive the attack! But take honour in knowing that they fought the end and saved many of our people" said Chief Danjuma

Safarhi dropped a few tears but deep in her heart she knew this was the case.

Then the Chief comforted Safarhi saying "I'll tell you this, you will see them again just in a different form"

"What d'you mean?" Asked a confused Safarhi as she wiped her tears

"In respect of their honour we gave them the accreditation of warriors, so rather than being buried they were Ascended and due to them being family to a Chosen One, I done a little extra just for you" said Chief Danjuma with a small smile on his face

"Extra?" Asked Safarhi

217

"Yeah I got tech to place them in The Source's database allowing them to be intwined into your SG Gem" said the Chief

"So you mean they're with me at all times?" Asked Safarhi

"Well not yet, but I have a feeling that when we unlock your ZuraGene fully you may be able to summon them in war and even life"

Safarhi gave him the biggest hug and said "You're truly the best"

Chief Danjuma Replied "I know, I know... now go enjoy yourself" then they rejoined the festivities.

Everyone continued to have a great time, but the Chief refused to let the Squad think it would be all fun and games! They were here for a serious reason, so at the end of the night he approached the teens, Tanya and Jay to let them know that intense training and development will begin first thing in the morning for all of them... even Tanya!

CHAPTER 10.5 – Gains No Games!

It was the crack of dawn and Chief Danjuma was ready to go! The Chief entered Squad Gigantic's quarters and shouted out

"EVERYBODY UP AND READY IN TEN MINUTES... TRAINING HAS NOW BEGUN!"

"Rahhhh what's wrong with donny? Moving like some alarm clock man" said Chunksta as he was abruptly ripped from his sleep "Man can't even press snooze"

Truth predicted the Chief would come first thing in the morning, so he woke up a few hours early and got ready, then he spent some time playing on a new console he discovered in Paradise Mountains, it was years ahead of anything he had ever seen in London.

Truth sensed when the Chief was coming over and knowing Pacer would be slacking, he went to his room just before the Chief made his presence known to make sure Pacer didn't embarrass them.

Pacer barely opened his eyes to see Truth standing over him

"Brooo, why are you here? Louw' me g" said Pacer

"Just shut up and get up, this ain't a holiday... find your manners and get ready!" Said Truth.

"Alright calm down bro" said Pacer as he wiped his eyes.

"I mean it G, no jokes... no games... no stupidness! Bring your A-game and show the Chief what we're really about!" Replied Truth, he knew Pacer would be the one to create an issue, so he made it his responsibility to go to him first and prep him.

Chunksta and Safarhi emerged from their rooms fully suited and ready.

"I've been ready Chief... let's get this work!" Said Safarhi as Pacer came running over too.

"You wash your skin yeah... I know how you move hahaha" said Chunksta to Pacer.

Safarhi laughed and said "Them man just dash a quick piece of water on his body then it's let the aftershave do the rest"

"SILENCE!" Commanded Chief Danjuma instantly shutting everyone up!

Gigantic and Tanya joined the congregation

"Morning everyone, Chief I don't fully understand why I'm here for training... I never go on the field"

"Training isn't just for the physical it's also for the mental too... today you're going to learn a few things too" replied the Chief

"Now everyone's here we can go" said Chief Danjuma then he teleported them all to the Paradise Mountains HQ

"This is our HQ, it's similar to your SG HQ but just a little bit bigger, better and advanced" stated the Chief

"OMG!!!" Shouted Tanya as she looked around "a little bit? This is a hundred times better! It makes our HQ look stupid"

"Glad you like it Tanya... as this is where you'll be spending your day, the funniest thing is majority of this equipment is millions of years old! We're gonna get you up to date with our level of technology and show you a few new tricks to put up your sleeve" said Chief Danjuma

Tanya was truly in Paradise, she couldn't believe how advanced everything was.

"I feel like a kid in a sweetie shop" said the astonished Tanya.

"Well come out of the shop for one second, I need you all to listen closely" said Chief Danjuma bringing Tanya back to Earth.

"As you know we've discovered that Zeitan is on Planet Zurakaya which he has taken over and named the Supreme Earth! Zeitan has it running as direct replica of Earth! This is crazy because initially for many years we believed that Zurakaya was made inhabitable by the original Gigantians in order to destroy him! However, we were wrong! We established that he survived the land purifications by managing to download the Earth's data and basically run it as a live stream... allowing the planet to be habitable"

"But how?" Asked Tanya

"Good question Tanya, as you may remember in the ancient tales of Gigantic and Lordisha, Zeitan was once gifted an extract of The Source when they believed his Zupremes were a creation made to help Zurakayans"

"Jay you made man trick you? And who's Lordisha... you got a side ting?" Asked Pacer

221

"No you fool, the original Gigantic and his wife Lordisha... are you stupid?" Gigantic was raged by Pacer's ignorance "You telling me you don't know your history?"

Pacer saw he took things too far and interrupted "I'm only Joking, I'm only joking... course I know I was just lightening the mood... louw' me man"

"This ain't the time for jokes, I'm telling you something serious... you pay for that later in Training!" Responded Chief Danjuma with the most serious look on his face. This scared Pacer, he stopped speaking immediately!

"As I was saying, Zeitan was able to hack into this extract of The Source and download many files! The Source holds all the information on... everything, Past and future! Zeitan used the data he ascertained to help ensure his survival, it has helped get him out of captivity, it has helped him stay one step ahead, and it has also helped him get close to taking your SG Gems and getting full control of The Source too!

Zeitan also used the information he pulled up to avoid full blown defeat many times, with the first time being when he used his Source Extract to essentially reboot Planet Zurakaya, after it was destroyed in order to get rid of him and his Zupremes!

However, we identified all wasn't lost and that a virus was placed in his extract that made it impossible for him to replicate Paradise Mountains, this has been our saving grace.

You see, there are other Gems that prophecy placed around the world, these Gems aren't as powerful as the SG Gems and although they are naturally fuelled by a

222

minimal amount of The Source's energy... they're neutral! Well they are neutral until touched by a force of good or evil!

Zeitan has managed to use people and Zupremes to gather these neutral Gems, which he eventually influences to become evil Dark Gems! Zeitan tricks the people he uses to find the Gems by making them believe that the Gem has a spirit which offers them the world if they allow themselves to be a vessel for its power, then when the time is right Zeitan appears and robs them of the Dark Gems before killing them! That's exactly how he manipulated Bang and many others in the past. Zeitan also uses these people to search for Paradise Mountains and destroy The Source, Bang was the closest ever and I truly believe Zeitan thought Bang would've been successful but obviously he was wrong!"

"So where does this leave us now?" Asked Gigantic

"Right now, we are in a tricky position, because not only are we fighting to ensure he doesn't get the SG Gems and take control over The Source! We also have to protect The Source from imploding itself as The Source has been used so many times over the years to stop Zeitan, that it has now become unstable! We need to leave The Source as uninterrupted as possible for many more years in order for it to stabilise and get back to full glory!"

"What will happen if The Source erupts?" Asked Truth

"Honestly... we don't know! It could be the end of life itself... it may unlock everyone's ZuraGene and cause universal chaos... it could kill all you Chosen Ones as your Gems are connected to The Source and you at the same time... we just don't know! So we have to play it safe, this time round we basically need to physically stop Zeitan, no land purification just a straight battle!"

"Is this why we're here now?" Asked Safarhi

"Yep! We need to attack very soon as we don't know how long The Source will hold out as every time Zeitan uses his extract, it has a knock-on effect on the main Source!

We think it's best to launch a two part surprise attack on Zeitan whilst he's still on Supreme Earth because one... he won't be expecting it and two... it'll be safer for Earth and its inhabitants if the battle takes place there!"

"Cool let's go SMASH CRASH on these pagans!!!" Said Chunksta

"Slow your role, in order to make this attack as effective as possible we need to fully open your ZuraGenes and have you all performing at your best abilities... we can't afford to lose! Today we train... Tomorrow we attack!" Said Chief Danjuma

Gigantic was dubious at how quick the training was going to be "And we'll be fully ready in just one day?"

"Hahaha Paradise Mountain's Training is a whole different ball game from the training you do in London" laughed Chief Danjuma

"You'll all come with me and I'll do the unlocking of the ZuraGene... then you'll experience some truly amazing scenarios where you'll test out your new skills and tricks. Tanya you'll stay here with my main guy from tech and learn how to use the SG Gems to their full capabilities, you'll also be able to grab some new equipment that you may want sent over to your HQ... that simple!"

Everyone stood around speaking amongst each other as they waited, they were all excited to see what they would become and what new things they'll be able to do.

"Ok who's first?" Said Chief Danjuma

Everyone went forward shouting out "ME"

Chief Danjuma smiled as he saw the Squad's enthusiasm.

"You know what, let's all go" said Chief Danjuma then he teleported them all to the forbidden area leaving Tanya behind in good hands.

The first thing the Squad noticed on arrival at the Forbidden Area was The Source, they couldn't recall ever being so close to it.

The glow omitting from The Source was almost hypnotic

"Beautiful ain't it" said Trapz who was on shift guarding The Source with his right-hand man 2's.

"Yeah" said Safarhi who was still in a slight trance.

"It's going a bit crazy though, there's a random kinda' interruption in its flow... it's never been this unstable, I'm a little bit worried... we need to do something or I'm not sure how long it will last!" Replied Trapz. Trapz and Safarhi seemed to have built a nice little rapport, Truth detected a little crush on both of their behalf.

"Alright sis calm down, I don't know what's gassin' you more... The Source or Trapz" said Truth telepathically into Safarhi's mind

"Shut up I'm just being polite" replied Safarhi in total denial.

"If you say so hahaha, remember when we snuck here and died that time" said Truth

"Of course, how can I forget I was shook! We were way too farse' as kids" said Safarhi, then the twins broke everyone's silence by what looked like a random burst of laughter.

"They doing telepathic chattings' again" said Chunksta

"Don't hate" jokingly replied Safarhi to her little brother and they all just laughed.

Chief Danjuma brought back order to the Squad, instructing them to all stand within arm's reach of The Source, the teens and Gigantic did as instructed. As they drew closer to The Source, their SG Gems ignited, then both the Gems and The Source began to behave erratically. The Source acted like a magnet to their SG Gems and whether they liked it or not they were being drawn into The Source... the Squad were scared but they obeyed the order.

"Stop being wussys' and get closer" said Chief Danjuma as the Squad tried to keep a little extra distance between themselves and The Source.

"You and The Source are ONE! How can you be intimidated by yourself? Your SG Gems are pure energy which is powered by The Source, a major extract that is directly connected to it... you are all basically walking, talking, portable versions of The Source!" Stated the Chief

This gave the Squad more confidence, Chunksta was the first to step right up to The Source and to everyone's surprise as he approached it calmed down and gave off an ora that welcomed his presence, this gave everyone else the confidence to follow.

"Yeah you know to follow bad man" gloated Chunksta

Chief Danjuma gave a little smirk, partly because he liked Chunksta's spirit, but also because he knew what was about to take place next.

"Let's still see if you're a bad man now, everyone step into The Source!" Said the Chief

"Whaatttt are you mad... I might not be the smartest, but I remember the stories Mummy G told me! Certain man just touched it and they got rubbed... nar mate I ain't stepping I'm good" said Pacer

"Well if you listened properly to all the stories you would know that Gigantians and Lords can touch it" stated Gigantic shutting Pacer up.

"Yeah but touching it and jumping in are two different things tho' big man" intervened Truth jumping to his brothers defence.

"Either jump in or get pushed in" bluntly said Chief Danjuma

"Trust in The Source... only The Source can fully open your ZuraGenes and take you to your ultimate levels, it's an honour we all wish for" said Trapz

"I think we should just do it" said Sarahi as she hung on Trapz's every last word.

"Yeah you would say that" said Truth, then he privately mocked her telepathically "Ohhhh Trapz anything you say Trapz" Safarhi had no response.

"You know what... you lot talk to much" said Chunksta, then he jumped right into The Source!

"In for a penny... in for a poundddddd" said Gigantic as he jumped in too.

Safarhi jumped in too "Ayyyyeeeeeee"

Pacer was still dubious, so just before Truth took his lunge into The Source, he pushed Pacer in then followed after.

The full Squad Gigantic were now immersed into The Source.

All their fear was lifted, and they felt a euphoric feeling run through their body as The Source unlocked their ZuraGenes to their full potential.

"I can feel my power uppin'!" Said Chunksta

"I feel it too son" replied Gigantic

Safarhi was loving all the positive energy she could feel from her family.

"I feel energy rushing through my body! I think I'm getting smarter too" said Pacer "Oi Truth I bet I'm smarter than you now fam"

"Don't push your luck bro" said Truth shutting his little brother down.

As they communicated with each other they started to feel the presence of their ancestors who had ascended into The Source... they felt the touch of every Gigantian and Lordisha from their heritage! This was a real honourable experience.

Then just as they got fully comfortable in The Source, they noticed the environment change!

It's was no longer calm and euphoric, The Source began to feel hostile and shaky!

"What's going on?" Asked Gigantic

Then from a distance they heard Chief Danjuma's voice shout "Congratulations your ZuraGene's are unlocked, TRAINING STARTS NOW!!!"

Then each one of them was shot out of The Source into an unknown land!

The Squad didn't know what was going on, but one thing they did know was that they were in this strange place alone... with the exception of Truth and Safarhi!

CHUNKSTA'S TRAINING

"Jerome... Chunksta" said a voice

"Yeah who's that?" Replied Chunksta

"I am Gigantic the very first Gigantian" said the voice

"And I'm Lordisha" said another voice

It was the spirits of the very first Gigantic and his wife Lordisha, Chunksta looked forward and saw them appear.

"You unlocked your full potential, are you ready to show us what you can do?" Said Lordisha and before Chunksta could reply Gigantic The First started to attack him!

Chunksta didn't know what to do!

"Use all your might and defend yourself!" Commanded Lordisha

Gigantic The First literally threw everything at Chunksta from Spaceships to Mountains! Chunksta punched through it all as he felt a new level of power and strength oozing out of his body.

"IT'S ONNNNNNN!" Shouted Chunksta as he continued to perform at a new level. Chunksta loved it, now he was on the attack and ran into battle.

Gigantic The First upped the ante by sending through an army of one hundred warriors with a similar power set to Chunksta! Chunksta was in problems now, he's never faced this much of a challenge before! The warriors surrounded Chunksta then laid into him.

Chunksta was on the floor taking a beating, he was trying to fight back but his efforts were useless! All he did was frustrate himself and get angry.

"You can't fight properly if you're angry, clear your mind and embrace the attack... turn the negative energy into positive" said Lordisha

Chunksta listened and as he calmed himself down, he felt his body begin to absorb the pain from the attack and transfer the energy into more and more power!

"MORE... MORE... BRUCK ME UP MORE!" Shouted Chunksta as he now laughed at the attack, then as soon as he felt he gathered enough energy, Chunksta jumped to his feet... drew back his arm.... Clenched his fist... then sent a mega punch into the ground!!!

"SMASSSSHHHH CRAASSSSSHHH!!!!!!!!!!!!!!" Shouted Chunksta as he punched through the ground and sent out the "Chunksta Booom!" which blew every last warrior off their feet leaving them either unconscious or dead!

"Well done, all the energy you absorb will be multiplied then released in whichever way you feel appropriate! EMBRACE YOUR PAIN" said Gigantic The First

Chunksta looked at the hole he left in the floor and felt unstoppable but this feeling was short lived as he looked back up and saw Gigantic The First had placed another hundred men in front of him, however they were now armed to the teeth with Guns, swords and even a Rocket Launcher!

Knowing he had he's suit on he was still slightly confident that he would be ok, then he noticed his suit beginning to disappear and transform into one of he's favourite tracksuits!

"Alright... you man are taking it too far now!" Said Chunksta, now he was worried! "These are bullets and blades now fam... you're gonna body me!"

Lordisha and Gigantic The First ignored his pleas and shouted "ATTACK!"

First the sword men attack him from all angles, Chunksta put up a good fight but there were just too many of them... eventually they got him! He was being stabbed from the front and behind, he tried to keep calm and absorb the pain but this was different he couldn't transfer stabs. Chunksta fell to the ground bloodied up and full of open wounds, he wondered when they would stop but the warriors were relentless! The sword men eventually left him alone but he wasn't given any respite, they just stopped to make way for the gun men, who stepped forward and emptied their clips on Chunksta with no sympathy,

"Stoppp please... STOPPPPP!" Begged Chunksta

"You think Zeitan will stop?" Replied Lordisha

Chunksta realised he was in this for the long haul, so once again he just embraced the attack and cleared his mind, then he had a moment of clarity

'How am I still awake begging for them to stop... surely I should be dead?!?' thought Chunksta.

Then he took a second and looked at his body, Chunksta was amazed to see that's his blood stop leaking, and his wounds were closing up one by one!

"MAZZZZAAAA!" Shouted Chunksta as he realised he could self-heal.

Chunksta also noticed that the bullets were not fully penetrating him, each bullet pierce his skin and flesh then simply fell off his body. Chunksta pick a few bullets off the ground and saw that the tips were dented... Chunksta was now bulletproof too!

The warriors disappeared into thin air as soon as Chunskta came to the realisation of his new abilities, then his tracksuit slowly transformed back into his SG Suit.

"You're lucky... thought we were gonna have to hit you with the rocket before you understood you new abilities"said Gigantic The First

"Well done Chosen One Chunksta, your training is over... now go save the Universe" said Lordisha and just like that Chunksta was back in the Forbidden Area.

PACER'S TRAINING

"Danny... Pacer" said a voice

"Yooo" Replied Pacer

"I am Gigantic the very first Gigantian" said the voice

"And I'm Lordisha" said another voice

It was the spirits of the very first Gigantic and his wife Lordisha, Pacer looked forward and saw them appear

"You unlocked your full potential, are you ready to show us what you can do?" Said Lordisha and before Pacer could reply Lordisha started to attack him!

"Rah what you on?!?" Said Pacer as he used his speed to dodge the oncoming assault

"I swear your like my great great great great granny or something, how you moving to man?" Asked Pacer

"Shut up and train!" Replied Lordisha as she placed twenty warriors in front of him, each warrior was armed with lasers and speed alongside the ability to shoot lightening... Pacer was more than matched!

"Let's see how quick you really are!" Said Gigantic The First

Arrogant as ever Pacer responded with a cheeky reply "Alright big man, watch this!"

Pacer's ignorance had him blinded to the danger he was in, he sent laser shots but they were too slow, the warriors just dodged them and sent back shots of their own! Pacer tried to use his speed to get round them and attack from behind but again this didn't work! They saw him coming and dropped him each time!

"This is pathetic!" Said Lordisha "You move quick, but your mind is slow... we can see everything your gonna do before you do it!"

Pacer was frustrated and this made his performance even worse, he was getting battered!

"STOP AND THINK!" Shouted Gigantic The First "slow your mind down and speed your body up!"

Pacer stopped for a second to apply the advice he was given, he fell back to create a plan of action but before he could figure anything out Lordisha came out of nowhere then grabbed him by his arms and ripped off the laser shooters that were attached to his SG Suit,

She crushed his laser blasters "You rely on these stupid things too much!" Said Lordisha.

Pacer started to panic "How am I gonna bust shots without it?" He asked.

"You're more than you're suit, all these attachments do is slow down your attack! PUT OUT YOUR HAND, THEN AIM AND SHOOT" instructed Lordisha.

Pacer did as he was told, he held out his arm and began to clinch his fist. As his fingers curled his hand to a ball, he could feel all the electrons in his bodily atoms excite themselves as they connected with his SG Gem, then BLAMMMMMMMMMM! As soon as his fist clinched fully, he shot out the most powerful Laser Shots ever which instantly vaporised three of the warriors in front of him

"WHAATTT! Ten trillion watts in less than a trillionth of a second.... that's what I'm talking about!" Said Gigantic The First.

"Now they can't see it coming hahahaha" laughed Gigantic The First as he gleamed with pride.

"Use that same feeling to boost your speed to another level and finish the rest of them!" Commanded Lordisha.

Something from within clicked with Pacer, he was experiencing a new feeling of power and speed running through his body. The Laser had merged with his blood stream and now he was able to create Laser Shots without any assistance... all he had to do was release what was within.

Pacer took to this new level of ability like a fish to water, he zooped around the remaining warriors and took them out in a second!

"Now you're ready" said Lordisha

"Ready for what?" Asked Pacer

"Ready to go home, you're training is over" replied Gigantic The First then he put his arm around Lordisha and simply walked of with his wife.

"Ummmm how? I don't even know where I am... you man brought me here!" Said Pacer

Then just before disappearing into thin air, Lordisha looked back and said "Teleport, you can do that too now, just think of where you wanna go, simple... bye" said

Lordisha then they disappeared leaving Pacer stranded and alone in the unknown land.

"Do they think I'm Truth or sut'um, how am I meant to do this science ting" said Pacer

Pacer spent hours trying to teleport and find his way back to Paradise Mountains, but he was doing it all wrong. Once again Pacer's simple mindedness had him doing things wrong, he mixed up teleportation with travelling through portals. Pacer shot out Laser Shots then tried to run through it as fast as he could! Which only led to him constantly shooting himself.

It just wasn't working however, he refused to give up no matter how frustrated he got.

After what felt like a whole day of trying with no success, he finally accepted he was never going to make it back home and sat down to take a rest, then he had a breakthrough,

He heard Gigantic The First's voice "slow your mind down and speed your body up!"

'I'm doing it all wrong! Instead of trying to shoot out teleportation and catch it like some portal, I gotta use my powers from within' thought Pacer then he jumped up to his feet with a new lease of life, finally he understood the difference between the two.

"Here goes nothing" said Pacer.

Pacer closed his eyes then held out he's hands and clinched his fist but instead of shooting out the Laser Shot he reversed it and shot it within, ZOOP!

Pacer felt something happen so he opened his eyes and was excited to see that he was back in Paradise Mountains.

TRUTH AND SAFARHI'S TRAINING

"Raheem... Truth" said a voice

"Rhiarn... Safarhi" said another voice

Safarhi telepathically asked Truth "You know what this is bro?"

"Nar, they too strong they've blocked me out" replied Truth

"I am Gigantic the very first Gigantian" said the voice

"And I'm Lordisha" said another voice

It was the spirits of the very first Gigantic and his wife Lordisha, Truth and Safarhi looked forward and saw them appear

"You have both unlocked your full potentials, are you ready to show us what you can do?" Said Lordisha and before the twins could reply the ground disappeared from underneath them and they fell deep into the Ocean!

Before they could even figure out where they were, Gigantic The First sent in an underwater army who started to attack them!

Springing straight into action Truth telekinetically created a path of air around him, by moving water from the Ocean's surface all the way down to him.

"You see these Ops in front of us sis, my hands are kinda tied right now you reckon you can take em?" Said Truth directly into his sister's mind

"Of course bro" replied a confident Safarhi

Safarhi began to choose which animal she should channel, her confidence dropped ever so slightly as the warriors came closer and she couldn't choose between the Pistol Shrimp or a Cardinal Fish then Truth whispered into her head "Choose both". Truth could sense that Safarhi's powers had developed to a level where she could channel multiple animals and elements of nature at one time.

Safarhi burst out a sonic boom which startled the warriors whilst creating a route for her to breathe out a fire ball that burnt the warriors under water!

"Madddd" said Truth, Safarhi was GASSED! She'd never done anything like that before.

"Let's get out of here" said Truth, then he used his power to push himself up to the surface whilst Safarhi swam up.

As soon as they got out of the water, they were greeted by thousands more warriors, they couldn't see no way out!

"These man are on us ennit" said Safarhi

"Only way out is to go through em! You ready?" Replied Truth

"Go Get Em!" Said the twins then they ran into battle.

Without giving it a single thought, they began using their powers at a new level. This is where their high level of intelligence helped them out, the twins naturally took to their new powers without any need for instruction from Lordisha or Gigantic The First.

Truth didn't need touch things to learn them no more... if he wanted to know something, his SG Gem would technically download it straight to his mind. He could also move anything now, even himself, as long as it was natural or made from this World or Zurakaya he could control it telekinetically, he demonstrated this by not only making himself glide through the skies but by also dropping everything from Buildings to Cars on his enemy!

Truth's new level of power was actually ground-breaking, no I mean it... he was literally lifting the ground! He ripped the concrete, tarmac and everything beneath it off the ground then used it to crush the enemies whilst simultaneously burying them under the Earths gravel!

Safarhi had at least three high powered animals running through her whilst creating isolated earthquakes and tornados which took out the opposition and as promised by the Chief, Safarhi was now able to summon Chalky and Greazy who stood by her side in battle tearing the opposition to shreds! Using her intelligence, Safarhi got to thinking about how she could manipulate nature to create weapons for battle, then she had a eureka moment. Safarhi drew the most minuscule water particles from the atmosphere and froze them into the shape of deadly icicles! She then compressed the air around her and used it to shoot the deadly icicles at the oncoming warriors at the speed of bullets.

"Bro you see that... I'm calling them Ice Shots" said Safarhi she was so excited by her new level of development.

"Don't get too gassed sis, cos there's more and more coming" said Truth

The twins were unstoppable but there were just too many warriors, every time one died two more respawned!

Truth then realised he could now speak into other people minds too!

"How long we gotta do this, surely you see were on job like a 9 to 5? You just wasting our time now"said Truth into Lordisha's mind

"I'm enjoying watching every last minute of this, but the only way to stop this is to fully work together!" Said Lordisha

"Sis we gotta do sut'um together to end this" said Truth to his sister

"What's you mean?" Asked Safarhi

"I reckon we need to combine our powers and do a madness!" Said Truth

"Yeah like... take em on a Truth Safarhi!" Said Safarhi

"I like that still... let's make sut'um happen" Truth

"I'm on it, don't hold back you know... rise the ting" said Safarhi

"Soufflé" replied Truth making an out of character joke.

Then the twins got serious! Truth focused deeply and Safarhi did the same, this intense level of concentration led to an almost cosmic experience as their SG Gems combined and let out a glow that shot into the sky where it was met by a similar glow that was shot out by The Source!

They recently discovered that their Pink and Purple Star Diamonds were pure forms of The Source's energy but they were still shocked at their ability to draw down on so much power. They had officially elevated to whole new level, like their siblings they were directly unified with The Source, but the difference was they had now established how weaponize it!

The Source created a Forcefield shield that omitted around the twins in order to protect them from the damage they were about to cause!

Truth and Safarhi looked at each other and smiled, they could feel it in their bones that they were about to do a madness! Truth started his attack without moving a muscle, the whole atmosphere changed to a dark Purple mist as anything in Truth's path of attack was obliterated! Cars were crushed and buildings came tumbling down as he used his powers to elevate every last one of the enemies into the sky. As the warriors helplessly dangled in the sky, Safarhi was ready to join the action! The Earth shook as she added a Pink mist to the atmosphere and formed thousands of Ice Shots what she lined up and blasted at the warriors hitting them all simultaneously! Each Ice Shot connected and slowly froze the floating warriors as Truth continued crushing them! Their two energies combined with The Source was way too much for any living organism to survive, the Truth Safarhi was slowly destroying the enemy from within... then the Truth Safarhi got stronger and stronger until BOOOOOOMMMMMM! The energy combusted and pulverised everything and anyone that was deemed to be opposition! Then the shield disappeared along with the Purple and Pink mist and all went back to normal as Lordisha said

"Well done Chosen Ones Truth and Safarhi, your trainings over... now go save the Universe" then just like that Truth and Safarhi was back in the Forbidden Area.

GIGANTIC'S TRAINING

"Jay... The new Gigantic" said a voice

"Yes" replied Gigantic

"I am Gigantic the very first Gigantian" said the voice

"And I'm Lordisha" said another voice

It was the spirits of the very first Gigantic and his wife Lordisha, when Gigantic looked forward he saw them appear and instantly dropped to one knee

"Get up! You don't bow to no one... you're the leader of prophecy" said Lordisha

"You unlocked your full potential are you ready to show us what you can do?" Said Lordisha, before Gigantic could reply, Gigantic The First placed him in what could only be described as a live action recording of a specific section of each teens training that had just took place.

At first Gigantic just watched as he tried to figure out what was going on,

"You better do something, or you and the Squad will die!" Said an emotionless Lordisha

"What's this all about?" Asked Gigantic

"I think it's obvious to see, you're the leader of the Chosen Ones... the chosen one who was chosen to directly lead the Chosen Ones! Whatever they can do you can do too, they have all been through these scenarios successfully using their abilities to overcome life-threatening situations... now you must do the same! Use the same or similar techniques as the teens to survive, or you will all die" said Lordisha

"You got to survive using their abilities, but you should know, you can only use one teen's power alongside your own at any given time... Go!" Said Gigantic The First then he threw Gigantic into specific segments of the teens training segments.

Gigantic found himself under water with Truth and Safarhi, he replicated Safarhi's abilities and summoned the abilities of a Shark in order to breathe, attack and then finally swim to the surface where he then shot himself out by replicating Truth's powers.

Gigantic now found himself in the battle on the ground moments before the Truth Safarhi took place, he continued using Truth's telekinetic power and threw the warrior enemies in the air then smacked them back to the ground before unleashing combos on them, coupling Truth's telekinesis with his immaculate close combat skills.

Gigantic was just warming and enjoying the battle when he was dramatically pulled out and thrown into Chunksta's training segment just after he released a Chunksta Boom!

Gigantic watched in amazement, proud of his son's ability, but this was short lived as he looked back at the enemy just in time to be riddled with bullets!

Gigantic let out an all mighty ROOAAARRRRRR as the shots came at him! Each bullet connected and dropped him to the ground, then he too noticed that he was still alive! Gigantic was also bulletproof, him and Chunksta got back to their feet and readied themselves to attack the warriors that were coming at them... then Gigantic was pulled out and thrown into the end of Pacer's training as he tried to teleport home.

Gigantic watched Pacer and laughed as he tried to figure out teleportation "Look at this doughnut, what's he trying to do?" Asked Gigantic

"He's trying to teleport home, just like you have to do" replied Lordisha

Gigantic wasn't really phased by the thought of teleporting as he had done it before, he focused and controlled himself then within seconds he teleported and was back at Paradise Mountains listening to the rest of the Squad comparing notes and sharing stories about their training sessions in The Source.

Back at Paradise Mountains

"We're all here, thanks for finally joining us Jay" said Chief Danjuma

"That was intense" said Truth

"Yeah that weren't no joke" said Gigantic

"Yes that was The Source's Training simulation what was designed by Gigantic The First and Lordisha with the intention of... well... you guys! It was specifically created millions of years ago to take the Chosen Ones to the highest level" said Chief Danjuma

"Okaaay, that's why they were in there" said Safarhi

"What... you got to meet them?" Blurted out Chief Danjuma who was slightly jealous and equally worried "No one's ever met them before... this must be serious!"

"Well boy, they don't play... they were moving like pagans in there" said Safarhi

"You get me, certain times things got peak and it was like they were just gonna leave me to get rubbed" agreed Chunksta

"They would've never made that happen... it was just tough love" said Truth

As they spoke The Source became more and more unstable, it seemed that the training sessions strained it even more. Trapz whispered something into the Chief's ear then the Chief shock his head and said "Anyway there's no more time to waste, the Chosen Ones most travel to Zurakaya right away before The Source self-destructs! Prepare a Galax for travel and let's get to the launch pad"

A Galax is technically a compact version of The Gigantor Galax, they looked very similar to the Aero Gigantor's and even though they were much smaller than the Gigantor Galax they were still bigger than the Aero Gigantors.

The Galax was loaded full of tech like the Gigantor Galax and able to travel around the entire Galaxy. A fleet of them were located in what was called the launchpad in the back end of the Gigantor Galax. The Gigantor Galax was located in Paradise Mountains behind the Tech Area where once again it was well disguised as a Mountain. Only a selected few were authorised to remove the cloak and access the Gigantor Galax.

Even though the Gigantor Galax was millions of years old it was still thousands of years ahead of our technology. The Galax fleet and the Gigantor Galax itself were the only way for Zurakayans to travel between Planets of the Universe, as the portal and teleportation abilities Zurakayans possess only allows travel within the planet they're situated in at that specific time. In the past a few had tried to go between planets using teleportation or creating portals, but they were unsuccessful in their travels and ended up either combusting or being lost forever between universes!

This was a disadvantage for the Squad Gigantic and all other Zurakayans, as Zeitan has access to EOTS technology that enables him to generate intergalactic portals and travel between planets whenever he feels like.

Chief Danjuma led the way to the Gigantor Galax, on route they passed through the Tech area to link up with Tanya and Boss Tekkie, in order to brief them on the mission they were about to deliver comms and technical support for.

Whilst everyone else was in training, Tanya was getting put through her strides too.

She spent the day with 'Boss Tekkie' - Chief Danjuma's Head of Tech and Communications. Tanya's mind was being opened to heights she never knew existed! The technology was literally out of this world and it was now all at Tanya's disposal. She was now like a child in Hamley's Toy Store! She picked up everything she saw and asked what's this? What does this do? Can I try it?

The team loved her enthusiasm and gave her free reign.

"Anything you want or feel you need... it's yours" said the tech guys, "Anything?" Replied Tanya

"Yep anything, this is all yours! If you like it, say it and it'll be in your HQ within seconds" said Boss Techie

"How would you get it there so quickly?" Asked Tanya

"Come let me show you" said Boss Tekkie then he took Tanya and showed her how to teleport items from the SG HQ to anywhere Squad Gigantic may be in the world.

"Remember each SG Gem is like a portable version of The Source, it possesses pure Source energy so basically anything The Source can do... so can the SG Gems! It can even be used to control and shut down parts of Earth but that's another story for another day" said Boss Tekkie

"I've been instructed to give you this bit of tech that possesses an extract from The Source, this machine captures whatever you're sending then effectively uploads the item by breaking down the particles, then it contacts and connects with the SG Gems which basically downloads the item that's been sent then rebuilds the particles making them ready for use... and the greatest part is that it does this in seconds" said Boss Tekkie

Tanya stood there in disbelief with her mouth wide open, all she could say was "Shuttt up!"

Boss Tekkie laughed and replied "It's true, this can be done in reverse too they can send things to HQ from wherever they are in that planet too"

"I've gotta try it" said Tanya as she grabbed things and started sending it through to her HQ using Boss Tekkie's larger equivalent to the SG Sender she was just gifted.

Tanya sent so many things that she got carried away and tried to send herself

"Oh my gosh I forgot my Safarhi Fly lip gloss in my room and I've been wanting to get it since we got here... I'm just gonna run through and get it" said Tanya as she tried to enter the Boss Tekkie's Sender

"Noooooo you can't send people! You will die if you're to be broken down!" Said Boss Tekkie

"Yeah that makes sense actually" said Tanya.

Tanya calmed down and continued to go through Paradise Mountain's catalogues of equipment and tech putting whatever she required through the SG Sender.

Tanya was now fully equipped, just as Boss Tekkie closed the session and sent the SG Sender through to the SG HQ, they were interrupted by the rest of the Squad who were on their way to board a Galax and travel to the Supreme Earth!

Chief Danjuma gave Gigantic the honour of revealing the Gigantor Galax

"What do I do?" Said Gigantic as he approached what thought was a Mountain

"You see this big Mountain in front of you, place your palms on it, your Gigantian DNA will do something magical... just watch" replied the Chief.

Gigantic placed his hands on the Mountain and as promised something amazing started to happen. Gigantic felt his DNA pass into what he thought was the Mountain Rock.

He stepped back in line with everyone else and watched as the transformation began, the Mountain shield declined and revealed the Gigantor Galax.

"Fammmmmmmm" said Chunksta in amazement

Truth and Tanya smiled as they enjoyed the intricacy of such a machine.

The Gigantor Galax was the size of a city! Once the transformation was complete, they all boarded the major Spacecraft. Chief Danjuma gave them a live interactive history lesson as he and Boss Tekkie toured them through the Gigantor Galax, eventually they arrived at the Launchpad where they were told to pick a Galax.

"That one... it looks mad!" Said Pacer as he ran towards the one that attracted him the most, but he was stopped in his tracks by his big brother.

"Don't know why your getting excited, we all know I'm gonna be the one to fly this thing so I'm choosing which one we go in... and I'm not choosing it by which looks prettiest" said Truth.

Pacer knew better than to argue with Truth, so he fell back and left his brother to make the choice.

Chunksta laughed and said "Always taking bad up" mocking his brother Pacer.

"And you would take the bad up too!" Said Truth to Chunksta stamping his authority as big brother.

"I don't have it from no one bro" replied Chunksta refusing to backdown

Then Safarhi put a stop to the childish squabbling "Arrrr all of you shut up"

Then Truth said "This one!" Picking the Galax that happen to be the highest spec.

"Good choice" said Boss Tekkie "This is one of the latest models it literally has... everything hahahaha, hop in and let me show you how it works".

Before Truth jumped in he looked at Boss Tekkie and said "It's cool, I already know how to... you either use autopilot after coordinates are locked in or you fly manually by combining you mind and hand movement"

"But... how?" Said Boss Tekkie in disbelief, Chief Danjuma gave Boss Tekkie a look and a hand gesture whilst saying "He's special mate".

"Here's the mission brief, this first part is not a mission of conflict, it is a mission to take and capture!" Instructed Chief Danjuma

"You want us to capture Zeitan?" Asked Chunksta

"Don't interrupt big man" said Pacer who was itching to get back at his younger brother for embarrassing him earlier.

"No Zeitan is not the target... his Source extract is! You only fight in life when you must, plus why just go for the burger when you can use the same money to get the whole meal?" Asked Chief Danjuma

Being food related, Pacer instantly understood that analogy.

"Getting Zeitan himself may stop him for a while but him and his creations will still be fully active due to them being powered by his extract of The Source, but if we get his Source extract and place it back in The Source, it will return back to positive energy, defuse Zeitan and exterminate all his creation".

"Makes sense" said Safarhi

"We'll aim to create minimal attention, you will travel to the so called Supreme Earth with the Galax in stealth mode so your entrance will be untraceable, the coordinates will be set to the perimeter where we believe The Source is being held but it is not the exact precise location but on arrival your SG Gems will lead you to the exact spot where it's situated then Gigantic... you will need to compact The Source and place it in your Fire Red Diamond" said the Chief

"Only me... or can anyone else do it?" Asked Gigantic

"No, it must be you, we don't know exactly how big The Source extract is so your Fire Red Diamond is the only SG Gem that we know is definitely powerful enough to hold the extract" responded Chief Danjuma

"Cool" said Gigantic as he accepted the responsibility

"It's important for you to know that even though we'll be here on comms, you will effectively be alone out there! We can't send in the SG Hit Squad or anybody else so easy, if it kicks off back up can only be sent in a Galax and even though travel will feel like a few hours in space, in reality it's a few weeks at least! So by time they arrive the battle would likely be over! GET IN AND GET OUT! CONFLICT SHOULD ONLY BE IN DEFENCE OR LAST RESORT... AGREED!?!" Stated Chief Danjuma

"AGREED!" Said Squad Gigantic

"Well say your see you laters and be on your way" said Chief Danjuma

They said their goodbyes and boarded the Galax.

As soon as Truth sat in the pilot's seat, he's Purple Star Diamond began to glow and the Galax identified him.

"Welcome Pilot Raheem aka Truth, the coordinates to an undisclosed area in Planet Zurakaya has been locked in... autopilot is engaged... initiating ignition".

Then everyone's SG Gems let of a glow sending out a quick glare that powered the Galax "Ignition successful,

Welcome Squad Gigantic we're now ready to take off" said the Galax then ZOOOOOOOOOOOMMMMMMM... They were gone!

CHAPTER 11 – The Supreme Earth!

Squad Gigantic were travelling through space and to top if off they didn't even need spacesuits... they couldn't believe it!

"Mans really cruising through space like say we're just in ends" said Chunksta

"Nuts ennit" said Safarhi "I thought being able to breathe under water was mad but we're really gliding through space and breathing like we're just in the yard".

The journey was going smooth, although Truth wanted to navigate the Galax himself he didn't see the point in interfering with things, so he left it in Autopilot and just enjoyed the experience with his family.

Meanwhile in Supreme Earth, Nefarious noticed something strange.

"Zeitan, come have a look at this" said Nefarious calling his boss over to the satellite screens

"The systems are identifying an anomaly! It's as if something is approaching but when I look at the satellites nothing seems to be there!" Said a confused Nefarious

Zeitan erupted in laughter "These little pest think they're smart, they forget I was around when their tech was created hahahaha I made the motion detector just for situations like this, what's happening here is someone's trying to approach in stealth mode hoping they can creep up on us"

"Who?" Asked Nefarious

"It can only be Squad Gigantic!" Replied Zeitan

"Shall I send some Zupremes to take em' out or shall I load up and shoot them down from here?" Said Nefarious as he awaited instruction

"Narrr, then their SG Gems will be lost in space forever! Let's play this out, wait for them to enter then shoot them out the sky and grab them and their Gems!" Said Zeitan as he walked off excited "Ohhhhhhh today is gonna be a great day!"

Squad Gigantic we're unaware that their cover had been blown, they were unknowingly walking right into Zeitan's trap!

Zeitan aimed to finish Squad Gigantic once and for all by luring them into his world then taken their SG Gems and their lives!

The vibes was up on the Galax, everyone was gassed about entering a new planet. The darkness of Space began to brighten up as they finally reached the final leg of their journey and approached the Supreme Earth.

Everything seemed to be going to plan but just as they burst into the Supreme Earth's atmosphere, Truth had a vision that sent chills through his spine!

Truth saw the Galax being blasted out of the sky with catastrophic consequences, he saw the whole Squad down and out being severely hurt from the attack! He calculated the likeliness of his vision coming true and knew they were in for a hard time when the results came back with a ninety nine percent possibility!

Just as Truth went to warn the others of the imminent attack, the Galax's comms stating "incoming attack detected, contact will be made in 3... 2..."

"Everybody brace and prepare to crash!!!" Shouted Truth!

Then BOOOOOOOOM!!!

The Galax was hit by a barrage of blasts that destroyed its shields and defence systems, they didn't even have the chance to shoot back, the Galax was reduced to pieces before it even fell out of the sky and crash landed on Supreme Earth!

"BULLSEYE!" Shouted Zeitan

"ALL HITS NO MISSES!" Gloated Nefarious

Squad Gigantic were in a bad way! The mission was already a complete failure, they were nowhere near Zeitan's Source extract and to top it off they were laying half dead alone in an alien land surrounded by the Galax's debris with no way to get home!

The comms system was going crazy, Tanya couldn't track their whereabouts and lost contact with the Galax as it was blown to pieces. The only access she had to the Squad with via their SG Suits and SG Gems, she checked each person's vitals and burst in to tears when she saw how low they were... they were all inches away from death! Chief Danjuma consoled her and told her to have faith in them and The Source.

Things were looking grim for Squad Gigantic! The glow in their SG Gems slowly began to disappear along with any sign of life! They were now easy pickings and Zeitan was ready to seize his opportunity to finish them once and for all!

Zeitan sent a fleet of a five hundred Zupremes led by Nefarious to retrieve the SG Gems and dispose of Squad Gigantic.

The Zupremes arrived at the scene of the crash and could see their prey in a near distance and started rushing towards them perform a swift execution!

However, as they got closer Chunksta woke up and slowly raised to his feet! His ability to self-heal allowed him to come round at inhuman speed. He was a bit disoriented and confused, as he tried to get his head around what had happened, but at the same time he could his body was filled with a high level of energy that he absorbed from the blast!

Chunksta looked up to see the Zupremes coming at him, he then looked around his immediate surroundings and saw his comrades were all out of the game!

"Oiiii wake up…. WAKE UP" Shouted Chunksta but he received no response, they were all still out cold!

Tanya noticed Chunksta's vitals had risen considerably so she attempted to make contact with him

"Chunksta can you hear me?" Asked Tanya

"Yeah, it's all mad out here!" Replied Chunksta

"I know and I'm sorry to say it seems like you're on your own... everyone else's vitals are dangerously low! What's happened?" Asked Tanya

"All I remember was we just entered this planet and was about to pull up... then I swear Truth tried to warn us both sut'um... then BOOOMMM!!! We got slapped out of the sky!" Said Chunksta

"Are you safe" Asked Chief Danjuma

"Boiiii it's kinda techie right now still... I'm the only one standing and I can see a bag of man coming at me as we speak!" Said Chunksta as he assessed the situation he now found himself in.

Chunksta tried to wake everyone up before the Zupremes got too close but again he was unsuccessful.

The Zupremes were basically in front of him and he had to make the choice fight or run... and you know Chunksta ain't from running no one!

Feeling attack was his best form of defence, Chunksta ran towards the oncoming Zupremes and shouted "IT'S ONNNN!!!"

As soon as the first line of Zupremes were within range he drew back his arm, clinched his fist and said "CRASSSSHHHH!!!" as he punched the ground releasing his built up energy sending out a massive Chunksta Booom that took out the first line of Zupremes.

The remaining Zupremes became a bit more cautious, as they realised they now have a fight on their hands. Chunksta clenched up and readied himself for the onslaught coming his way.

Miraculously the Chunksta Booom sent a vibration along the ground which woke Safarhi. She got up and saw her brother readying for battle, she ran to his side prepared to take on the Zupremes with him

"Sis don't even make no sense you fighting these tings with me right now, I'll be cool one way or another" said Chunksta

"What d'you mean, we ride together!" Said Safarhi

"Yeah, I hear that but best thing you can do is go heal them lot… we'll be back at full strength then we can deal with these Op boys properly" said Chunksta

"Well I ain't leaving you alone" said Safarhi then she summoned Chalky and Greazy to ride with her brother.

Safarhi knew Chunksta was right, she ran over to her father and other brothers, then used Bear strength to drag and place them side by side, Safarhi then stood over them and let off her pink glow which went into each person and slowly began to heal them all at the same time.

Chunksta found himself surrounded by Zupremes whilst Safarhi healed their injured teammates!

He went to war with the help of Chalky and Greazy, he was fighting with all he had as he created a safety barrier between the Zupremes and his family enabling Safarhi to save them, but there was just too much of them, every time he dropped two Zupremes, at least four more came! Zeitan watched with joy as his creation got the upper hand on Squad Gigantic! Chunksta, Chalky and Greazy put up a good fight but now Chunksta was taking a severe beating.

Safarhi had no choice but to watch her little brother get beat down as she tried to heal the others as quick as possible!

Chunksta was bloodied and nearly finished as Nefarious came through the crowd of Zupremes to administer the final death blow to Chunksta and take his SG Gem!

All except two of the Zupremes surrounding Chunksta stepped back, the two who remained picked up Chunksta and held him by his arms leaving his body open for Nefarious to beat the last piece of life out of him.

Nefarious gave Chunksta three heavy blows to his chest and face! Chunksta tried to absorb the energy but it was useless he didn't have enough strength in him to break free from the Zupremes and do a Chunksta Boom! Finally, Truth and Gigantic was awake and they came rushing over to aid their brother as Safarhi continued to heal Pacer! Gigantic's head wasn't in the right place to teleport as he just came round so they ran as fast as they could, but they were still to slow!

Nefarious gripped Chunksta's SG Gem with one hand and drew his other arm back with the intent to deliver the final life ending blow to Chunksta then………
BLLLLAAAAAAAMMMMMMMM!

A blast came out of no where and blew Nefarious's arm right off! Then BLLLLAAAAAAAMMMMMMM! Another shot hit Nefarious and dropped him!

Then a voice screamed "LORDS ATTACK!!!" An army of Lords jumped out of an Aircraft whilst another one hundred plus more came from behind the Zupremes and started putting in work!

The tables had turned! Pacer woke up and Zooped in to battle, Safarhi followed... Squad Gigantic was back in full effect! The Zupremes were getting terrorised, the remaining AI's were no match to Squad Gigantic who were also backed by The Lords!

Yep you heard me right... the Lords!

Gigantic couldn't believe his eyes as he stood side by side with descendants of Lordisha's warriors

"Gigantic get your guys back to your Galax and try your hardest to find a part called the Source Connector, when you find this you can place it in our Lord Ship and travel back to Earth" said The new Lord Commander.

"We need to get Zeitan's Source extract" said Gigantic

"Forget it... that's not gonna happen today! We're seriously outnumbered and we'll only be able to hold them off for a while... you must do what you need to do to get home and fight another day!" Said the Lord Commander.

Knowing Truth and Safarhi are the most intelligent in the Squad, Gigantic sent them to search through the Galax's debris for the Source Connector whilst the rest battled alongside the Lords to hold off the Zupremes.

Zeitan's smile was now completely wiped off his face as he saw his main guy Nefarious left for dead on the battlefield.

"I guess if you want something done you got to do it yourself" said Zeitan Supreme then he opened a portal and walked right into the middle of the battle.

"ZEITAN IS HERE" Shouted the new Lord Commander "Lord's focus your attack on him... Squad Gigantic...GET OUT OF HERE!"

"Big man I ain't running from no one" said Chunksta who was almost back to full power.

"You get me bro" said Pacer as they worked together to tear through the Zupremes.

"If you don't go now you will never get back home!" Said the new Lord Commander

"Truth, Safarhi where are we on that Source Connector?" Asked Gigantic as he ripped off a Zupreme's face.

"Found it but it needs fixing, gimme a few minutes" said Truth as Safarhi ran back to battle with her war pets standing by her side.

Zeitan was effortless killing any Lord that got in his way, he was an unstoppable force.

The new Lord Commander couldn't see this ending well, so she decided to go to her back up plan

The Lord Commander grabbed Kon-X one of her new aged Lord warriors "Kon-X get to the base and grab our Lord Gems" instructed the new Lord Commander.

Kon-X possessed some amazing abilities, not only was she able to generate emojis and weaponize them she was also able to travel through social media and internet locations online.

Kon-X location surfed to the base, grabbed the Lord Gems then came right back and handed them to her Commander.

Whilst Kon-X went for the Lord Gems, Truth delivered some bad news "This Source Connector ting is dead out! There's no way of fixing it"

Upon hearing the news from Truth, The Commander pulled Gigantic and Kon-X to a side and said "I had a feeling this would happen, the only way out of this will cost us Lords our life's but luckily the Lords are not new to sacrifice for the greater good! We can get you out of here on our Lordship without the Source Connector"

"How?" Asked Gigantic

"Basically, by jump starting the Lord Ship with our Lord Gems but we'll need to have the Lord Gems on the Lord Ship whilst a big force of energy acts as a catalyst and blasts the ship in to action" replied the Lord Commander

"No problem, I know exactly where we can get the energy" said Gigantic then he called Chunksta and Pacer over and whispered a plan into their ears.

"One more thing" said the New Lord Commander "This is Kon-X, there's a major chance that she will survive the sacrifice which will put her at Zeitan's mercy! We can't let that happen, I need you to take her with you... Chief Danjuma is fully aware of this"

"No problem she's family!" Said Gigantic, Then he called over Truth and Safarhi and instructed them to go with Kon-X to the Lord Ship and prepare for travel, they did as they were told and boarded the Lord Ship, Truth got familiar with its systems in order to fly it back home.

Now Gigantic was ready to put his plan in place, Pacer took the Lord Gems from the Lord Commander and patiently waited for Gigantic's word.

Chunksta got Zeitan's attention by taunting him "Oi likkle man, stop acting like you're bad and really do me something"

Zeitan took the bait without any hesitation he mustered up a mega shot and blasted it right into Chunksta's chest.

"PACER NOW!!!" Shouted Gigantic, then Pacer paced into the Lord Ship with the Lord Gems and placed them in the aircrafts system.

The remaining Lords launched an attack on Zeitan to keep him occupied as Gigantic placed himself behind Chunksta who was now filled with an enormous amount of absorbed energy, Chunksta released his biggest Chunksta Boom to date which connected with the Lord Gems and kick started the Lord Ship, whilst creating a major explosion which unfortunately killed every Lord and Zupreme in sight!

Zeitan was down and seriously hurt too, he couldn't do nothing but watch with his half open eyes as Truth launched the spacecraft. As soon as Truth took off Gigantic grabbed Chunksta and teleported them both on to the Lord Ship which was already mid-air!

Zeitan played right into Gigantic's plan and now he had lost his best chance so far to grab their SG Gems!

Zeitan summoned Zupremes to retrieve both him and Nefarious and take them back to his HQ where he could recuperate.

Truth made contact with Paradise Mountains and informed Tanya they were on their way home with their new comrade Kon-X.

Chapter 11.5 – Lords Be My Saviour!

That was a madness" said Pacer

"Yeah, they had me on the ropes, couple times I thought I was a goner!" Said Chunksta

Squad Gigantic took a moment to reflect on what had just took place, that was their most challenging battle to date.

Knowing that they would've be exterminated if it wasn't for the Lords saving them and making the fatal sacrifices, Gigantic said "Kon-X I can't explain how grateful I am that you all intervened, I promise that the sacrifice was not made in vein, this war with Zeitan has just got even more personal now... he's gotta go!"

Kon-X gave him half a smile, she was dealing with the fact that she had just lost all her family and friends.

"You ain't in any debt to us, our main purpose is to protect the Chosen Ones with everything we have... this was fate" replied Kon-X.

As insensitive as ever, Pacer joined the conversation and said "I know you probably don't wanna talk and all that but I'm baffled, I need to know sutum' I thought the Lords didn't exist no more, didn't they all die like millions of years ago... wha gwarn for that?"

"Don't answer him if you don't want to, this boy don't have no filter or self-awareness!" Said Gigantic

"Nar he's cool I don't mind explaining but I can show you better than I can tell you" said Kon-X, then she cleared a space and began to project something from her hand.

The projection looked like the end of the battle between Zeitan and Equinile just before he released the first ever land purification.

"LOCKDOWN THE ENTRANCE" Demanded the Lord Commander,

All the Zurakayans except the defending Lords were on the Gigantor Galax ready to escape. The Lords put a wall of guards in place to create a barrier between the Zupremes and the Gigantor Galax but two Zupremes managed to breakthrough and were a few steps away from entering the Gigantor Galax before The Lord Commander noticed them then flipped over the wall of Lords and ripped the heads off both AI's bodies before battering them down to cubes and sealing the ships entrance to ensure the safety of all. Knowing her and her warriors were on a suicide mission, she took a look at her brave and loyal warriors fighting with honour, giving every last thing they had and refused to let them all die! The Lord Commander completed her mission by locking down the spacecraft and allowing it to take off.

Kon-X interrupted the projection and said "This is where everyone got the story wrong! They believed once the land purification was performed only Zeitan made it to safety and survived"

Everyone looked around in shock and surprise, then begged Kon-X to continue the viewing

The Gigantor Galax was taking off, Zeitan was down and so at this point the Lords were just wasting their time beating up Zupremes.

The Lord Commander had a moment of enlightenment, she thought back to a secret base Gigantic and Lordisha once took her too, then Lordisha's voice ran through her mind as she remembered her saying 'Never forget this place, it's been built specially for you to take the Lords forward and eventually save the Chosen Ones when the time comes... and don't worry you'll know exactly when that time to come back here is!'

The Lord Commander had no doubt that the time was now! She spoke directly into her remaining warriors minds and gave instruction "This whole planet is gonna be purified... it's either we pointlessly stand and fight Zeitan's minions or you lock in this location and follow me to this secret base built by Lordisha".

The Lord Commander sent the location, then they all teleported to the safety of the purpose built base to ensure the Lords would survive the land purification and continue to a form of defence for Zurukayans.

"Generations of Lords stayed in this secret base for years upon years... until they deemed it safe to touch road again. However, when they finally came out of hiding Zeitan reigned and he had already downloaded the Earth file and changed Zurakaya to Supreme Earth! The Lords had to retreat back to base and live life in the shadows for many generations more. As time went by things improved but only slightly! The Lords found a way to communicate with Paradise Mountains and even managed to capture some Zupremes and rewire their mainframes to make them obey Lord Commanders instead of Zeitan. This allowed the Lords to infiltrate Zeitan on many occasions and help Paradise Mountains halt many of his attempts to take over or destroy The Source, but they were still heavily outnumbered and outgunned on his Supreme Earth, so we always make sure that when we strike it's swift, effective and untraceable, we only ever come to the surface for real serious purposes! We became a pain to Zeitan, he spent so much of his resources trying to find the base and destroy the Lords but the same virus that hid Paradise Mountains from Zeitan also removed the Lord's base location too, that was the only upper hand we had on Zeitan.

The Lords resistance existed and survived up to this day but the end is not a sad occasion, when The Source gifted us the Lord Gems it came with a prophecy that informed us that the day will come when we will have to make the ultimate sacrifice to protect in order to save the Chosen Ones and The Source" bravely stated Kon-X.

"I guess that day was today!" Said Gigantic

"Exactly, so as mad as it sounds this is a joyous occasion. My family will ascend and receive all the good that's been promised" Replied Kon-X

"This might come out wrong but I'm not being disrespectful... what made you so special?" Asked Truth.

"Nar that's a fair question" said Kon-X

"Once again you don't have to answer if you don't want to, these youths are too nosey! Your Commander said Chief Danjuma knows your situation and that's good enough for me" said Gigantic making sure Kon-X was completely comfortable.

"It's cool, my story's a mad one still... like I really been through it" said Kon-X, once again she had the full attention of the Lord Ship.

"Might as well get straight to it, the reason I'm 'special' is cos I'm half AI half Lord" said Kon-X

"What d'you mean you're a cyborg... like Zeitan?" Asked Safarhi

"Nar, I'm different unique one of a kind. My Mum was a Lord, and my Dad was a Zupreme!" Said Kon-X causing a state of confusion on the Lord Ship.

"How, I swear them man are robots... how they breed a ting... like a real woman?" Asked Chunksta

"Remember I said that the Lords managed to capture and rewire Zupremes" said Kon-X

Everyone replied "Yeahhh" then continued to listen

"Well over the years, Zupremes developed to levels you wouldn't believe, they were already advanced from the beginning, you seen how human like they look, it's only little subtle things like their eyes and that tint of colour their synthetic skin has, that really allows us to identify them. This is because the AI's adapt to their surroundings, first they progressed to a level where they managed to breed amongst themselves and being AI's they don't have to wait nine months to give birth its basically just a week or two, that's why Zeitan's numbers are so high.

Anyway, let me get back to my point, as I was saying they adapt to their surroundings so once they were recalibrated to be amongst Lords they began to think, act and you could say... become Lords. This introduced love and emotions to the mainframe of the Zupremes under our control, eventually they started to live, love and recreate like us. Cut a long story short, my Mum and a Zupreme got close and fell in love. The Lord Commander at the time wasn't having none of it, not knowing my Mum was pregnant she ordered the execution of my Dad for what was seen as outrageous out of character behaviour. My Mum and Dad fled the base deciding to take their chances on the Supreme Earth's mainland, this was easy for my Dad to do but not long after I was born my Mum got noticed on ends and a Zupreme reported her to Zeitan! Zeitan was so intrigued by the fact that a Zupreme and a Lord could make life that he done an investigation operation on my household, then once he was satisfied with his findings he personally came to my house with Nefarious and slaughtered my parents in front of me!

Just as Nefarious and Zeitan grabbed me, the Lord Commander and a few of her warriors breached my front door and entered my house, word got back to her that my Mum was at risk and you know the rule... a Lord can never intentionally leave a Lord behind, so she came to rescue my Mum but she was too late. I can remember the shock in the Lord Commanders face when she took a brief look around the room and saw my toys, she genuinely didn't know I existed! She attacked Zeitan hoping to get me out of his hands but that didn't work! Zeitan and Nefarious were too powerful they destroyed the Commander and her warriors then took me anyway." Explained Kon-X

"Arrr that's horrible" said Safarhi "so how did you end up back with the Lords?"

"When the Commanders predecessor examined her place of death, they saw all the evidence of my existence and she made a vow that one day I will be saved and brought home to the Lords" said Kon-X

"Cool then they got you?" Asked Pacer

"Yeah, but don't get it twisted it took them a long time to find me!" Replied Kon-X "I went through a madness, I was basically raised by Nefarious... if that's what you wanna call it! They held me like a prisoner until they realised what powers I had!"

"I saw you do a few things in that fight... looked MADDD" said Safarhi "what can you do?"

Kon-X Replied "They call me a new aged Zupreme because my ZuraGene blends with my AI capabilities. In a nutshell, I can bring any emoji to life and use it in the real world, more time I just use it in defence and create weapons but sometimes I had to use it to create food and Earth when then had me captured... that's actually how they saw my abilities, they kept on finding chicken bones and cake crumbs next to me hahaha. All jokes aside though, the main ability they abused of mine was my ability to travel through online locations... if you put a location on social media or even show me a location or address online in can travel through data and pull up in minutes sometimes even seconds" said Kon-X

"That's nuts" said Chunksta

"Yeah, real crazy! Nefarious used me to sell Glitches online, he forced me to deliver Glitches to Zupreme's all over Supreme Earth and to make sure I didn't try escape he put a tracker on me that would kill me if I ever took it off" said Kon-X

"What's Glitches?" Asked Chunksta

"It's basically like drugs in our world, certain times things get a bit mad for Zupremes and rather than recode them and give them resources to deal with stress, Nefarious created Glitches that they use as a vice to temporarily forget their pains and issues but like drugs Glitches are bad for them! It slowly eats them from within, plus it's highly addictive and expensive so they start doing crazy things to be able to afford it! Like any other drug it eventually kills them! But Nefarious don't care bout that by then he wouldn't got his P and taken full advantage of the control he had over them... then he just disposed of them and used their parts!" Explained Truth

"So the Zupremes on Glitches are basically crackheads!" said Pacer

"Maddd, some intergalactic crackheads you know!" Joked Chunksta

"Yeah exactly that... they're the feens of Zupreme Earth! Truth, how you know all that... are on it?" Asked Kon-X, surprised that Truth had so much knowledge of Glitches.

"No way! Drugs are for mugs!" Said Truth

"He can learn anything about anything in seconds love, he's just showing off" said Safarhi

"Ohhh phew, cos' they ain't a game! I've never used it in my life but selling them for N's had me in some horrible environments doing madness just to survive and protect myself. N's had me running nuff' different Traps for him and the crazy thing was I wasn't only good at it, I actually started to enjoy at times." Said Kon-X as she hanged her head in shame

"How could you enjoy that life?" Asked Pacer

"What you have to understand is, I didn't know no different. I was taken so young that I grew up thinking N's was my Dad... I didn't know I was a Lord! I didn't remember anything about my parents, they fully hid my history from me.

As far as I was concerned, this was my family and this is my life, like any other kid I craved the love and attention that you get from your family, but the only time I ever received anything close to this love was from N's whenever I made bank in the trap or mashed works on someone who tried to Glitch without paying, that's the only time I ever got any positive form of attention at all.

They had my mind tapped, I was on constant crud! If you needed road doing in anyway... shout me, I would make it happen!

I didn't find out who I really was until one day The Lords launched an attack on Zeitan and caught him slippin'! They caught him so off guard that N's had to draw us youngers in to defend him, but when I pulled up, the Lord Commander saw my Mums resemblance in my face and right there and then she changed their attack to a rescue mission.

I was baffled I thought I was the Lords target until I saw Zeitan and N's switch on me... they started shouting out things about my history then Zeitan looked at me and replied 'I should've killed you when I killed your parents' then they tried to kill me!

I didn't know who to trust but what I did know was the Lords where attacking to protect me and the Zupremes were attacking me... so my choice was kinda made.

I escaped with the Lords, they removed my tracker and took me to the base. The Lords ran a few tests and discovered Zeitan interfered with my memories forcing me to forget my parents and background, the Lords reversed the procedure and open my memory bank.

Not only did I realise I was home, I also realised that the life I lived was never meant to be the path for me.

I've been with the Lords ever since, they trained me to become a warrior by teaching me the moral codes and the disciplines of a Lord along with developing my abilities and enabling me to use my powers to my full capabilities.

My unique way of travel was handy in so many ways from getting supplies to gathering info before an attack, but it's been risky! N's tried to set me nuff' times, certain times he caught me... mashed me up then, was close to recapturing me but the Lords always popped up and dealt with him!

That's another reason why today was so special, it was the first time I was able to come at him head on and I can't lie it felt good to whip up those Comet emojis and smash him to pieces with it" said Kon-X

"Ohhh you sent them shots, luv fam you saved my life" said Chunksta

"Yeah I was gonna send a whole Train bro but it would've hit you too hahaha" said Kon-X

They all laughed then kicked back and rested listening to music as they travelled through space back to Paradise Mountains.

MEANWHILE BACK ON ZUPREME EARTH

Zeitan was hurt badly but he was not destroyed.

The explosion from the Chunksta Boom colliding with the Lord Gems energy really knocked him for six, whilst on the ground he managed to call in a support team to collect him and Nefarious who took him back to his HQ where he planned to rest and heal. Zeitan knew he had to bring Nefarious back to life to eventually perform the most dangerous procedure he had ever done to date! Zeitan felt he had no choice but fuse his Source extract into his mainframe, so once he felt he was recuperated he vowed he was going to take his power to a whole new level, doing a drastic move that'll ensure that as long as he was alive neither him or the Zupremes could be compromised!

It would be a bold move that would come with many risks but if executed correctly it would also come with many rewards for the evil Zeitan Supreme!

CHAPTER 12 – OWNERSHIP!

The Squad's trip back to Paradise Mountains was successful, upon arrival they were met by Chief Danjuma, Jenay, Mummy G and Santago. Gigantic felt ashamed as he gave the Chief a debrief of the failed mission but the Chief reassured him that he had nothing to be embarrassed about, not only did he bring the Squad back safely from a situation what could've easy had a devastating outcome but he also managed to deliver Kon-X to Paradise Mountains, this keeps the Lords bloodline in existence.

"This was just prophecy fulfilling itself once again, this mission may not have went the way we wanted it to go but as they say when we plan and the powers above laugh" said Chief Danjuma, his words brought comfort to Squad Gigantic.

The training was complete and each member of Squad Gigantic was now at their pinnacle so there was no reason for them to stay at Paradise Mountains any longer. Chief Danjuma knew that Zeitan would not take this defeat lightly and taking Kon-X also added insult to injury!

Chief Danjuma instructed Squad Gigantic to go back to London as he could sense that an attack from Zeitan and his new companions was imminent!

Kon-X took an instant liking to the Squad and was slightly hoping she would be ordered to go with them too.

279

However, Chief Danjuma had different plans for Kon-X, she was sent with Trapz and 2's who welcomed her into the SG Hit Squad.

Squad Gigantic said their goodbyes and farewells to everyone on Paradise Mountains.

Little Stompy came running out of now where and gave Chunksta a massive hug which he awkwardly accepted. Santago opened a portal which led the gang into the SG HQ and just like that Squad Gigantic was back in London.

Squad Gigantic got home to find out things had drastically changed! They couldn't understand how quickly everything was turned upside down. They felt as if they were only gone for a few days, but this was because they didn't take all the space travel into account, the truth was many weeks had flown by.

With Squad Gigantic out of the way Bangz Army had full reign of the streets, Officer KK and the Mayor were fully under Bang's thumb, London was being ran under what the streets called Bang's Martial Law!

Bangz Army linked up with the Unknown Hittaz and took over the underworld with no resistance from the LCP, in fact the LCP colluded with Bangz Army and Unknown Hittaz by applying pressure to the other gangs and criminals in order to create a clear pathway for Bang's takeover!

London was in a bad way and the only resistance was Thug Rock and his crew, but every time they gained any momentum the Mayor enforced new laws on the City to purposely cripple their movements. The Mayor's latest enforcement was a City wide lockdown and anyone who disobeyed the new rules was met with extreme force.

Another part of Bang's masterplan was to take over and run all the main estates in the area, Bang used the Mayor's influence to take control of the major block without having to invest a penny or make any formal commitments, Bang aimed to gentrify the estates so from the outside looking in it looked to be a safe and thriving community, whilst in reality he ran a heavy criminal underworld in secret with fake businesses washing his illegal money from the inside.

Initially residents welcomed the proposed changes and were on side with the Mayors plans. However, Bang being Bang he wasn't patient enough to execute such a complicated plan so he ended up reverting back to his old ways and within days these blocks were infested with serious crime! Residents were either pushed out or scared to leave their homes, flats were turned into Traps and it was no longer safe for children to play in communal areas, as gang members basically used their parks and play areas to do deals or whatever else they wanted to do, within a week or two the blocks became inhabitable for the residents as Bang's Gang members ran wild.

Ironically the only block that Bang was unable to take over was the 'Bang Block'. Bang tried to actually buy this block but was repeatedly denied. He couldn't understand why his offers kept being refused! Every time he pressured the Mayor regarding this area, the Mayor would communicate with his superiors only to be told an undisclosed property developer had already proposed a development plan for this estate which had been accepted.

Bang hated the fact he couldn't have his way, so on the day he saw works beginning in the area he sent some of he's soldiers to vandalise the construction ground, he hoped he would eventually scare off the developer, which would result in them putting a halt on the development but when his guys arrived, they were surprised to be greeted by Rock Ard Thugs who were sent to protect the area!

Bang couldn't do nothing about the development taking place.

Londoners didn't know what to do! They were living in constant fear, things were so bad that even Sandra Patty was begging for the return of Squad Gigantic.

The morning after arriving home from Paradise Mountains Gigantic sat in his office with a bowl of fruits and his daily SG vitamins, Gigantic always liked to start his day eating breakfast whilst watching the news.

Gigantic almost spat out his multivitamins as her saw Sandra Patty make a direct plea for Squad Gigantic to come back and save the day! The outspoken news reporter had taken a complete U-turn in regards to the Heroes from the ends, she spoke on how bad things had got in London, then she went on to run a special on how the Mayor's false promises of hope to the estates which he snatched back as soon as he got the opportunity. Sandra 'Chatty' Patty and the rest of London had finally found out that the Mayor wasn't who he claimed to be.

Sandra Patty released a secretly recorded three-way phone call between the Mayor, Officer KK and Bang which she received from Angel... the Mayor's daughter! Angel saw her father's corrupt ways on a daily basis and had enough of the injustice so she sent over a recording of them briefly speaking on their underhanded plans, they gave brief mention of their leader Zeitan Supreme which left Sandra Patty asking the question "Who's really running our city? And even more importantly... Who is Zeitan Supreme?"

Jay Gigantic just laughed as this was old news to him, as he finished his breakfast he mumbled to himself about how lucky she was that he put plans in place.

Jay Gigantic got up, placed his bowl in the kitchen, washed his hands then returned to his office to make an important call.

"Yo bro, it's me" said Gigantic

"I was waiting for your call, you took your time" replied the person on the other end of the phone

"Yeah space travel and them ting deh' madness still but forget all that, how we looking?" Replied Jay Gigantic

"Real good, the deal is sealed... payments gone through, the work is almost complete just how you requested it... and hear this... even the gang truce is in place" replied the person on the on the phone

"What no resistance?" Asked Jay Gigantic

"Yeah, a little but nothing we couldn't handle, everyone fell in line except Bangz Army and them Unknown Hittaz but that was expected. In regards to the block stuff, your guys from the government kept the Mayor in his place and putting up one hundred million instead of sixty knocked any other offer out the equation! With regards to the road ting... we made sure Bang's joke army couldn't mash no work round here!" The person on the phone was Thug Rock!

Before travelling to Paradise Mountains, Jay Gigantic and Thug Rock spoke with each other and held a secret meeting which led them to striking an even more secret deal.

Thug Rock was in agreeance with every point Jay made on the news, something about it all just made sense to him, at the time he already had a weird feeling inside making him want to reach out to Jay Gigantic but at that point of time there was too much bad blood between them but having Chief Danjuma inform him of his true past allowed Thug Rock to understand why he felt that strange feeling, he realised it was his destiny to stand with Squad Gigantic and fight for good over evil, so he contacted Jay Gigantic with a proposal.

First Thug Rock asked Jay if he was serious about buying the block, when Jay replied 'as serious as a heart attack' Thug Rock pledged his allegiance and then they made history!

Jay Gigantic put up the eighty million pounds to buy and develop Bangs Block.

Jay decided to rename it 'Gigantic Block' a.k.a 'G Block'.

The only issue was that Gigantic was about to travel to Paradise Mountains and with Bang hot on his heels he knew that time was of the essence!

Not looking to let this opportunity pass him Gigantic connected Whipz with Thug Rock and instructed him to get all his affairs in order whilst he travelled, Jay Gigantic briefed Whipz on all the main points making it clear that there were three simple but highly important stipulations that he wasn't willing to compromise on:

1. WE RUN THE WHOLE BLOCK AS OUR OWN ENTITY AND HOW WE SEE FIT

2. WE HAVE OUR OWN POLICE AND EMERGENCY SERVICES

3. WE HAVE OUR OWN EDUCATION PROVISIONS

Thug Rock was fully in board with Jay Gigantic's plans and promised to do whatever was needed to ensure the success of the deal. Thug Rock only had one request which was his part of the proposal, Thug Rock wanted to take lead in policing the area with his Rock Ard Security firm, they all knew that they couldn't trust the LCP whilst it was under Officer KK's command, so the only way to protect the ends was to take full control of this area themselves.

Thug Rock was already on a journey of self-enlightenment, and hearing of his true history made him search even deeper into his culture and soul. He now wanted to use his abilities to protect his people and ensure growth rather than inflict the pain and destruction he usually caused.

Whilst away, Jay Gigantic left the negotiations in Whipz hands with Thug Rock providing any muscle and support he needed, this worked well allowing the deal to be sealed before Jay made it back from Paradise Mountains.

Jay Gigantic was now the official owner of Bang Block... sorry I mean G Block!

Jay Gigantic and Thug Rock's relationship had flourished to a real bromance, it was crazy how two sworn enemies could now laugh and joke like brothers. They continued their conversation in their usual serious but somehow still jokingly manner

"I was just about to get a briefing from Whipz, you two worked well together yeah?" Asked Jay

"Yeah bro he's a real brudda, no nonsense he went in and got the job done" replied Thug Rock

"Sounds like Whipz, what else has been going on? Out there seems crazy bro!" Said Jay Gigantic

"Arrrr mate where do I start, as I said before the truce is in place with every one we expected on board... we knew Bangz Army and Unknown Hittaz would never be apart of it but my guys, Da Grabberz and Spade Gang are all with us... actually speaking of Spade Gang this might make you laugh. Imagine, after Dealer died that nasty ting Elisha had the cheek to place herself at the top of Spade Gang claiming Dealer promised everything to her but after the solicitor read the will and all that, we found out Dealer actually left everything to me!

Anyway to cut a long story short, true she didn't get nothing she tried to work brain when I pulled up to kick her out of the club, telling me that she's always wanted to be with me and how we'll be good together... blood I couldn't believe it" said Thug Rock

Gigantic was in stitches "She ain't got no shame fam... you didn't fall for it did you?"

"Boooyyyy I did a quick little ting then told her to duss' hahahahaha" said Thug Rock

"You're a wrongen mate" said Jay Gigantic

"She tried to take me for a fool, so I took her for an eediot" Replied Thug Rock

"Well you're not the smartest person I ever met mate hahaha" joked Jay Gigantic but many true things are said in jest.

"Fam that's not even the end of it, who d'you think she ran off to after?!" Said Thug Rock

"No way, not Bang... he could never have taken her back!" Said Jay Gigantic

"Yes way, her and Bang are back together hahaha the doughnut not only took her back she told him Dealer had her under a spell hahahahaha... and he believed it! Fammm he's tapped she all had him calling my phone sending threats talking about what he's gonna do to me for disrespecting his woman, this guys lost the plot" said Thug Rock

"They deserve each other mate, leave em' to it! Anyway, let's not waste any more time on these fools we got much bigger things on our hands and you know what they say... small minds discuss people whilst great minds discuss ideas! And bro we ain't only discussed an idea... we made it happen!" Said Jay Gigantic, he became more and more excited each time he thought to himself 'I Own The Block!' he knew he was about to change many people lives for the better, he was so gassed that he added Whipz to the call to hear first-hand where they were at.

"Yo bro, I've been hearing good things... what you telling me?" Said Jay Gigantic to Whipz

"My family, it's good to go! Everything's in your name, your accountants a bit worried at how much you spent but he gets it hahahaha. All the residents will move back into their fresh new apartments and properties in the next two weeks, all retail units and community spots will be filled by the end of the month, the sports and recreation areas are ready too, street lights, road signs, street names, everything is ready bro... the only thing left to do is set the launch date." Said Whipz matching Jay's excitement.

"Cool, we gonna do this big the ends needs it bro! Get on to that Chatty Patty and let her know we got an exclusive for her. I wanna give her a tour of the area before the launch and let's show everyone what we got going on" said Jay.

The block was now Gigantic's and he vowed to do it big!

Things were quiet over the next few weeks, a little bit too quiet for Jay's liking. He knew Zeitan would need some time to recuperate from their last fight but there was no word from Bang, Officer KK or even the Mayor... it was strange!

The good thing was this period of silence allowed Jay and his team to complete G Block ahead of deadline.

As promised, they called down Sandra Patty and took her news crew on a tour of G Block before the launch, all the residents were back living there and every business was open.

Sandra Patty was amazed at what the block had become, what was once a dark and dingy hell hole plagued with nothing but violence and crime, was now a bright and thriving community filled with love, happiness and opportunity.

"A lot of people spoke a good one but they either weren't willing to put their money where their mouth is or they didn't have truly good intentions and would've had the block running the same or even worse than before!

I refuse to let that happen, so I personally raised the funds and bought back the block! My sons friend got killed out here with another yout' not too long ago, to me was the final straw something had to be done! This isn't how we were raised, and our children shouldn't be made to live like that.

What I want to make clear is that the block doesn't have to be a place of doom and gloom, unfortunately a lot of the time that's just how the powers that be had forced us to live. The block ain't a place of crime it's actually a place of manners, culture and respect that became plagued with crime! The block is where we learned how to live together as one and share what we have, no matter how big or little it is, we learned to respect our elders and to show love to our community and everyone around you. The block is also a place where we manifest untold talents creating many styles and cultures that's embraced all over the world whether it be music, fashion, dance, art... you name it and we make it" said Jay Gigantic to Sandra Patty as they walked through the G Block Sports and Recreation Area

"Here's the Sports area, we got bored of seeing them same old metal back football goals with a caged net and some dead basketball hoop on top... fam you score a goal and the ball just fires back at you! We can't be having that, so we switched it up! Kids in the hood want to be more than just footballers too, so as well as full size multi-sport grass and 6G pitches which residents can use for anything from Football to Lacrosse, we've also got Tennis Courts, Basketball courts and a full Athletics Track. Also, if you look just behind it, we got a brand new Gym and spa with state-of-the-art equipment... Jacuzzi, Steam rooms, Saunas and Olympic size swimming pool, you name it! The best part is if you live in the block, memberships included in your rent. No expense has been spared simply because fitness, mental and physical health is highly important to us."

"I'm actually speechless" said Sandra Patty,

"I've never seen you speechless before" joked Jay "Come let me show you more"

Jay took Sandra to another section of G Block and began to point out its amenities

"Here's our very own Police station which we staff and control ourselves, there's a GP which also has an A and E Trauma centre attached for emergencies, there's a Dental Surgery, Pharmacy, Therapy Centre and an Elderly and Disability assistance unit."

Before Sandra could catch her breath she was in another section

"Here's our Education quarters, we got a Montessori Nursery and pre-school, The Marcus Garvey Primary school named after one of my heroes, The Gigantic Academy Secondary school and The Gigantic Futures College. My Son's Music Studio and The G Block Youth club are also in this area as we believe informal learning is just as important as academic learning too."

Whilst Jay walked Sandra Patty over to the Food and Shopping quarters, he looked just outside of G Block and noticed a few of Bang's guys snooping around, without raising an alarm he signalled to a few of Thug Rock's men to go check it out. As soon as Thug Rocks men approached them, they drove off, Bang's men were sent to spy and see exactly who the buyer of Bang's Block was.

Jay wasn't fazed by the slight interruption, he continued to show Sandra Patty the final section of G Block

"I would show you the apartments and houses, but I wouldn't want to invade the resident's privacy like that, just know they're something special too! All original residents are on reduced rent rates with OAPs and disabled residents completely rent free." Jay wanted to make sure Sandra didn't notice anything around the situation with Bang's guys.

He swiftly diverted her attention and said

"Here's the Food and Shopping quarters, the best thing about this area is that all the shops are either owned by or staffed with the local residents, we're all about keeping the opportunity and money within the community but don't worry we welcome people from everywhere to come and shop with us. We got the Gigantic Supermarket, a GastroPub, a Caribbean Takeaway, a Vegan Food Spot and even StackTown has moved from being a takeaway spot on the street to a full blown restaurant inside G Block, we got a butchers, a Fishmongers, a Newsagents and of course a spot thats close to my heart The Safarhi Fly Fashion & Beauty Emporium which is actually my daughters store that she named after her favourite superhero." Said Gigantic ensuring no link is to be made between Rhiarn and her hero form Safarhi!

Not knowing if there was going to be any backlash from Bang's guys, Jay quickly ended the interview

"Remember we have a Family fun day and Block party this Saturday from 12pm, everybody is welcome. We're not only celebrating the new G Block but were also marking a momentous time for everyone from this area... a gang truce has been called between The RAT's, Spade Gang and Da Grabberz, so we're celebrating that too" said Jay then he thanked Sandra Patty and sent her on her way.

Sandra Patty didn't want to leave, she was in love with G Block and she even took a liking to Jay's charismatic ways, she tried to stall by letting Jay know that the news piece would air on the Six O'Clock news that evening.

As Jay walked away he shouted "Thanks that's great, I'll be sure to watch it... I'll see you on Saturday"

"You certainly will" muttered Sandra Patty, she was smitten. The irony was that she had a vendetta for Squad Gigantic and everyone in it but she fancied Jay... you couldn't make this stuff up hahaha.

Bang's men finally arrived back to his HQ with the information on who the owner of G Block was, Bang was furious when he found out Jay Gigantic was the person who snatched the block from him! Bang called the Mayor and let him have it! He couldn't believe the Mayor allowed this to happen, but the truth was there was nothing any of them could do about it. Seeing that he was wasting his time on the Mayor, Bang decided enough was enough, it was time to speak with Zeitan and put an end to Squad Gigantic once and for all!

Luckily for Bang, Zeitan had the same thoughts too!

ZEITAN'S BOUNCE BACK!

Zeitan used the last few weeks to recover after the defeat he suffered at the battle. Zeitan and his fleet took a hit, his numbers had not been this low for years.

Zeitan had to drag Nefarious from death's door and bring him back to life with a complete new rebuild. Zeitan was no fool, he knew that something had changed with Squad Gigantic, he could see they had hit a new level of power and strength, he was in trouble and the only way he would be able to go against them would be by taking drastic measures! Zeitan previously vowed that he was going to do a bold move that will take his power to new heights once he had recuperated.

Zeitan decided he was going to place his Source extract directly into his Cyborg anatomy, this was risky in many ways as just touching the extract incorrectly could kill him! He also knew that if he placed The Source into himself, he becomes the direct source of energy for all his Zupremes and even the Supreme Earth... so if he dies, they die do! Zeitan was willing to take this risk, after all if he died there would be no reason for them all to exist anyway.

Zeitan racked his brain trying to figure out ways to plant the extract in his body, then he remembered seeing Truth trying to fix The Source Connector from the Galax whilst they were in battle. The Source Connector was effectively a conductor that was able to contain and carry the Source's energy long enough for it to be transferred to another entity.

He sent a few Zupremes to retrieve the pieces from the debris, they did as commanded and carried the pieces back to their master.

This was exactly what Zeitan needed! After a few hours of manipulating the piece of technology he finally had it ready to transfuse The Source's energy into his mainframe.

Nefarious had to perform the nerve wrenching three hour procedure, the delicacy of The Source meant his hands had to be extremely steady and accurate. Luckily for them both it was a success, The Source Extract was now a part of Zeitan, Zeitan instantly grew to an even bigger stature with his powers and abilities advancing highly! Although he felt more powerful than ever before Zeitan refused to rush his attack, this had to be the big one! He thought it'll be wise to wait a few weeks using this period of time not only to train but to also build his army of Zupremes to at least five hundred.

Just as he hit the target of five hundred Zupremes he received communication from Bang.

"Boss it's me Bang, we need to talk right away mate"

"What's the issue today Bang?" Asked Zeitan in an exhausted tone, "It's seems all you ever call me with is problems... never any good news or successes".

Zeitan was getting fed up with Bang's failures

"It's like no one's taking me serious out here, the Mayor, Officer KK, Jay Gigantic... none of them! They're doing things and getting away with it, I know you said we should lay low for a bit whilst just running our normal services, but I think they're feeling that we've fell off! They need to know I'm not a joke mate... Boss I can't fallback no more... I'm ready to do a madness!"

"Usually I would tell you to shut up and relax but you've caught me in good mood today... IT'S TIME!" Replied Zeitan Supreme

"What d'you mean?" Said Bang with the biggest smile on his face

"It's time we put an end to all this nonsense! Time we destroy Squad Gigantic... take over Earth and most importantly get The Source!" Responded Zeitan.

This was music to Bang's ears, all he wanted to know was when and where!

"They brought the war to my world... now I'm taking it to them on their ends! Let's make a spectacle of them, Jay Gigantic wants to play community leader and protector... let's put him to the test! This weekend at his launch and block party we're gonna spice things up! All men, women and children will either bow to my reign or be exterminated! Simple as that... no more games, this weekend London... Paradise Mountains... Squad Gigantic and The Source will all fall!" said Zeitan

"Sounds good to me, just let me know what I gotta do" replied Bang

"To get the games started send some men down to the G Block launch event and spray it up! Flood it with bullets... spare no one! Seeing all their precious residents in a pool of blood should get their attention, then they'll fall right into our hands..." Zeitan then went on to tell Bang the plan of action.

Bang loved the ruthless plan. He jumped around full of joy, finally he had been given the go ahead to fully unleash his new powers on London and he was going to relish every last piece of this opportunity!

"This weekend everything changes mate!" Said Bang

CHAPTER 13 – Gigantians VS Zupremes!

Weekend had finally arrived, and the Gigantic household was amped up and raring to go.

Gigantic and Tanya done a once over of the entire block ensuring that the residents and volunteers were happy and that all businesses were in order and ready to trade.

All was well, everything was running smoothly... almost too smoothly! Squad Gigantic were unaware of the dramas that were about to take place on what should be the greatest day ever for the community.

Safarhi had her Safarhi Fly store stocked full of clothes, accessories and beauty products. She was so excited to bring her Safarhi Fly Lip Glosses to the ends, Tanya also connected her with some of her associates from the fashion industry which led to Safarhi's first range of T-shirts and Hoodies. Safarhi was ready to make her mark in the world of fashion and beauty, she wanted to show females all over the world that they can be successful at anything in life, she always said "You can't tell me the sky is the limit... I've been to space!" And she weren't lying!

Chunksta had Dj's playing music for the block party directly from the studio, everybody was requesting his songs and going mad when they dropped! Chunksta's music received nothing but love from the hood.

Finally, it was time to cut the ribbon and officially open G Block to the World.

This was usually an honour held by the Mayor of a city but in the spirit of bringing true change to the area, Jay Gigantic proudly done the honours as the residents cheered and labelled him as the People's Champion. Although he was embarrassed the Mayor still stood next to Jay for a photo opportunity, Jay could see the anger hidden deep within the Mayor's eyes, Jay just laughed and whispered in his ear "You're lucky I even let you in here!" As he gave him a hard squeezing handshake.

The launch had started, and everyone was having a great time, Stacktown provided free food for everyone, the Barbers and Hairdressers were given out free haircuts and styles, there was multiple sport competitions going on and Safarhi's team were giving out goodie bags. The vibes were nice, and the community was one. As promised, the gangs upheld the truce and were even working together either as security or volunteering help wherever they were needed.

It was truly amazing but unfortunately this was never going to last as Zeitan and Bang has different plans.

Truth was running a Gaming Competition in the Youth Club when he got a scary vision! He immediately dropped the controller, ran out and discreetly suited up!

Truth sent an alert through the SG Watches, one by one they went to a side to read and respond.

"Yo SQUUUAAADDDD UP! Somethings mads about to happen, you lot suit up and link me at the entrance... NOWWWW!" said Truth into his comms.

However, Jay Gigantic was surrounded by reporters and residents, he felt his watch alerting him but couldn't do anything about it as there was no way he could react without exposing his identity.

All the teens suited up and made their way towards the entrance whilst Tanya got to comms, something was about to go down and all the Squad minus Gigantic was ready!

Pacer got there first, he noticed a few tinted cars lurking and decided to check them

"Wha gwarn, why you man lurking... what is it?" Inquired Pacer

The car closest wound the tinted window down half way, and said "Don't ask bad man question!"

Chunksta stepped in and said "Bout bad man... get out the car and let me show you badman!"

The guys just laughed, "Why you laughing, what is it... You Bangin' or You Squad G?" Asked Pacer once more but this time there was clear.

"WE'RE BANGIN' G!!!" Then the car tyres screeched as the tinted windows rolled down and then BANG BANG BANG BANG BANG BANG BANG!

A flurry of machine gun shots came flying at Squad Gigantic.

Truth stopped the majority of the first shots whilst Safarhi and Pacer fired back with Ice Shots and Pacer Lasers!

The whole of G Block went into a frenzy, people trampled over each other as they tried to find safe spots to seek refuge from the array of gunshots. This was the perfect time for Jay Gigantic to make his escape and suit up, Whipz and Thug Rock played the role of security and took him away acting as if they were protecting him but really it was a decoy so he could suit up and join the Squad.

As Bang's men let off shots, Chunksta lost his temper and fearlessly ran straight at the car!

"Chunksta GET BACK!" Shouted Safarhi worried for her brother's safety but Chunksta ignored her and carried on going at them. He was a few metres away from Bang's men and ready to attack when he looked over his shoulder and noticed that a kid had strayed from the crowd walking right into the line of fire!

The little boy was oblivious to the danger he was in, Chunksta knew he had no choice but to abort his attack and remove the child from harm's way but before changing his path Chunksta grabbed one of the cars from underneath and tossed it in the air taking out three gunmen and a driver, then he turned his back to the shooters and ran over to the little boy.

The teens watched as Chunksta became a human shield taking a number of shots in his back, but this was cool as they just bounced of his SG Suit.

Chunksta picked up the boy and literally threw him over to crowd of people who caught him, the boy was safe but Chunksta wasn't!

Just as he spun back around to get back into the battle he was hit right in the forehead by a bullet!

"CHUNKSTAAAAAAAAAAA!!!!!!!!!!" Screamed Safarhi as she watched her little brother drop to the ground. Gigantic teleported in behind the gunmen, as Safarhi ran over to try and heal her brother. Gigantic beat the living daylight out of each gunman in his reach! Then he scooped two of them off the ground and threw them in front of Truth

"Find out where Bang is... we end this TODAY!" said Gigantic.

"Chunksta's been hit with a head shot, check he's vitals... there's no way he'll survive that" said Pacer to Tanya as his eyes filled with tears, Pacer and everyone else G Block thought Chunksta was dead for sure!

As Safarhi leaned over Chunksta to begin using her healing powers, she saw the bullet pop out of Chunksta's head.

"Huh" said Safarhi she was bewildered, then Chunksta's eyes opened, he jumped to his feet and nonchalantly said "Oh yeah... mans bulletproof still".

The biggest gasp of relief travelled around the whole of G Block.

"Them man almost bodied a yout' on our block, that's disrespectful! We gotta go for him today... immediate retaliation!" Said Chunksta then he gripped and lifted one of the men in front of Truth and started roughing him up saying "Tell me where Bang's at!" Chunksta almost beat him to death as he released the energy he absorbed from the head shot.

"Stop bro... STOP! Dead men can't talk fam" said Truth "Plus they were never gonna tell us... I done read his mind and got the drop already! What you saying Gigantic we pulling up on them?"

"Deffo, lets go!" Gigantic decided it'll be best to ride out rather than teleport, so he spoke into his comms "Tanya send in my SG Quad... please" asked Gigantic knowing better than to forget his manners.

"And my SG1000 too please" added Truth

Then within a matter of seconds Truth's SG1000 came shooting out of his Purple Star Diamond and formed right in front of everyone's eyes, Gigantic's SG Quad done the same via his Fire Red Diamond and now they were ready to go!

Gigantic led the way on his SG Quad as Chunksta hopped on the back of his brothers SG1000 whilst Safarhi hit the sky and Pacer... well he just Paced!

Little did Squad Gigantic know they were heading right into Zeitan's trap, Zeitan knew they would want to know where Bang was and once they found out they would be sure to attack him for doing something as drastic as shooting up a family day! Zeitan planned to lure them up the motorway to some open land on the outskirts of London where they will be met by an overwhelming amount of Zupremes and soldiers from Bangz Army.

Zeitan's plan was falling into place but what he didn't expect was the numbers Squad Gigantic would have! Tanya communicated with Squad Gigantic as they hit the motorway

"Are you guys seeing this?" Asked Tanya

"Seeing what?" Replied Gigantic

"Look behind you!" Said Tanya

The whole Squad looked back to see an entourage following behind them! There was at least two hundred people in Cars, Vans, 4x4's, Motorbikes, Quads and even mopeds!

"Who's that?" Said Chunksta

"It's The Truce! Looks good, that's Thug Rock leading them" said Tanya

Squad Gigantic couldn't believe the whole ends was riding with them!

Whilst the confrontation between Squad Gigantic and Bang's was taking place, Thug Rock gathered together Rock Ard Thugs, Da Grabberz and Spade Gang.

"The time for talking is done! You see what these Bang boys are doing!?" Said Thug Rock to his congregation.

"We really gonna sit back and accept it? No bro...NOOOOO! We're all here together cos' we called the truce, that means we are one gang now... now we ride together!" Said Thug Rock as he made it clear to everyone that they were now one!

"It's simple as this either You're Bangin' or You're Squad! And if you're Bangin' you better get out of here NOW! But if you're Squad... load up and let's get ready to ride... this is for the hood!" Said Thug Rock

"The TRUCE!" Shouted Thug Rock then I'm solidarity everyone shouted back "The TRUCE!"

G Block erupted in roars and cheers... the gangs joined together for good and named their new force The TRUCE!

The TRUCE! Was Squad and they refused to let Bangz Army run the endz!

A change for the better was in the air and they were ready to put everything on the line to make sure their children can grow in a safe world whilst aspiring to be whatever they wanted to be.

Squad Gigantic and The TRUCE! Pulled up to see Bang fully gassed standing in front of hundreds of Zupremes. Plasma was violently running through the veins in his arms, he was ready for war!

Gigantic and Bang caught eyes, this time there was no exchange of words... it was straight action!

Bang sent a massive thermal blast through the ground in attempt to take out a high number of his opposition! However, this didn't work, Chunksta clocked the play and counteracted with a Chunksta Boom that sent the blast right back and took out a got number of Zupremes instead!

"You're gonna have to do better than that fam" shouted Chunksta as Gigantic teleported over to Bang and unleashed a combo on him with no reply... the war had officially started!

Truth broke his serious and silent stance by shouting "MAN DEM.... ATTACK!"

SQUAD GIGANTIC

Squad Gigantic and The TRUCE! Charged at Bang and the Zupremes as they charged back!

It was a mazza.., both sides were getting it!

In a strange twist of events Chunksta and Thug Rock stood side by side and created a powerhouse which tore through the Zupremes! Chunksta was punching through their faces whilst Thug Rock hit them with Rock Shots and boulders!

Safarhi attacked from the sky whilst sending Chalky and Greazy out on the ground! She hit Zupremes with Ice Shots and used her abilities to manipulate nature and create mini earthquakes that dragged Zupremes underground then crushed them when she closed back the cracks.

The Zupremes were being taken out in multiples of tens whilst casualties were minimal on the other side.

Gigantic was relentless, he kept applying the maddest of pressure... Bang couldn't get no respite! Once again Bang was being overpowered and out skilled by his nemesis. Bang managed to hit Gigantic with a few of his Plasma Burst Bangs but with little effect, Gigantic sucked them up and just went at him even harder!

Mechanics tried to come to his rescue too but Gigantic just ended up punching them both up!

Bang was out of ideas and to make things worse Truth partnered up with Gigantic, now Bang couldn't even get close to his enemy! Truth crushed Mechanics Gun then controlled Mechanics and Bang with his telekinesis, Bang had no control of his body. Truth repeatedly tossed them up in the air then pulled them back into Gigantic's punches, then once they were bored he just threw them away like a dolly, it was hilarious.

"Enough is enough!" Blurted out Zeitan, The Zupremes numbers were low once again and Bangz Army were useless, Zeitan couldn't watch no longer!

"Nefarious send in another hundred more Zupremes and prepare for travel!" Said Zeitan

"I can't watch this atrocity no more… you want something done properly, you gotta do it yourself! I want those SG Gems and I Want Them TODAY! We're going in!" Said Zeitan Supreme.

Squad Gigantic and The TRUCE! We're running a mockery on the battlefield, Bangz Army and the Zupremes were truly done out there!

Only one thing could save the day… ZEITAN SUPREME!

Suddenly an enormous portal cracked open the Earth's atmosphere and another hundred Zupreme's came running through led by Nefarious. However, this time they were not alone! After the infestation of Zupremes come flooding through the portal the colossus and menacing figure of Zeitan Supreme slowly walked through making his presence known!

"Rah I don't remember him being that big" said Gigantic as he realised that they now had a real fight on their hands!

A few members of The TRUCE! wasn't on no long ting… they ran forward and let off shots at Zeitan.

"You little fools, you think that can harm me?!" Gloated Zeitan as he soaked up the bullets. Then Zeitan's rib cages opened up and four blasters came out firing at The TRUCE's shooters! Each shot connected and burnt them to ashes!

Pacer paced round and shot his Lasers at the blasters managing to damage one before Zeitan retracted it into his anatomy.

"That was quick, well done but know you won't get that opportunity again" said Zeitan

"Fammm, stop talking" said Pacer.

Nefarious went straight for Thug Rock punching him in his face with a powerful left hook that sent Thug Rock across the field. Chunksta weren't having that, he instantly retaliated with an even bigger right hook to Nefarious's face dropping him too!

Now a new rumble started as Chunksta and Thug Rock took against Nefarious!

Chunksta and Thug Rock started stamping out Nefarious whilst shouting at him

"You pulled up on the wrong two brudda!"

Nefarious took at least twenty kicks before he managed to activate his drone setting and rocket away from under their feet. Chunksta and Thug Rock refused to let him get away, they ran him down and slapped him out of the air with Rock Shots after getting a little assistance from Safarhi who sent a bolt of lightning that struck Nefarious!

Thug Rock and Chunksta took turns punching Nefarious back and forth to each other

"Oi this is like playing Bang's at school bro" joked Chunksta

"Yeah but I'm getting bored" said Thug Rock

"Well let's done him G" said Chunksta

Ready to put Nefarious to sleep, Chunksta unleashed a devastating combo! Thug Rock just stepped back and watched as Chunksta let Nefarious have it! Chunksta worked him... left Jab to the eye, right hook to the cheek and a left uppercut across the chin followed by six body blows which dented Nefarious's abdominal area! Chunksta dropped the big bad N's with a kick to the shin, then Thug Rock took over and pounded Nefarious into the ground before dropping a boulder on his legs

"You can chill for a little bro" said Thug Rock, then they walked off laughing as they left N's on the floor defeated.

Pacer continued to pace around taking out Zupremes with his Laser shots whilst Gigantic, Truth and Safarhi took on Zeitan!

Truth tried to lift Zeitan off his feet using his telekinesis powers, but it didn't work!

"Sorry mate, that don't work on me! My body isn't built from resources that originate from Earth or even Zurakaya, so you don't have power over me hahahaha" said Zeitan as he rubbished Truth's attack and lifted him instead!

Zeitan threw Truth across the field, Safarhi went mad and sent Ice Shots but they couldn't penetrate Zeitan's armour! She tried to freeze him... he heated up his body, she tried to burn him with volcanic lava... he sprayed out liquid Nitrogen and solidified it! Their powers weren't doing a thing... the only thing they could use was brute force!

Gigantic said "A Drop Of Rain Is Nothing On It's Own, But When They Form Together..."

"...It's A STORM!!!" Replied Truth and Safarhi!

Then they ran at Zeitan and attacked... unfortunately Zeitan read the play and smacked down each one of them!

BLAOOOOW!!! Truth took a full blow to the face...

BAAMMMMM!!! Safarhi went flying after receiving a shot to the stomach!

Gigantic kept teleporting in and out trying to catch Zeitan off guard but every time he did so, Zeitan caught him and gave him a couple blows for his troubles, Zeitan was in full control and now he had the upper hand!

Tanya could see that the tables had dramatically turned, she decided it was time to call in the cavalry! She made contact with Paradise Mountains and Chief Danjuma responded immediately!

A bright and colourful portal appeared and before it was fully opened, 2's Force Swords flew out and glided around effortlessly beheading every Zupreme that came in their path. The Force Swords returned to 2's as him, Santago, Trapz, Kon-X and the rest of the SG Hit Squad came rushing out of the portal!

"IT'S ONNNNNN!" Shouted Chunksta he was mad happy to see them, things were looking bleak for Squad Gigantic ,this was the lift they needed!

"AIM FOR HIS NECK!" Advised Kon-X, exposing Zeitan's only weak spot!

Zeitan's neck area was where his head and his impenetrable body merged together, this is where all Zeitan's main connectors are housed. For there to be any chance of stopping Zeitan physically... destroying the technology in his neck was it!

Squad Gigantic changed their attack strategy, they fell back and joined together "The only way to beat him is by working as a team!" Said Truth

"Strike hard, strike accurate and strike as one!" Instructed Gigantic as he led the new approach.

It was a beautiful sight to see as they all worked as one to take down the mighty Zeitan Supreme. Kon-X was whipping up Comets and Fireball emojis then firing them at Zeitan's neck, whilst 2's sent out his Force Swords to destroy and kill annihilating the Zupremes! Then to top it off whilst all this was going on Truth, Safarhi and Gigantic were smothering Zeitan.

Zeitan was doing everything within his power to protect his neck but he was being bombarded!

Trapz created the coolest portals ever seen by literally punching them into existence! In an effort to even the numbers Trapz punched a combination of portals around the Zupremes and forced them into it sending them to the bottom of the ocean where the water pressure was so fierce that it crushed them.

Squad Gigantic were back on top!

Knowing they were now fighting a losing battle, Mechanics decided it was time to make his exit

"Im-a outta here-a mate" Shouted Mechanics as he ran off to hide like the coward he is.

Bang tried to follow his pal but found himself confronted by Chunksta and Thug Rock who were ready to put a serious beating on him for their own personal reasons.

"Mechanics come and back it!" Shouted Bang

"No way matey, you're-a on-a your own my friend... ciao amico" replied Mechanics

Mechanics was not coming back, and Thug Rock was blood thirsty!

"You killed my friend" said Thug Rock

"And your boys killed my friend too!" Added Chunksta

"And what are you two muppets gonna do about it?!?" Said Bang then punched Chunksta in his mouth with a powerful Plasma Burst Bang!

"Silly move!" Said Chunksta, as that was the worst thing Bang could've done as he placed all that energy into Chunksta which he gladly absorbed.

Now it was Chunksta and Thug Rock's turn!

Rather than one big Chunksta Boom! Chunksta decided to let the energy out bit by bit so he could slowly inflict the maximum amount of pain on Bang!

Thug Rock put Bang in a head lock and hit him with rapid Rock Shots to the side of his face! Bang took the shots and managed to reverse Thug Rocks headlock by putting him in a backwards suplex.

Chunksta didn't jump in straight away, instead he laughed saying "Don't have that big man!"

Thug Rock didn't have it! He jumped back to his feet, dived at Bang and took him down. Bang pounded on Thug Rocks back trying to get him off him.

Thug Rock head butted Bang on the bridge of his nose which dazed him for a bit, Thug Rock use this opportunity to pick Bang up, spin him upside down and give him a Piledriver, Bang was out cold!

"Bout time fam, I thought I was gonna have to save you hahaha" said Chunksta

"Save who? Im a bad man" replied Thug Rock.

Then Thug Rock joined the rest of The Truce! and Trapz to tackle the Zupremes as Chunksta joined the fight on Zeitan.

"Look at him, its working! His dance soon done!" Said Chunksta as he noticed Zeitan weakening, however Zeitan was still far from defeat, even though he was clearly being beaten he was still giving as good as he got!

"Squad stay patient and continue doing what we're doing, make every shot count and don't do no crazy moves that'll take you out of the formation" instructed Gigantic, he was well aware the risk was still there!

Nefarious finally broke free from the boulder and came to his master's aid with a few Zupremes by his side.

Chunksta and Trapz took on Nefarious and his small team of Zupremes whilst everyone else continued to break down Zeitan.

Then in a moment of stupidity Pacer changed everything!

After clearly being told to be patient and stick to the plan, Pacer allowed his arrogance get the best of him and decided to do otherwise!

The structured attack finally began to take toll on Zeitan but rather than continue with the strategy Pacer chose to use this moment as an opportunity to be the hero!

Pacer devised a plan in his mind...this never goes well!

'I can Pace madddd fast and creep up behind Zeitan then BLAMMM him in his neck with a Laser Shot from a point-blank distance that will kill Zeitan and make me the big man!' Thought Pacer.

Unfortunately, in real life Pacer's plans never run as smoothly as they do in his silly brain.

Acting as if he didn't see Pacer lining up his attack, Zeitan continued battling with the others with one eye slyly watching Pacer's every move, then BOOOOOOOMMMMM!!!... In less than a split second everything changed and somehow Zeitan had Pacer dangling by the neck!

Zeitan waited for Pacer to make his move, he anticipated Pacer's speed and grabbed him just as he got close enough to shoot his Pacer Laser out!

Pacer's plan didn't work one bit, all he managed to do was put Squad Gigantic and their SG Gems in jeopardy!

"What the F....!" Said Gigantic, as he saw his son hanging in Zeitan's hands!

"Hahahahaha there's always one" said Zeitan as he held Pacer by the scruff of his neck.

"HOLD YOUR FIRE!" Commanded Gigantic "He's got Pacer!"

Zeitan knocked Pacer out, then took his Chain and Golden Beryl SG Gem.

Zeitan placed Pacer's Chain over his neck then said

"One down... Four to go! This is how life goes I guess, one minute everyone's coming for your neck then the next minute your decorating it with jewels and gems... bet you won't aim at my neck now hahahaha!" Said Zeitan Supreme.

With Pacer's life literally dangling in his hands, Zeitan was now in the position of power!

He knew Pacer's life held a lot of value and he was definitely going to take full advantage of it.

"Now we play this my way... is this where we start negotiating Gigantic?" Mocked Zeitan

"Bout negotiation... you're gonna have to kill us all!" Said Chunksta but Gigantic knew the true danger at hand. Zeitan is an evil and ruthless man, shouting threats won't work in Squad Gigantic's favour.

"What do you want in exchange for his life?" Asked Gigantic

"It's simple, gimme all your SG Gems or I'll rip him in half!" Demanded Zeitan.

Gigantic was lost, he didn't know what to do! Giving Zeitan the SG Gems would give him control of The Source and the whole world, but not giving him the SG Gems means the death of Pacer! Gigantic look over to his father for answers.

Meanwhile in Paradise Mountains

The Source was going crazy! It became more unstable the moment Zeitan put Pacer's SG Gem on his neck, and with Trapz & 2's both being at the battle nobody was guarding or watching over it, The Source was like a ticking bomb waiting to explode!

Back at the battle

Santago looked Gigantic straight in the eyes and said "Do it, give him your SG Gems!"

"But then life as we know it is over! We'll all die here on Earth and Zurakaya!" Said Gigantic

"Have faith in The Source son... whatever's meant to be will be! Maybe he will take over the world and maybe we will all die... but that's maybes, what we do know is that he has Pacer there right now and he WILL definitely kill him! Just give him what he wants!" Said Santago.

"So what's it gonna be, your Gems or his life" said Zeitan in the most arrogant tone ever, he knew he had them over the barrel and was going to get exactly what he wanted!

SQUAD GIGANTIC

Gigantic pulled Truth, Safarhi and Chunksta to a side then told them to hand over their chains. Each teen handed over their chains without any argument or hesitation knowing it was the only way to save their brother.

Before taking the Chains and SG Gems over to Zeitan Gigantic made a promise to the Squad "One way or another we will get these gems back and make everything right in the world!"

The teens stood in solidarity and agreed with their father.

"Smart decision" said Zeitan as Gigantic reluctantly walked up and handed over the Chains with the SG Gems attached.

"Don't be so upset, Maybe I'll keep you all as my personal slaves once this is over, it'll be better than dying right?!?" Said the even cockier Zeitan.

Nefarious stood to the left of his master and laughed.

"Here hold this" said Zeitan treating Pacer like an old rag as he threw him into Nefarious's arms

"Give him to the Black Lion once you see I have all the Chains" instructed Zeitan.

Gigantic approached Zeitan and went to hand him the Chains

"Place them on my neck one by one, I want to savour this moment" said Zeitan

Refusing to give him the pleasure of placing them on his neck Gigantic threw the Chains in front of Zeitan and mumbled "You must be mad you Pom Pom" under his breath as he left the Chains on the floor in front of Zeitan.

Seeing that Zeitan was in possession of the SG Gems, Nefarious tossed Pacer to Gigantic.

Gigantic took Pacer and slapped him back to consciousness once he was back with Squad Gigantic, the SG Hit Squad and The Truce!.

The SG Gems being in Zeitan's possession made The Source go really out of control! The Forbidden Area became dark with random lightning storms momentarily flashing light in the darkness as The Source behaved more erratically.

Feeling something wasn't right, Chief Danjuma rushed to the Forbidden Area but there was nothing he could do! Every time he got near to The Source it shot him away, The Source was very close to being fully consumed by darkness!

All Chief Danjuma could do to protect the people of Paradise Mountains was evacuate the area.

"Clear the area and make sure not one soul comes within five miles of the Forbidden Area!" Instructed Chief Danjuma.

"Is this the end sir?" Asked one of the Chief's warriors.

"Not yet, it's not totally dark yet... we still got one more trick up our sleeve" replied Chief Danjuma.

The same darkness and lightning storms from the Forbidden Area was now taking place above Zeitan Supreme on Earth, he could feel The Source's power bursting into his body!

"It's working, it's working! I have all the power now... feed me Source... FEED MEEE!" Shouted Zeitan as he gladly welcomed everything The Source was giving him.

Then all of a sudden everything stopped! The darkness above went away taking the lightning storm with it, Zeitan felt the same power he was just receiving begin to leave his body.

"Huh, what's happening?!" Said Zeitan "NOOOOOOO! Where's all the power going?" Asked Zeitan as he looked up to the sky.

"I told you have faith" said Santago to Gigantic "Get your guys ready... it's about to go down!"

Gigantic was lost to what was going on but rather than waste time looking for an answer he just did as his father told him and prepared them all for battle... well everyone except Pacer who was still a little worse for wear and discombobulated.

"What have you done... why is this not working?" Shouted out Zeitan.

He had spent millions of years fighting just to get to this moment, and now he's finally here nothings happening!

Refusing to give up Zeitan placed the SG Gems directly over where he fused The Source extract into his anatomy, this seemed to have done the trick! The darkness came back carrying the storm with it, this time it was more violent and volatile... Zeitan may just be getting his way!

Things were looking dire! Understanding it was now and never Santago knew that he no choice but to attack!

"WE GOTTA PUT A STOP TO THIS... SEND HER NOWWWWW!" Screamed out Santago

"Send who now?" Asked Gigantic

"MEEEE the first Chosen One!" Said Mummy G as Chief Danjuma sent her through a portal from Paradise Mountains! She gave Zeitan a round house kick to the back of his neck whilst he was still distracted... Zeitan went flying!

Mummy G stepped on Zeitan's chest, then she placed her hand over his face and water forcefully came rushing through her palms into Zeitan's mouth slowly choking him as the water poured down his throat.

"It was never gonna work, you haven't got this!" Said Mummy G as she brandished the Queen of all Gems the Black Fire Pearl!

Mummy G has the ability to control, manipulate or even become water in any state. She was the first ever Chosen One born with the Black Fire Pearl. Paradise Mountains kept her as a secret just in case a situation like this would ever arise. Mummy G's SG Gem is held deep under the seas in the underwater world of Gigantis! Where it is protected by her people... the Gigantians of Gigantis.

"It was never just five Gems... it's six!" Said Mummy G, as she froze Zeitan's head protection and ripped it off!

"Your parents never teach you not to teef peoples tings" said Mummy G, as she turned her flow of water to a massive sharp icicle and pointed it at Zeitan's neck as she took back the Chains with her other hand.

Nefarious snuck up behind Mummy G and swung his fist at her!

Just before he was able to make contact, Chunksta caught his fist with his left hand and banged him with his right hand!

"You really try sneak up on mans granny fam, you mad!" Said Chunksta as the power of the blow made Nefarious begin to malfunction.

Mummy G gave Zeitan a quick but brutal ground and pound aiming a majority of the blows to the weak spot in his neck!

Chunksta wanted to join in but it felt weird beating up someone with his grandmother, so he just stepped back and watched in amazement like everyone else.

"Tanya, we need to make my mum a SG Suit, she's really up here fighting man in her Sunday best... this is embarrassing" joked Gigantic through the comms.

Mummy G got off the ground and fixed her hair as she walked over to her son and the other grandchildren with Chunksta close by her side. Mummy G hugged each person as she gave them back their Chains and SG Gems.

Mummy G thought she had Zeitan defeated, she shouted out "Someone tie him up, we can decide what to do with him after!" One of the SG Hit Squad members went to apprehend Zeitan but Zeitan wasn't done!

All in one motion Zeitan hopped up, grabbed the warrior and snapped his neck! Then he aimed his blasters at the back of Mummy G's head as she obliviously walked away with her back to the most dangerous being on Earth!

Truth noticed but he wasn't fast enough to warn her

"Mummy G DUCKKKKKK!" Shouted Truth as Zeitan sent his shots!

Mummy G couldn't get out of the way quick enough but luckily Gigantic could get in the way! Gigantic grabbed his Mum and teleported her a few metres away to safety.

Zeitan was back with a vengeance! His second breath had kicked in and he wasn't holding back!

Thug Rock and his guys attacked Zeitan but got dealt with horribly!

Everything that was thrown at Zeitan was shut down, he got Nefarious functioning then they ran riot together!

"Yo bro, there's only one thing that we haven't done to this guy" said Safarhi, speaking into Truth's mind

"I was thinking the same thing sis... let's take him on a Truth Safarhi! We need to get close up and personal then let him have it!" Replied Truth

"Let's go!" Said Safarhi then her and Truth charged through the Zupremes and arrived in front of Zeitan.

"Arrrr how cute, sibling love aye? You come to take me on together as one?" mocked Zeitan

But Truth was never really one for the talking! They ignored Zeitan and powered up whilst he insulted them.

Zeitan stopped his noise and dressed back once he saw the Forcefield shield appear around Truth and Safarhi as they connected with The Source!

Zeitan tried to penetrate the Forcefield but failed! Every time he hit the shield it slammed him backwards!

The colour of the sky started to change, and The Source shot down from above and combined with the SG Gems which omitted a shine like never before... something major was about to happen!

Back on Paradise Mountains

The Source became fully unstable and was about to blow! The Truth Safarhi was drawing too much power from it... one wrong move and The Source was going to erupt!

Back at the battle

"Pssst psssst hey Bang, come on-a-man let's get out of here, the sky outside is new bloody colour this-a ain't-a normal... its-a home time pal, Zeitan can deal with this" whispered Mechanics to Bang, his guilt made him come back for his friend but refused to stay and fight.

Bang saw things were extraordinarily crazy and agreed! Him and Mechanics jumped in a random 4x4 and drove far up north to a spot he had.

Truth and Safarhi caused carnage all around them as they built up their Truth Safarhi, the whole area around them became Black, Purple and Pink! The floor was cracking and the atmosphere around them had become unbearable for the average human.

"Whatever it is your doing, just hurry up and do it!" Said Zeitan as he too loaded up his own weapons to fight back! Zeitan grew even bigger now that he was at capacity and he's attack on the Forcefield shield was no longer slamming him back... he actually managed to pierce a small hole in a section. However, Zeitan's efforts were pointless and all growing bigger done was make him a bigger target! Truth and Safarhi were ready! They were about to let off a something so powerful that it had to come with catastrophic consequences!

"NOOOOWWWWWWWW!" Shouted the twins then BOOOOOOOOOOMMMMMMMMMMMMM! The Source's energy flowing through their bodies reached its ultimate pinnacle and blasted out their Truth Safarhi!

It was a truly amazing sight! In one swift motion Safarhi discharged a colossal Shockwave that was matched by Truth's mega eruption of pure energy from The Source!

The Truth Safarhi destroyed everything in its path! The whole city was illuminated Pink and Purple for around five to ten seconds, whilst something resembling meteor like rocks fell out of the sky hitting random people.

The Truth Safarhi drew so much energy from The Source that it combusted!

Nobody predicted that Truth and Safarhi's link with The Source was this powerful!

It didn't only tip The Source's unstableness over the top... it fully erupted it!

THE SOURCE EXPLODED AND SHATTERED THE SOUL DISC INTO PIECES!

"What's going on? I'm getting crazy readings on the SG System! Some explosion just took place and for like five to ten seconds random portals opened between London and Supreme Earth! Also, at the same time some

Comet like energy rocks fell out the sky and hit at least ten random people in and around London... I don't like this something ain't right!"

"Tanya that's not even the worse thing" Replied Gigantic

"What d'you mean?" Asked Tanya

"We can't find Kon-X or Safarhi, they've just disappeared... THEY'RE GONE!!!!!" Said Gigantic

TO BE CONTINUED...

SG Merchandise and much more available at:
www.SQUADGIGANTIC.com

.

"A Drop Of Rain Is Nothing On It's Own, But When They Form Together... It's A STORM!!!"

-J. Andrade